The
Honorable
Mr. Darcy

A Pride & Prejudice Variation

A Meryton Mystery: Book 1

Jennifer Joy

"The Honorable Mr. Darcy: A Pride & Prejudice Variation"

Published by Jennifer Joy

Blog: jenniferjoywrites.com

Facebook: Jennifer Joy

Twitter: @JenJoywrites

Email: contact@jenniferjoywrites.com

ISBN-13: 978-1-944795-93-1

Table of Contents

This book is for you.

CHAPTER 1

Fitzwilliam Darcy glared at the insolent man before him— the man who had become a plague to his family and a threat to his little sister. "Why are you in Hertfordshire?" he demanded, pulsing his fists at his side.

George Wickham sat at a table near the cot in his assigned tent, polishing his pistol with booted feet propped lazily on top of the rugged wood. "What? Is it not obvious?"

"My father paid off your debts before his death. I owe you nothing— especially after what you attempted at Ramsgate." Darcy's teeth clenched. He could not bring himself to say his sister's name before the blackguard. How could Georgiana possibly have believed Wickham loved her when he had proved time and again that he loved no one but himself?

Wickham chuckled menacingly. "How unfortunate you discovered my plan. You have to admit it was clever. Georgiana certainly had thought so before you showed up."

"Do not say her name," Darcy growled. He wanted nothing more than to disturb the smirk on Wickham's face, but he was a Darcy and would not give Wickham the satisfaction of a lost temper… unless he was so foolish as to mention Georgiana again.

Wickham took him seriously. He lowered his feet to the floor and straightened his posture.

Assuming a bored tone which ran contrary to the fire coursing through his body, Darcy continued, "In every way, you have acted with deceit and treachery. I would be remiss to call you clever."

Raising his unloaded pistol, Wickham slowly inspected it, rubbing his thumb over his engraved initials on the sideplate. With a sneer, he said, "Where is your sense of humor Darcy? You take yourself much too seriously, and your pride will be your downfall. I came to Meryton with the sole purpose of making you miserable." Wickham's cackle shot a shiver down Darcy's spine. "I had these glorious plans of ruining the villagers' opinion of you, while gaining their favor for myself… and what do I find?" Standing up and leaning across the table, his hand still grasping his pistol, he said, "They already despise you. They believe you to be an arrogant snob who considers himself much too good for the likes of them."

Gossip. Darcy despised the harm it caused, and knew all too well how easy it was for others to be influenced by Wickham's charm. "I do not care for the opinions of others. Of what import is it to me?" he asked, slowing his breath to calm his agitation.

With a scoff, Wickham set the weapon down. Bringing himself to his full height and raising his chin so that he stood eye to eye with Darcy, he said, "So long as your pride prevents you from allowing your precious little sister's reputation to be ruined— thus casting a shadow over the otherwise perfect Darcy name— I intend to profit from it."

Darcy held his gaze steady, though a bead of sweat trickled down his back between his shoulder blades. "You will get nothing from me. I saw to your commission and arranged for your independence from my household. You have benefited from my assistance to the fullest degree, and your insults and threats will get you nowhere."

Wickham's eyes flickered in mischief. "Ah, but is that true? How can you prevent me from relating how eager your innocent sister was to elope with me? She practically begged me to take her to Gretna Green."

It was as if the scum were begging for Darcy to rearrange his face. Would Wickham's charming influence lessen if he had a flattened nose or missing teeth? Darcy's fists clenched and his blood boiled, but he did not lose control. It was what Wickham wanted. He would see it as a weakness and use it against him.

Forcing his fingers to relax in an admirable display of self-possession, Darcy said, "Nobody would believe you. It would be your word against mine, and I could readily supply witnesses to testify to your true character."

Wickham harrumphed, but he took a step back. "That would take too long and the damage would be done. Besides, do you really think the people of Meryton will believe your word against mine when you have done everything possible to insult them? I hear that you did not condescend to dance at their assembly." He paused, seeking affirmation.

Darcy gave no answer. He had refused to dance when it soon became clear that the maidens he would have to partner were only interested in his fortune. Whispering fathers and ambitious mothers paraded their daughters in front of him like peddlers desperate to sell their wares.

Wickham continued, "And I have it on good authority that you openly insulted a lady's vanity. A lady who is as pleasing to the eyes as she is to the ears."

Miss Elizabeth Bennet. Darcy winced before he could stop himself.

With a self-satisfied grin, Wickham said, "I see that the rumors are true. Really, Darcy, I had thought that a lady such as Miss Elizabeth would turn your eye. She is of the intelligent type you have always preferred without degrading herself to the level of a bluestocking. Need I mention her fine eyes?" he added in mockery.

Darcy glared at Wickham. If he showed any sign of his regard for Miss Elizabeth, it would only make her his next target. He deeply regretted the cut he had made her close to two months before at the Meryton Assembly. He had not known her character, and had assumed that she was no better than Mrs. Bennet with her presumptuous claims that Bingley, with his five thousand a year, would soon propose to her eldest daughter. It was one of the rare times Darcy had to admit to making a mistake, and he was not too proud to admit it— if only to himself. However, he was unwilling to admit as much to Wickham. Best to change the subject.

"The fact is that my sister did not marry you. You did not get her dowry. This is only a desperate attempt to leech off the fortunes of others so that you may continue in your vices. I will have no part in it."

Wickham sneered, not having the decency to be ashamed of his reprehensible conduct. "I thought you would say as much." Shrugging his shoulders, he continued, "It is of no concern to me. I already have the ear of the more respected members of Meryton society."

Society? In Meryton?

Any humor Darcy found in the contradictory terms soon shriveled up as Wickham added, "When the time is right, I will reveal the truth about your sister, and it will not take long for word to spread. 'Society', be they of the upper or the lower classes, has one thing in common: They love to gossip, and they glory in the denigration of one who believes himself so far superior to themselves as to make his fall all the more spectacular. It is your choice, Darcy. I would take great pleasure in ruining you, but my silence can be had for a price."

Darcy's breath trembled in his effort to control it. How could he protect Georgiana without bending to the will of a man undeserving of his cooperation?

He needed to distance himself. No good decision was ever made at the height of emotion. "You have said enough. I will hear no more." He turned to leave.

"I will see you tonight, Darcy," Wickham called out from behind him, the laughter in his voice darkening Darcy's mood as he smacked the canvas of the tent aside to depart.

Blast Wickham! Blast Bingley for arranging a ball and inviting the devil!

He stomped to his horse, ignoring anything but his purpose. He had to rid himself and his sister of Wickham's influence.

***

Elizabeth Bennet watched Mr. Darcy burst out of a tent between the rows of white canvas. His shoulders tensed up to his ears as he jammed his hat onto his head and stalked away in the opposite direction.

"That is Mr. Wickham's tent. What business could Mr. Darcy have with him?" asked Lydia, peering at the flapping canvas left in Mr. Darcy's wake.

Indeed. Elizabeth knew of the so-called gentleman's unjust behavior toward the lieutenant. Mr. Wickham had confided in her— her already poor opinion of Mr. Darcy justified when she heard how he had failed to honor his father's wishes upon his death, and how he had cast Mr. Wickham out as of no consequence. Had the miserable man come to gloat?

Jane, Elizabeth's eldest sister, spoke, interrupting her own accusatory thoughts toward the unpleasant Mr. Darcy. "Lydia, how do you know which tent is Mr. Wickham's?"

Elizabeth had been so upset about Mr. Darcy, she had overlooked that important detail.

Lydia was the youngest of the five Bennet sisters and renowned for her coquetries. Her eyes flickered over to Kitty, her partner in crime. Kitty ought to have been more sensible, being a year older than Lydia, but she seemed pleased to follow the lead of her troublesome sister. It was a pity. Kitty was as kindhearted as she was gullible.

Wrinkling up her button nose, Lydia said, "Do not alarm yourself, Jane. It is not as if I have been inside Mr. Wickham's tent."

Mary, the middle Bennet sister, and the polar opposite of Lydia in matters of morality, huffed out of flared nostrils in righteous indignation. "I pray that no sister of mine would commit such an act of impropriety. It would reflect poorly on our entire family, and what would Mr. Collins think of us then?" she said through pinched lips.

For Elizabeth, Mary put too much importance on what their boorish cousin, Mr. Collins, thought. Just because he was to inherit the estate did not give him the right to occupy her thoughts nor those of her sisters, one of whom he was determined to marry. Elizabeth shivered in revulsion.

"Of what import is Mr. Collins to me?" asked Lydia, voicing Elizabeth's opinion. "With so many handsome officers about, I flatter myself that I may handpick a dashing husband of whom you will all turn green with jealousy," Lydia giggled, flashing her pretty dimples and looking down the row of tents.

"Will you encourage Mr. Wickham then? He is exceedingly handsome," said Kitty, watching Lydia intently.

Lydia lifted one shoulder up and at an angle, reaching up to twirl a tendril of hair near her collarbone. She need not have concerned herself with her provocative posture. There were no gentlemen about to admire her at that moment. "I would look well on his arm, would I not? We would be the most handsome couple in London, I should think."

Elizabeth scoffed. "And what makes you think that he could take you to London— or would even propose marriage to you when you have no dowry to recommend you?" Really, Lydia needed a healthy dose of reality. Gentlemen became officers when they did not have a fortune on which to live. When Mr. Wickham married, it would be to a lady with a fortune. Neither she nor her sisters had been blessed with such an allurement.

Kitty's eyes clouded over, and she sighed. "How romantic it would be to live on love."

"It would stop being romantic soon enough when your stomach growls with hunger and the landlord demands the rent," said Elizabeth.

Lydia huffed. "How dull you are, Lizzy. I suppose you would marry someone like Mr. Darcy then, with his fortune and grand estate. I suppose his wealth would tempter his frigid manners?"

Kitty jabbed Lydia in the ribs. "You are only put out because he did not dance with you at the Meryton Assembly."

With a frown, Lydia lashed out, "At least he did not dance with anyone at all, and he did not openly snub me as he did Lizzy."

Jane reprimanded her. "Lydia, you ought not speak of such things as brings one pain. Especially to your own sister."

"I am sorry, Lizzy," Lydia said with a pretty pout. "You do know that I love you. I can imagine how I would feel if a handsome gentleman of fortune were to insult my vanity. I declare that it would cut me so deeply, I might not ever recover."

Choosing to laugh rather than take Lydia's thoughtless words to heart, Elizabeth said, "Then it is a good thing he insulted me and not you. I have since decided not to allow anything Mr. Darcy might say or do to affect me in the least, and I am determined to refuse to dance with him should he ever condescend to ask me. Now, let us proceed to the shop as we set out to do or else we shall have no ribbons to braid through our hair for the ball tonight."

The mention of ribbons distracted Kitty and Lydia, who accelerated their pace and discussed which colors would best suit their complexions and match their gowns. Mary, who spent much time studying the virtue of self-sacrifice, accompanied them, no doubt believing it a penitence with which she would improve her standing before God. Only Jane held back, reaching her arm out for Elizabeth to take.

"I wish Lydia would learn some discernment. She does not mean any harm, but she could benefit from some discretion," Jane said.

"And she exercises a poor influence over Kitty. How I wish Father would find a way to check them. If he is unwilling to do so himself, he ought to see to a companion." Elizabeth's pleas over the years had fallen on disinterested ears.

Jane, understanding her frustration, nodded. "Father has always allowed us more freedom than most ladies. Since you and I turned out well enough, he hoped all of his daughters would follow suit. Now that he sees how his lack of interference has affected them, he considers it too late to do anything."

Elizabeth sighed. "And so he does nothing." She dearly loved her father, but he had never been one to take action when it was needed. He was of the mind that fate sorted things out anyway, so why bother?

Elizabeth did not believe in fate. "No, Jane, I fear the responsibility lies with us. We must see that our younger sisters are properly guided before they ruin our chances to make good matches. Mr. Bingley admires you greatly, but his sisters will be quick to bring up our family's shortcomings to discourage him."

Jane's eyes widened, and her cheeks flushed at the mention of Mr. Bingley. Her reaction confirmed what Elizabeth suspected. She would allow no one to interfere with her dear sister's happiness. Especially the senseless behavior of their sisters.

CHAPTER 2

"Mr. Denny!" shouted Lydia eagerly as they crossed the street, waving her hand back and forth. As if it were possible for him not to see them in the empty square.

"There is never occasion to shout, Lydia," observed Mary, determined to impose her upright views on her errant sister.

Lydia stuck her tongue out at Mary, then returned the sweet smile to her face before turning back to Lieutenant Denny.

He swept his hat through the air in a dramatic bow, resting it against the breast of his red regimental coat. "How delightful to see the Misses Bennet this morning."

"And we are equally delighted to see you, Mr. Denny," purred Lydia.

Elizabeth linked her arm through Lydia's and held her firmly to her side. Perhaps her closeness would calm her. Her efforts were thanked with a sharp jab of Lydia's elbow to her ribs. Elizabeth bit her tongue to keep from yelping, tightening her grip on Lydia's arm both to keep her in place and to prevent her from repeating the gesture.

"Are you coming to the ball tonight?" Kitty asked.

Mr. Denny smiled. "Indeed, I am. I do believe Mr. Bingley invited the entire regiment! It promises to be quite the crush."

"What of Mr. Wickham? Does he plan to attend?" asked Lydia, tugging her arm to free it from Elizabeth's vice-like grip.

Mr. Wickham was a happy addition to any party, and while Elizabeth harbored no amorous feelings for the gentleman, she did look forward to dancing with him. He would make for an increasingly diverting evening and an excellent dance partner.

Mr. Denny leaned forward, his eyes darting about. Cupping his hand around his mouth, he said, "I only inform you because I know our friendship with Mr. Wickham is mutual and, since you asked directly, I see no harm in telling you…." He paused, again looking around.

"Well? What is it?" voiced Lydia, stamping her foot like an impatient filly.

Elizabeth could not criticize her overmuch. Her skin prickled with anticipation and, if Mr. Denny paused any longer, she did not know if her curiosity could bear it.

"I will not insult your sensibilities by giving you details, but suffice it to say that if Mr. Wickham chooses not to join us at the Netherfield Ball, it will be the doing of a certain gentleman who is presently residing as a guest there." He dropped his hand and stood somberly.

Mr. Darcy. What a dreadful man. It seemed that the more Elizabeth knew of him, the less she could find to like about the gentleman.

"I am certain there is a reasonable explanation for their manners. If they were to discuss their problems openly, they would soon enough find a satisfactory solution," said Jane. She was too kind to imply bad motives to anyone.

Mr. Denny clucked his tongue and shook his head. "I am not so certain. Only minutes ago, I saw Mr. Darcy storm out of Wickham's tent in a high temper."

"We saw that too," Elizabeth acknowledged.

"He must feel wretched. A call from us would soon cheer him," whimpered Lydia, looking longingly toward the tent.

Before Lydia could arrange a party to visit poor, abused Mr. Wickham in his tent, she added, "We are on our way to the haberdashery to buy some ribbons."

"Then, by all means, let me escort you. I am in need of a new buckle and shall be the laughing stock of the regiment if it is not seen to before the entertainments of the evening," replied Mr. Denny, holding his arm out to Kitty, who gratefully accepted it.

Lydia glared at Elizabeth, who had yet to loosen her hold.

The inside of the shop was a menagerie of notions and fripperies. Drawn to a stack of magazines in the corner, Elizabeth left her sisters to look at the snuff boxes, hair clips, silver combs, and various adornments on the glassed shelf. Streams of ribbons hung from the ceiling in a long rainbow of color.

After a half of an hour, during which Lydia managed to spend everyone's pin money, as well as her own, they continued to Aunt Philips' home, leaving a contented Mr. Denny to return to the barracks with his newly acquired buckles.

Elizabeth noticed how Kitty's eyes followed his progress down the footpath until he disappeared from their sight.

"You like Mr. Denny?" asked Elizabeth quietly, falling into step beside her. He seemed like an amiable gentleman, and his friendship with Mr. Wickham could only serve to recommend him.

Kitty sighed. "He looks handsome in his uniform. Do you think he notices me? It is difficult with Lydia around. She always insists on being the center of attention." She spoke sincerely, without the bitterness of envy.

Wrapping her arm around Kitty's shoulders, Elizabeth said, "Let us first determine Mr. Denny's character better before you set your heart on him. Or is it already too late?" She hoped not. Having never fallen in love, she would not know how best to help Kitty.

Kitty's forehead rumpled in thought. "No, I do not think it is too late. I suppose you are right. I would never want to marry a gentleman who proved to be unkind— although I find it difficult to believe that a gentleman as handsome as Mr. Denny could ever behave in a manner unworthy of an officer."

Elizabeth shook her head, breathing deeply in her relief, and moved her arm to wrap it through Kitty's. "Looks can be deceiving." Mr. Darcy was perhaps the handsomest gentleman she had been privileged enough to gaze upon, and yet his manners did nothing to recommend him.

Kitty said, "Life would be much simpler if everyone acted according to their appearance. Unlike Mr. Darcy, for instance."

Elizabeth nearly tripped over her feet. She had not spoken aloud, had she? Fortunately for her, Kitty continued, "He is pleasing to the eye, but I could never admire a gentleman who has offended you." She squeezed Elizabeth's arm to her side in sisterly support.

"Maybe he will bald with age," Elizabeth replied, causing Kitty to cover her mouth and giggle.

Though she said the words, Elizabeth did not think them possible. Mr. Darcy's hair was as thick as it was curly. Nor would his teeth fall out. They were as straight and white as pearls strung on a necklace. Bothersome snob. Were he not so disagreeable, she could see herself admiring him a great deal.

Lost in her contemplations and determining to her chagrin— for it was the height of injustice that a man so beautiful and masculine should also be so unforgivably proud— that Mr. Darcy suffered no physical flaws observable to the eye, Elizabeth followed her sisters to Aunt Philips' where they were led into the drawing room directly. And just in time. There were better things to ponder than Mr. Darcy's features.

Aunt rose to greet them, with her hands reached out to embrace her nieces. "Oh, girls, how fortuitous you should visit me today! I have made a new friend I should very much like for you to meet."

A lady with light brown hair pulled away from her face joined Aunt. Her dress was the same unimposing mauve color as Aunt's carpet. She blended in with the room so well that if she stood still, Elizabeth doubted she would have noticed her. The lady's only adornment was a warm smile which reached her brown eyes as Aunt introduced them.

"Mrs. Yeats is looking for a position. Her charge married and there were no other children in the home. She is now, unfortunately, without employment." Aunt clucked her tongue and shook her head. "There is no loyalty anymore. The home she had known for these many years is denied her in spite of it being her efforts which arranged the daughter's successful match. It is shocking how some of these highborn families believe themselves above common decency."

"I am certain it sounds that way, Mrs. Philips, but I must assure you that I spent several wonderful years with the family, and I am pleased to know their daughter married very well. I only wish I could have been there for the wedding," said Mrs. Yeats in a soft voice, clasping her hands together uncomfortably.

"If the subject is disagreeable to Mrs. Yeats, perhaps we might change it," suggested Jane.

Mrs. Yeats smiled gratefully at her. "Thank you, Miss Bennet. I am certain your governess can look back on her influence on your delicacy with a good deal of pride."

Lydia scoffed. "Governess? We never had one."

Confused, Mrs. Yeats asked, "No governess? Then surely you have had a devoted nurse or companion to help guide you?"

All in the room kept silent except for Lydia, who blurted out, "Not at all. Father felt we did not need one when Jane and Lizzy turned out so well. And with the militia stationed in the village, I am sure to marry soon. I only have yet to choose who best suits me."

Mrs. Yeats did a masterful job of controlling her expression, though Elizabeth was certain she must have been shocked. As for Elizabeth, she wanted to groan, cry, and laugh all at the same time.

As she was about to change to a more pleasant— and much safer— topic, Mrs. Yeats said, "I will admit to my ignorance then. Your father must hold to more modern views of which I am unaware, having only lived in one household."

"You are very kind, Mrs. Yeats," said Elizabeth, pleased how the woman had glossed over her father's oversight in their education.

This was the kind of companion her sisters needed. One look at Jane told her that she agreed. "Aunt said you are currently seeking a position?" she asked, trying to sound more helpful than desperate.

"I am. I only arrived to Meryton two days ago, and I do not have any acquaintances outside your kind aunt and the innkeeper. My hope is to find a position with a family who spends most of their time in the country. I have no desire to return to town. I could not bear to see my young miss, and that is precisely what would happen were I to accept any of the other offers from amongst her circle."

It was perfect! If Elizabeth could convince Aunt Philips to help them, Aunt would persuade Mother of their need for assistance with her youngest daughters. Mother would not let up on the subject until she made Father so miserable he would agree to the scheme, or else risk suffering from another bout of Mother's nerves.

Looking between Aunt Philips and Mrs. Yeats, she said, "I am sorry it is a painful memory to you, but your ability to assist your previous charge make an advantageous marriage highly recommends you.

You did say she married very well, if I am not mistaken?" Elizabeth asked. Mothers of unmarried ladies would seek out a governess known to have had any part in a successful match, no matter how loyal they may be to the family for which she formerly worked.

Mrs. Yeats blushed and lowered her voice, "I should say so, though I cannot take all of the credit for it. While it was I who arranged for them to meet, it was the charming qualities my dear, young miss displayed which won over the earl."

That got Aunt's attention and exceeded Elizabeth's hopes for a favorable answer. "An earl? She married into a title? That is high praise indeed for one in your position. You should have no trouble at all securing a place."

Apparently, Elizabeth had not made her hint obvious enough.

A shadow passed over Mrs. Yeats' face. "It would be if only it could be known. I have not been allowed an audience with the family, and they have yet to answer my letters. I do not understand it." She dabbed at her eyes with a handkerchief. "I apologize. It is not proper for me to burden you with my troubles, nor just of me to speak anything but kind things toward my young miss. They really were very good to me."

Jane, in her tender voice said, "I am certain it is all one unfortunate misunderstanding."

Mrs. Yeats' eyes sparkled with unshed tears as she looked up at Jane. "Thank you, Miss Bennet. I take great comfort in that thought. It has occurred to me that in the chaos of the wedding, I was simply overlooked."

Aunt tapped her fingers against the cushion of her armchair. "Miss Stallard, our magistrate's daughter, is the only lady who comes to mind, but she has a companion. A young, widowed cousin left without twopence to her name… Hardly appropriate if rumors are to be believed…"

With her gaze fixed firmly on her aunt, Elizabeth said more pointedly, "That hardly helps Mrs. Yeats. She needs to begin life anew with a family who will treat her kindly. All we need to do is find a place with a family with an unmarried daughter. Or several…." Addressing Mrs. Yeats, she explained, "The difficulty you may encounter here would be to find a position with only one daughter. Unlike the Stallards, most of our families are quite large, and some have several daughters out."

Aunt Philips' expression underwent the most delightful change as she finally realized what Elizabeth had taken great pains to make obvious to her.

Mrs. Yeats said, "That would be no trouble to me. I would rather keep my mind occupied by staying busy."

Aunt clapped her hands. "I have had the most splendid idea! What if we could convince Mr. Bennet to take on Mrs. Yeats?"

Elizabeth tried not to look too excited. "Father has not agreed to any such arrangement before, I am sorry to say," she said to deepen Aunt's support.

Aunt Philips waved her hand in the air. "You leave it to me and your mother. Mark my words, Mrs. Yeats, you will soon have a place in a household with five unmarried daughters!"

Mrs. Yeats did not look in the least bit overwhelmed. "If what you say can truly come to pass, I would be eternally grateful."

"Good! We will leave for Longbourn immediately." Aunt called for her carriage, not wasting any time.

"Well done, Lizzy," whispered Jane as they clambered down the road. "I daresay this plan will work."

Elizabeth squeezed Jane's hand. "I do hope so for your sake, Jane. With Mrs. Yeats to check Lydia and provide what is proper for our sisters' education in society, an attachment with a respectable gentleman is much more likely to occur." She dare not presume to say that an attachment to Mr. Bingley was infinitely more possible, but Elizabeth could not prevent herself from thinking it. She would count how many times Mr. Bingley danced with Jane at the ball at Netherfield that evening.

As for herself, she would dance and enjoy herself in the knowledge that Jane's chances were vastly improved with Mr. Bingley. She would also take a stand for justice on behalf of the unfortunate and afflicted by refusing Mr. Darcy if he dared ask her to dance.

CHAPTER 3

The evening was all wrong. Why Elizabeth had believed that the simple act of hiring Mrs. Yeats would cause her mother and sisters to behave with more decorum had been a serious breach in her reasoning.

Father had sent their carriage to collect Mrs. Yeats' things from the inn, but by the time she had returned, she was fatigued and it was too late for her to ready herself to join them at the Netherfield Ball. More was the pity. Of course, Mrs. Yeats would need to settle in at Longbourn before she could give her full attention to their deficiencies — deficiencies which were painfully blatant that evening.

Mother bragged too openly of Jane's imminent engagement to Mr. Bingley. It did not perturb her at all when Elizabeth reminded her that the gentleman had yet to ask.

Mr. Collins, on hearing Mother's implication that Jane was soon to be engaged, had redirected his amorous attentions to Elizabeth. He followed her everywhere and made his presence a tiresome bother she could not shake. Like a burr on a wool stocking.

Mary, who did wish to receive the attentions of their clerical cousin, had determined to show off her self-taught musical accomplishments in the drawing room where the pianoforte sat. Elizabeth did not venture to enter that room so that she would be spared the cacophony her well-intentioned sister would produce from the instrument. Just the thought of the pounding keys made Elizabeth pinch the back of her neck.

Lydia and Kitty, contrary to her warnings that they behave as proper ladies ought to, flirted with the regimental officers in such a way as to cause the gossips to whisper behind their fans. To be fair, Kitty directed her attention entirely to Mr. Denny, and the couple seemed oblivious to anyone outside their enamored bubble. The attention Mr. Denny bestowed upon Kitty only made Lydia laugh louder and hold her pointy chin at the best angle to elongate her neck and draw attention to her shoulders.

Mr. Wickham had not made an appearance, and at that late hour, he was unlikely to do so. No doubt, as Mr. Denny had suggested, it had something to do with Mr. Darcy. The insolent man.

To make matters worse, Mr. Darcy had cast his sight in her direction several times during the night, and Elizabeth feared he would ask her to dance. While he would make a graceful partner, and she dearly loved to dance, what in heaven's creation would they find to discuss which would not lead to him discovering yet another fault in her or her family's character? She was not intimidated by him, but she would not make it easy for him to criticize her and those whom she held dear. Not if she could prevent it. Besides, she had decided she would not dance with him. It went against her sense of integrity to those whom he had oppressed.

So she had avoided him, feeling very much like a mouse pursued by a cat as the evening wore on.

Elizabeth's heartbeat pounded in her ears, and the pressure at the base of her neck grew unbearable. She smiled and nodded when addressed, but she felt as if she stood in the middle of a bee hive. She needed fresh air. However, it was late, and she did not want to separate Jane from Mr. Bingley merely to ask if she would accompany her out of doors in the cold night air.

Weaving her way through the crowd in the ballroom and out to the entry hall where a group of people had gathered, she saw Mr. Collins bump clumsily into Miss Stallard. The glass of ratafia she held emptied its burgundy liquid down the front of her cream silk gown, staining the ornate embroidery in its descent. A shriek being imminent, especially when Mr. Collins reached out to her bodice with a handkerchief in his hand, Elizabeth gritted her teeth and continued down the hall and past the stairs.

Wall sconces lit her way to the library. It was a room she had become familiar with during her brief stay nearly a fortnight before when a chill had overtaken Jane and she had had to accept the hospitality of the Bingleys. The music and the buzz of conversation quieted into a soft lull the closer she got to the doorway.

She held her breath as she tested the doorknob. Elizabeth would not put it past Miss Bingley to lock rooms in an effort to prevent the locals from stealing something of value. As if anyone in Meryton had the audacity to steal a book from a library which was, as yet, poorly stocked.

The door opened with a click, and Elizabeth stepped into the dark, quiet room. Leaning against the heavy wood with a large sigh, she rested her head against the smooth oak, its coolness soothing to the touch.

Moonlight poured through the window overlooking a fountain in the middle of the gardens and cast its relaxing glow through the center of the room. A welcoming couch in a dark corner beckoned to her, and she curled up on it, melting into the cushions and closing her eyes for a moment. The pounding in her head slowed to a soft drum. She would stay for just a few minutes. The tension slowly melted away from her body. It could not hurt to stay just a short while longer. That fleeting thought was the last she could remember as she drifted off…. Just a short while.

***

Darcy slipped down the hall, taking care to avoid drawing attention— especially that of Miss Bingley. He had felt her eyes on him the whole of the evening.

After hearing Wickham's basis for threats, he had been on his best behavior. He had listened to conversations he never would have made himself endure the day before, he had danced several times with various ladies— even participating in the pointless chatter expected of him between jumps and turns…. He had hoped to dance with Miss Elizabeth, but when it became apparent that she was purposely avoiding him, his good humor took a turn. His patience had reached its limits, and he could no longer pretend to be sociable when everything and everyone irked him.

With one final glance over his shoulder, he opened the door and looked around the dark library. Nobody was there to bother him. No presumptuous clergyman assuming a friendship for which he had no desire. No red militia uniforms to remind him of Wickham— the thorn in his side. No snide comments and condescending remarks to endure from Miss Bingley. No tactful cuts from Miss Elizabeth. Those smarted the worst, for he knew himself deserving of them.

He crossed the room, content to be alone with his thoughts for a while. Sinking into a tall, velvet upholstered chair facing the giant window overlooking the Netherfield grounds, he pondered his options. How could he protect Georgiana without giving in to Wickham's demands? Would he never be rid of the greedy leech?

Dreams of sending the knave off to the New World or to Australia cheered him. Now, that was not a bad idea.

Unable to keep still, Darcy rose from his chair and stood in front of the window. His library at Pemberley had glass doors which led out to a fragrant rose garden. In the summer months, he often kept the doors open to better enjoy the perfume of the blooms while indulging in a newly acquired novel or book of poetry. He could never do so in Bingley's library. While the room enjoyed a large window with a glorious view, it was positioned high off the ground to give more space to the kitchen and the other rooms below that the servants used during the day.

A rustle in the corner of the room startled Darcy from his thoughts. Squinting his eyes against the darkness, he saw a lump on top of the couch.

He drew closer, his steps hushed against the carpet. When he saw that it was a young lady, he started. He ought to leave the room. But something about the lady made him peer closer.

Her dark hair blended into her surroundings. However, the familiar curve of her lips and the mischievous arch of her brows— even in sleep— identified her. It was Miss Elizabeth Bennet. She had avoided him all evening, and now here she was. He would have enjoyed her conversation.

Leaning down, he appreciated how peaceful she looked in slumber with her eyelashes spread across her cheeks. She sighed and shifted her weight, freezing Darcy in place. He had already stayed too long. He must leave.

Slowly and deliberately, he shifted his weight to his toes so that he might depart without waking her. He took a step back and lost his balance when he stumbled on an object lying on the floor. Flailing his arms out to avoid toppling over, his hand caught against a vase or lamp or something inconveniently placed. It clattered to the floor in the one place not covered by a rug to soften its fall just as the clock struck. Darcy reached for the offending object which had caused his stumble and soon held one of Miss Elizabeth's slippers in his hands.

"Who is there?" asked Miss Elizabeth in a startled voice.

Darcy groaned. "I apologize, Miss Elizabeth. I was not aware anyone else was in the library. I shall depart."

He had closed the library door behind him. If anyone chanced upon them alone in the dark room, Miss Elizabeth's reputation would be compromised.

"What time is it?" she asked, looking around her frantically.

"The clock just struck midnight."

"Midnight? Oh bother, I must have fallen asleep. I must go."

She scrambled to her feet, her stocking toes searching for her slippers. Darcy reached down and placed the one he held before her.

The door widened and Bingley's housekeeper peeked in. "Is anyone in here?" she asked.

Miss Elizabeth moved forward. If they were seen…. Darcy clamped his hand over her mouth, pulling her against him and drawing them deeper into the shadows.

With a click, the housekeeper closed the door, locking it behind her. They were stuck.

CHAPTER 4

Elizabeth's immediate inclination was to bite Mr. Darcy's thick fingers, which she did with wholehearted enthusiasm.

As her teeth sank into his flesh, she heard him suck in air sharply. However, his solid arms did not loosen from around her. She would scream if only she could breathe.

"Hush!" he hissed, his breath tickling her ear and annoying her further.

She found herself stuck in Mr. Bingley's library with Mr. Darcy. Alone. Together.

The clattering of the housekeeper's keys stopped and after a few seconds, Mr. Darcy released his hold on her.

Taking a large step away, she spun around to face him. "Why did you prevent me from leaving? Now, we are locked in!" She ought to have stomped on his foot.

Taking off his glove and rubbing the finger she had bitten, he visibly regulated his breath. Only one angry tremor marred the control in his low baritone, "If Mrs. Harris saw you, she may very well have seen me too. Can you imagine the consequences to your reputation had she seen me attempting to hide from her in a dark library with you— an unmarried lady?"

His smooth voice and sound reasoning stood no chance before her ire. "And can you imagine the consequences when I am missed and it is discovered that both of us have gone missing from the ballroom?"

Mr. Darcy paced, reminding Elizabeth of a black panther she had seen at an exhibition once. "If we are caught here, you will be compromised, and I will have to make an offer for you."

"You would act honorably toward me when you have failed to do so for others?" she spat.

Running his uninjured hand through his perfect hair, he said, "I can only guess that you refer to Mr. Wickham. Let me assure you, Miss Bennet, that there is more to that tragic story than he would dare admit to you. He is not to be trusted."

"And I am to trust you?" She poured as much sarcasm as she could muster into her tone.

"Trust is earned, not seduced with charm."

She scoffed. "And what do you know of charm, sir? Perhaps you can enlighten me as I have yet to see its display in your behavior."

He closed the distance between them with one step. His dark eyes lit with a smoldering fire which made her skin tingle. She crossed her arms in front of her chest and lifted her chin before her thoughts muddled.

"Of what use is charm when it is used to disguise one's flaws?"

"Of which you have none, I suppose?"

"I have faults enough, but they are not, I hope, of understanding, nor so grave as those of Mr. Wickham."

"You believe yourself more honorable than he when you are the one locked in a dark room with an unmarried lady?" It was a low blow, but the irony of his claims and their present situation was too great to ignore.

"I will marry you if it comes to that." He sounded as thrilled about it as she did.

"And what makes you think I would accept your offer? Nay, Mr. Darcy, neither of us wants to be trapped in a loveless marriage. No more than we want to be trapped in this room. There must be a way out."

She pulled out a hairpin and scurried to the door.

"You must be quiet lest someone pass by," ordered Mr. Darcy.

Annoyed, she answered, "I suppose you have a better way?"

The doorknob rattled and Elizabeth jumped back, clamping her hand over her mouth to keep from exclaiming aloud. Jovial voices on the other side of the door conversed loudly.

Mr. Darcy tugged his hand through his hair, resting it on the back of his neck. "This is lovely," he mumbled.

Elizabeth remained by the door, hoping that the gaggle of people on the other side would leave.

"We must find another way out," said Mr. Darcy. He turned to the window, pulling the curtains aside.

"I could climb out of the window," she suggested, opening the glass and peeking out. Nobody was about.

"Absolutely not!"

Crossing her arms, she asked, "Why not? I am light and can easily fit through the opening."

"What if you fall?"

Must he object to her every idea? What an agitating man. "There is a nice ledge running around the house, and I am certain it will be no more difficult to jump down from it than from the branch of a tree."

Mr. Darcy looked shocked. "You have experience climbing trees?"

Squaring her shoulders, she said proudly, "I have had sufficient practice over the years." What did she care if he thought her a hoyden? His opinion meant little to her.

"Why does that not surprise me?" he smiled, disarming Elizabeth's witty retort. He had a nice smile. A beautiful smile. She nearly smiled back at him before she remembered she did not like him. Not in the least.

He continued, "I do not doubt your skills, Miss Elizabeth. I do, however, doubt you have attempted the feat in a gown and slippers. Were you to return to the assembly with your dress torn, it might prove difficult to provide a satisfying answer without compromising yourself further."

There was that. She dearly wanted to contradict him, but she could find no fault with his reasoning.

"What do you propose then, Mr. Darcy?" She looked him squarely in the face, determined he not see how greatly his smile had disturbed her.

"I will do it."

"But will you fit through the opening?" His superior height and wide shoulders would not allow it. Only the most agile of men could make such a climb without his size hindering him.

"I can squeeze through the side. Do you doubt my abilities?" he asked, his eyes full of... mischief? Mr. Darcy knew how to tease? He even appeared to look forward to the risky descent. Elizabeth did not know what to make of him, and it grew increasingly difficult for her not to smile.

"Who am I to doubt you, sir? The fact is that we need to leave this room before we are discovered, and our only other escape is blocked," she said, keeping her voice down. She still held the hair pin with which she had planned to pick the lock. Frustrated and confused, she shoved it back into place, jabbing her scalp.

Oh, how she wished she did not need Mr. Darcy's help. She could manage well enough on her own.

"I will enter the house again as if I had merely stepped out of doors for some fresh air, and I will ask where you might be so that I may request a dance."

So much for refusing to dance with him. She really had no choice now. "Ask Jane. She will know to look for me here."

"It is the first place I would have thought to search." He looked at her as if he expected her to say something, but his understanding of her only made her wonder why he would remember that unimportant detail. During her stay at Netherfield Park to care for Jane, he had given no indication he had noticed her at all.

Accepting her silence, for which she was grateful, he bowed. "Very good. Now I must be on my way." Like a cat, he hopped up and through the window, his coat slipping across the frame as he squeezed through in one smooth motion. "Please be so kind as to close the window," he said as he inched across the ledge and leapt down to the ground with ease.

Elizabeth reached out to the glass, letting the cold breeze cool the spark of admiration and flame of curiosity. Tugging at the curtain, she paused. Was that a shadow behind the fountain?

***

Grateful that his years of climbing rocks and trees with his Fitzwilliam cousins had not failed him, Darcy stood up from the crouch he had gracefully landed in and looked up at the window where she still stood. He had hoped to see a smile. Instead, her widened eyes looked toward the fountain in the garden.

His pulse raced as he followed her gaze. He saw nothing. Nor would it be wise to risk discovery by investigating the shadows of the fountain for witnesses of his exit through the window. Looking back up at Miss Elizabeth, he saw her shook her head at him and heard her close the glass.

Deeply relieved, he swallowed hard. Marriage to Miss Elizabeth would be an uphill battle. She seemed determined to mistake his character, and while he trusted her, he could not yet share with her the truth which would surely clear her vision. Not until he was certain she would protect Georgiana's reputation as vigilantly as he did.

He walked around the side of the house, pausing at an illuminated window to assess any damage done to his ensemble. Smoothing his cravat and puffing out the creases, he strolled into the house.

Miss Bingley was the first person he saw on crossing the threshold.

"Mr. Darcy, there you are. I had wondered where you had gone to. You simply must keep me and Louisa company or we shall perish from boredom. There is no worthwhile conversation to be had in this crowd," she complained in her stuffy voice.

He would much rather escape outside again than endure their insipid conversation. "I would very much like to dance."

Perhaps it was evil of him to ignore her pleased reaction, but he needed to get to Miss Bennet so he might inquire after Miss Elizabeth, and thus fulfill his obligation in the ruse. And so he asked, "You have not seen Miss Elizabeth, have you? I have not yet asked her to dance with me this evening, and do not wish to be remiss to Bingley's guests."

Miss Bingley's nostrils flared and her skin mottled. "No, I cannot say that I have."

"I shall ask Miss Bennet," he said, as the same lady had the good grace to appear in the archway of the ballroom leading out in to the entrance hall at precisely that moment. Bingley followed her, clearly smitten with the fair beauty.

"Pray excuse me," Darcy mumbled to Miss Bingley, leaving her to her own miserable company.

"Miss Bennet," he bowed. "I have not yet had the pleasure of dancing with Miss Elizabeth. Do you know where she is?"

He heard Miss Bingley huff behind him and, out of the corner of his eye, he saw her storm away. Better to risk her anger than to encourage her curiosity. Darcy had another secret to keep.

CHAPTER 5

Elizabeth leaned against the wall, contemplating whether it would be better for her to return to the couch or stay where she was. Mr. Darcy seemed to be in no hurry to return. She knew it was her own impatience making the time crawl, but it felt better to cast the blame on him.

Had she truly been alone in the room, what would she have done to escape? She grumbled to herself for not thinking of it sooner. She did not need Mr. Darcy's help at all. She would spare herself an unwanted dance with Mr. Darcy and free herself from the dark library before he bothered to inquire after her.

Pounding on the door, she shouted through the keyhole, "Is anyone there who can help me? The door is locked, and I am trapped!"

The chatter on the other side of the door quieted as she banged against it again, louder this time.

"I say, is there someone in there?" asked a masculine voice. It was most likely an officer. He and his friends would have a good laugh over her predicament.

"Yes, I am locked in the library," she shouted, hoping they could hear her through the sturdy oak.

"I will inform Mr. Bingley directly," said an authoritative voice. Elizabeth could imagine him clicking his heels before marching to find Mr. Bingley.

Not five minutes later, Elizabeth heard a ring of keys jingling and the glorious sound of the lock turning.

The housekeeper apologized immediately. "Miss, I must beg your pardon. I did not know you were here."

An inquisitive officer with a roguish grin peeked into the room. "Is anyone else trapped in here with you?"

Mr. Darcy had been correct in his assumption. She was grateful to honestly say, "It is only me. I had a headache and fell asleep on the couch. It is no wonder you did not see me," she added to reassure the housekeeper.

Mr. Bingley, with Jane and Mr. Darcy by his side, was beside himself. "I do apologize, Miss Elizabeth. I hope you were not frightened. May I offer you a refreshment?"

She smiled at his kindness. "Thank you, Mr. Bingley, but it was my own doing." She laughed.

"This will be nothing but a silly story to relate to my sisters over the breakfast table."

Jane moved to stand beside her. "When Mr. Darcy inquired where you were, I knew that if you were not in the ballroom or drawing room, then surely you would be in the library."

"How fortunate for me to have such predictable tastes and habits," Elizabeth said in good humor. The officers had their laugh, as she had suspected they would. She did not care. The final laugh was hers. She and Mr. Darcy, by all appearances, had successfully avoided a compromise.

She sensed his gaze on her, making her skin burn, but she knew herself too well to allow herself to return his look. Her expression would tell on her somehow, and they were so close to a clean escape from what would have been a disastrous match.

Mr. Bingley added, "Although, we would have found you soon enough. Just as Mr. Darcy asked about you, an officer informed me that a young lady was trapped in the library. I sent for the housekeeper directly."

Miss Bingley sauntered up to their group just as they neared the ballroom. "What has happened? Did I miss the only diversion to take place since our arrival here?" she asked.

"The housekeeper locked Miss Elizabeth in the library by accident. We have only now freed her. You do not know why the door was locked, do you, Caroline? I remember leaving it open," said Mr. Bingley.

All eyes turned to Miss Bingley as she hesitated to answer. "Well, I...," she began. With a haughty toss of the head, she continued more confidently, "I cannot say for sure. How unfortunate."

Elizabeth bit her lips together to keep from laughing. So, she had been right about Miss Bingley. If she only knew what her interference had nearly caused...

Mr. Darcy bit his lips as well. Was he thinking the same thing? Unable to repress the smile in his eyes, it struck Elizabeth that he might be in possession of a sense of humor after all. It suited him. People would think more kindly toward him if he smiled more often.

He bowed to her and held out his arm. "Miss Elizabeth, may I have the honor of your next dance?" he asked jovially.

At that moment, it did not occur to her to refuse.

***

"I apologize for taking so long," he said.

"I hardly expected you to ask me to dance this evening, Mr. Darcy. We have successfully avoided the activity until now," she answered dryly.

"You know what I mean."

Lowering her voice, she said, "Yes, I do, and I thank you to speak no more of it. Unless you do not fear discovery?"

He could read the anxiety in her eyes as plainly as if she spoke the words aloud. If their compromise were found out, they would have little choice but to marry. Why was the idea of a union with him so repulsive to her? Even worse, why could he not shrug her poor opinion of him off as he did with everyone else in society?

It pained him to know the relief he would see in her widened, dark brown eyes. "I think you are safe, Miss Elizabeth. Only Miss Bingley noted my reentry into the house." He wished he could have looked away, but he saw it nonetheless. The profound relief.

"Then we are safe. She would be the last person in the world to reveal her suspicion if, indeed, she puts all of the pieces together."

Darcy doubted Miss Bingley capable of such strenuous mental exercise.

He winced when their gloved hands touched. Miss Elizabeth's bite had been as sharp as her mind always was.

"Are you quite well?" She narrowed her eyes, her eyebrows furrowing in concern.

"I am, thank you."

"I do not believe you, sir," she said softly.

"Do your sympathies always extend to the injured?" Maybe she would like him better were he to adopt a limp.

"Someone ought to champion their cause. Too often, the defenseless suffer meaninglessly at the hand of the powerful. It is an injustice I despise." Her eyes sparked, and her voice trembled with the depth of her feeling.

"We are not so different then," he said under his breath. She would not understand him, but he so badly wanted her to.

He saw the curiosity spread over her expressive face. He also saw her chew on her upper lip before her jaw opened completely. "Oh! It is my fault. How could I have forgotten so quickly?"

Giving a quick look about them to see if anyone could overhear, he said softly, "That you bit me?"

She nodded her head, bowing it lower than she needed to. "I am sorry."

"Miss Elizabeth," he said her name to gain her full attention. "It was nothing more than an instinctive reaction, and one of which you should feel no shame. If anyone were to attempt something so foolish as to assault you, I have every confidence you would soon free yourself."

"But you did not let go."

If only he could tell her how it had taken every ounce of strength in his possession to hold her as he did, she would take more confidence in her tactics. Though her teeth sunk through his glove and bruised his fingers, he had been proud of her. Only the greater fear of compromising a lady whom he had begun to admire— a lady whose favorable opinion he was determined to win— had prevented her from shouting aloud and revealing their compromise. He could not do that to her. Not even when she fit so perfectly in his arms…

Clearing his throat, he said, "You would have lost your freedom to choose. What is a bruised finger in comparison?"

He could not read her expression. It was not one he had seen before.

She took care not to jostle his hand as the dance continued, and her care warmed Darcy's heart. It carried him through the next few hours of tortuous socializing until Bingley's ball came to an end.

***

Mother insisted they be the last guests to leave. However, when the sun dawned a new day and the other guests had gone, she could no longer postpone their departure.

Their wraps procured and their carriage ready to convey them home, Elizabeth paused in the entry hall while Mother dawdled. Through the open door, she saw three riders approaching at a rapid clip.

It was difficult to mistake Mr. Stallard, with his prancing blood horse and gleaming beaver hat. Joining him was Colonel Forster, also easily identifiable with his decorated scarlet regimental coat. The other rider was the village constable and innkeeper, Mr. Tanner, who sat atop a black horse as large as he.

Father greeted the gentlemen as they stood on the threshold. "You have arrived late for the festivities, but I daresay there is still some punch to be had."

Mr. Tanner said in his rough baritone, "I was not invited." He seemed pleased to cause discomfort and offered no further explanation.

Mr. Bingley joined them. "An oversight I shall not repeat again, sir."

"I am accustomed to being overlooked, Mr. Bingley. It is my lot," Mr. Tanner said bitterly, looking to the gentlemen accompanying him to speak.

Colonel Forster cleared his throat. "Ah, yes, we have come here to inquire if we might have a word with Mr. Darcy. Privately."

On hearing his name, Mr. Darcy stepped forward.

Again clearing his throat, Colonel Forster said, "You see, sir, we require your assistance in a matter of grave importance and extreme delicacy." He looked at the crowded threshold.

Elizabeth, taking his hint, encouraged her sisters to continue down the stairs.

Mr. Tanner, impatient, added, "Can you account for your whereabouts last night, Mr. Darcy?"

Mr. Stallard shot him a disapproving glare. "Calm yourself, Mr. Tanner. No accusations will be made until we gather more information, and I thank you to allow your superiors to ask the questions."

Mr. Darcy's brow furled, his eyes darting between the two men. Addressing Mr. Stallard, he said, "I was here all evening."

"As I suspected, Mr. Darcy. Now all we need is for someone to serve as a witness you were here at the hour of midnight. I trust that we will have no difficulties doing so," Mr. Stallard added with a smile of relief and an assured look at Mr. Tanner.

Elizabeth held her breath, her foot pausing over the last step. She knew exactly where Mr. Darcy was at the hour of midnight. He shot her a look so fierce, she clamped her lips shut.

Mr. Collins stepped forward eagerly. "As the rector of Mr. Darcy's beloved aunt, Lady Catherine de Bourgh, I can vouch for his superior character."

"Can you vouch for his presence?" retorted Mr. Tanner.

Mr. Collins' stature shrunk before the intimidating presence of Mr. Tanner, but to his credit, he did not back down. "If it pleases Mr. Darcy, I would be honored to stay behind to offer my full support and insight."

Colonel Forster, motioning to the rest of their group, said, "Perhaps we should allow Mr. Bingley to see to his guests before we continue with our questionings. This is a sordid affair and not fit for the ears of the ladies."

Elizabeth's skin prickled. Sordid affair? What had happened? Why had they come to question Mr. Darcy? She looked at him again, but he offered his arm to her and handed her into the waiting carriage in silence. Nor did he give an answer to Mr. Collins, who remained behind, content to be of service to

Lady Catherine's relation whether he was given leave to do so or not.

Mr. Tanner did not hold by such delicacy of manners. He called out loudly enough for her to hear, "Take care to watch over your household, Mr. Bennet. There is a murderer among us." He looked pointedly at Mr. Darcy.

Elizabeth felt Mr. Darcy's hand tense before he let go of her and saw her own astonishment reflected in his expression before the coach pulled away.

CHAPTER 6

Darcy watched the Bennet's carriage roll down Bingley's drive.

"Bingley, may we use your study?" he asked, his voice sounding strange and distant in his own ears.

Bingley nodded his head enthusiastically. "Of course. This does not seem to be the sort of conversation to be overheard by the ladies or the servants."

"As you please, sirs, but I would wager that most of Meryton believes Mr. Darcy guilty," said Mr. Tanner with a smirk.

Darcy tried to remember Mr. Tanner. He did not have the rough features of a commonplace man. His straight nose and high cheekbones looked more aristocratic. To Darcy's knowledge, he had done nothing to deserve such Mr. Tanner's derision. He had not conversed with the man. If only his manners matched his appearance.

Leaving the Hursts and Miss Bingley to do what they would, the men sat in a circle around the fireplace in Bingley's study— all except Mr. Collins, who hovered in the center of the group.

"Will you not take a seat, Mr. Collins?" suggested Bingley.

The clergyman bowed. "I thank you, sir. Your offer is most affable, but I feel that it is my duty to observe every detail and would be hard pressed to do so from a seated position."

Mr. Tanner said, "Take care not to stand too close to the fire lest you scorch your breeches."

Clearing his throat, Colonel Forster said, "We have come here this morning merely in a search for information. No accusations are being made." He looked pointedly at Mr. Tanner, who crossed his thick arms and sat back with a scowl.

Colonel Forster continued, "A soldier under my charge, Lieutenant George Wickham, was found murdered in the barracks."

Darcy froze. While a weight lifted off him, his stomach clenched at the loss. This was not the manner in which he wished to be free of Wickham. "George Wickham?" he asked, to be certain.

Mr. Tanner's stare bored into him. "Yes. One of the soldiers on duty heard a shot fire at midnight. He performed a search in the area from which the shot sounded and found Lieutenant Wickham dead— shot in the chest."

"Was nobody else around? Not all of the officers were here last night. For a certainty, someone must have seen something significant," suggested Bingley.

Colonel Forster shook his head grimly. "The lads who were not here with us were equally occupied at the tavern. Most did not even hear the shot."

Mr. Stallard added, "Too many of them were in their cups to offer any assistance at all. One detail worthy of mention is that upon searching through his officers' kit, we did not see his pistol. We are left to assume Mr. Wickham was shot with his own weapon."

Colonel Forster shifted in his seat. "It is our understanding, Mr. Darcy, you had an altercation with Mr. Wickham in his tent yesterday. Do you remember seeing his pistol?"

"Yes. He was polishing it. Who witnessed our disagreement?"

Shoving his head down so his double chin pressed against his chest, Colonel Forster said, "Mr. Denny, who is— er, was— a close friend of the deceased, saw you enter the tent."

Darcy's pulse drummed in his ears. "Did he tell you what he heard?" He had been careful to keep his voice down, but Wickham had not.

"He did not. Mr. Denny only mentioned hearing Mr. Wickham's voice raised and seeing you depart in an agitated manner for the stables."

"Is that why you killed him? Over a quarrel?" accused Mr. Tanner openly.

Mr. Collins tripped over his feet as he turned too rapidly to face the constable, nearly landing in the man's lap. "My good sir," he said, righting himself, "it is preposterous you should come here to question Mr. Darcy when it is apparent that this is the first he has heard of the unfortunate incident. As a member of a highly esteemed family, I would think him above suspicion."

"You do, do you?" boomed Mr. Tanner. "You assume that Mr. Darcy is incapable of committing a crime merely because he has been fortunate enough to be born into a wealthy family in the first circles? You must not read the paper, Mr. Collins, or you would know that those in the highest positions of society are the very ones who commit the most heinous acts."

Puffing up like an agitated rooster, Mr. Collins replied, "Let me assure you that as one charged with maintaining the delicate balance of moral purity in my parish, as entrusted to me by none other than Lady Catherine de Bourgh, I am well aware of the current events which might tarnish their minds. It is my duty to know of such evils so that I may protect my parishioners from their influence. However, I fail to see how you have the audacity to come here and accuse Mr. Darcy of a sinful act he could not possibly have committed."

Though grateful for Mr. Collins' blind faith in his innocence, his arguments stood on fickle ground.

"Can you personally account for Mr. Darcy's whereabouts at the hour of midnight? Can you swear on it before God?" asked Mr. Tanner. "Can you, Mr. Bingley?"

"Of course, he was here all evening," offered Bingley. "He danced with several ladies during the evening. However, you will be hard pressed to get anyone to say with absolute certainty that they observed any one person at a particular time at a crowded ball."

Mr. Stallard sighed loudly, "I agree that we ask what is impossible, Mr. Bingley, but it is the only way we can clear Mr. Darcy of suspicion. It is believed throughout Meryton that Mr. Wickham suffered a grave injustice at his hand," he paused, holding his hands up. "Whether it be true or not is beside the point. We only seek the truth where it bears insight on the murder of Mr. Wickham. I see no merit in it, but the villagers hold strong prejudices against you, Mr. Darcy, and we would do well to clear your name of any blame before the inquest. There are some among us who would not hesitate to send a gentleman of the first circles to the gallows."

Some, like Mr. Tanner.

Darcy held his breath. Only one person knew where he was at that hour.

"I did not kill George Wickham. On my word as a gentleman—"

"A gentleman?" Mr. Tanner scoffed. "Are we to accept your word merely because it is you who gives it? I think not, Mr. Darcy. The fact is, you are our primary suspect. We know all about your confrontation with Mr. Wickham the very morning of the ball. Several villagers watched you storm out of the barracks and many of them have agreed that you appeared infuriated enough to act in a passion."

"We had a disagreement. That much is true." He forced himself to breathe slowly, though his blood pounded in his head.

"What was the disagreement?" asked Mr. Tanner.

"I am not at liberty to discuss the matter, but Mr. Wickham was alive when I left him," Darcy said, leveling his glare at Mr. Tanner and holding it in a battle of wills which the constable seemed determined to win.

"Gentlemen, as of yet there are no accusations being made. Might I remind you, Mr. Tanner, that as the magistrate, I am in charge of this investigation with the collaboration of Colonel Forster as the commanding officer of this regiment? You are to assist me in your role of village constable, but I will conduct matters as I see fit. You answer to me."

Thank God the magistrate had some sense.

After a grudging nod from Mr. Tanner, Mr. Stallard continued, "Now, Mr. Darcy, do you have anything to say about your whereabouts at midnight? Are there any witnesses who might vouch for your presence here, at Netherfield Park, within fifteen minutes of that hour?"

Darcy would not lie, nor induce his friends to lie. Nor would he involve Miss Elizabeth in the infuriating mess either. "I did not leave Netherfield Park. You may question whom you please."

"I am relieved to hear you say that, Mr. Darcy." Colonel Forster turned his attention to Mr. Bingley. "Do you have anything to add?"

Bingley's ears turned bright red, but to his credit, his complexion remained cool. "I saw Darcy throughout the evening, but I cannot say precisely where he was at midnight. I am certain that he was here just as I am certain that you will find someone to confirm it." He looked apologetically at Darcy, but what else could he have said? Nobody save Miss Elizabeth knew where he was. And why should they? Who watched the clock so closely at a ball?

"Very good, Mr. Bingley. Now, may I ask if we might question the females in your household— with your presence, of course? Or would you prefer that we return at a later time?" asked Mr. Stallard.

"We had best have it done now. If anybody noticed Darcy's whereabouts, it would be my sister," said Bingley with a confident smile.

Darcy tried to look as pleased as his friend felt. Miss Bingley had noticed him enter the house after being out of doors. Her testimony may prove more detrimental than helpful.

They stood, everyone excepting Darcy and Mr. Tanner in high humor.

As they neared the door, Mr. Tanner said, "Might I suggest, Mr. Darcy, that you not attempt to travel beyond Meryton? It would be particularly unwise for you to depart until we have brought the murderer to justice. And trust me, sir, I will see the guilty party hang."

"As will I," Darcy growled back. He had bigger concerns than the threats of Mr. Tanner. He had to discover who murdered Wickham or else take the fall.

***

Elizabeth paced around the drawing room at Longbourn. She could not sleep as her sisters did, nor could she sit quietly enough to suit her father. Banned from the study and unwilling to wake Jane in their bedchamber, Elizabeth paced around the drawing room.

Had her thoughts not taken such a serious turn, she would have laughed at the irony of her anxiously awaiting the return of Mr. Collins. Of course, it was not the man himself she wished to see, but rather the information he possessed. She could only hope that his presumptuous over-importance would allow him to share what he had overheard.

The soft crunch of gravel in their drive alerted her to the arrival of a carriage. It was Mr. Bingley's. How good of the gentleman to lend the use of his carriage to Mr. Collins. He would make a kind husband to Jane… if he had not been offended by her family's outrageous behavior of the evening before. Elizabeth shivered at the recollection. Mr. Darcy had heard it too. He had looked on in acute disgust. And yet… he had asked her for a dance, and he had been amiable.

Hastening to the couch, Elizabeth grabbed the needlework near her and pretended to occupy herself with it. The door opened, and Mr. Collins entered the hall. He saw her.

"Cousin Elizabeth, might I inquire if Mr. Bennet is awake?"

"He is in his study. Might I inquire why?"

"There is a matter of grave importance which I wish to discuss with him. No time must be wasted." He marched down the hall and knocked on Father's door, leaving Elizabeth aching with anxiety.

Falling in behind him, she thought to gain entrance into the room. Indeed, when Father answered the door, he opened it wide enough she felt her presence welcome. However, Mr. Collins was not of the same mind.

"Cousin Elizabeth, what I have to discuss with Mr. Bennet is of a delicate nature and will be best seen to between gentlemen. I would be remiss to burden you with information which hardly pertains to a gentleman's daughter."

Balking at the idea that a gentleman could attend to a 'delicate' matter better than a lady, she opened her mouth to protest.

"Lizzy, dear, perhaps you had best go upstairs for the time being. You must be tired." Father arched his eyebrow and winked at her.

Her insult ran harmlessly through her mind, forgoing her tongue. She would do exactly what her father suggested she do. Elizabeth knew very well what his wink had meant, and she was glad to have received his permission to eavesdrop.

Going up the stairs, she sat three steps down from the top and settled in to listen by the hole between the bookshelf and the stairwell.

She slouched down, bringing her ear as close as she could without causing the wood step to squeak.

"Mr. Bennet, you are aware of my purpose in visiting you and my fair cousins," began Mr. Collins.

"Yes, you made your intentions clear in your letter. You wish to marry one of my daughters."

"It is the wish of my patroness, Lady Catherine de Bourgh, that I marry, and I felt it my duty to choose first among your daughters, since they stand to benefit the most from such an advantageous alliance."

"That was generous of you." Elizabeth could hear Father rolling his eyes.

"Yes, I think so. And it was gracious of Lady Catherine to agree to my plan. However, I fear that with the occurrence of recent startling events, my initial purpose must be postponed. You see, the nephew of my esteemed patroness is under suspicion of murder."

Now that had gotten Father's attention. As it had hers. Elizabeth stopped breathing so as to hear better.

"What? Of whom?"

"None other than Mr. Wickham."

Elizabeth went numb. Poor Mr. Wickham. Who could have done such a thing? Mr. Wickham was the most charming, interesting, affable man in the militia. Everyone thought so. Everyone except Mr. Darcy.

Oh no! Mr. Darcy. Had Elizabeth not known him for a fact to be innocent, she would have believed him capable of murder after witnessing his stormy departure from Mr. Wickham's tent the day before. How many villagers had seen him too?

Mr. Collins continued, interrupting her disbelief that one so vibrant and young should now be dead, and her dread that the wrong person was a prime suspect. "Yes, it is a serious affair. It is known that Mr. Darcy quarreled with Mr. Wickham the very day of his death and, apparently, it is known throughout Meryton that they have been longtime enemies."

So everyone knew how Mr. Darcy had wronged Mr. Wickham? While it had not struck Elizabeth as being improper when Mr. Wickham had revealed his tale of woe to her in confidence, it seemed wrong that so many people should be aware of it.

Mr. Collins continued, "As you know, I stayed behind to offer my counsel when Mr. Stallard, Colonel Forster, and the constable arrived at Netherfield Park. Two of the gentlemen were sensible and agreed with me that a gentleman such as Mr. Darcy, a man descending from a grand family, could not possibly have committed such a mortal sin against his fellowman. However, the constable's manners filled me with unease, and I feel it my duty to get to the bottom of this affair before unjust accusations are made against a family undeserving of reproach."

The constable? What could Mr. Tanner have against Mr. Darcy— other than his position in society? Elizabeth knew Mr. Tanner's feelings on the subject, but she had never known his prejudice to blind him. If he was the one to accuse Mr. Darcy, on what did he base his suspicion? Elizabeth bit her lips to prevent herself from shouting what she wished her father would ask.

"I see."

"I am relieved you do. My affection and future happiness must take a secondary place to the reputation and good standing of the relatives of Lady Catherine. I feel certain she would advise me to act in the manner in which I have done, were she here to bestow upon us her wisdom and counsel. I would write to her immediately of the situation, but Mr. Darcy instructed me not to reveal anything to her until he gives me leave."

"A sensible recommendation, by all means. There is no reason to cause alarm just yet, I should think. Now, perhaps you can tell me, Mr. Collins, on what grounds Mr. Tanner's suspicions lie?"

Thank you, Papa!

Mr. Collins clucked his tongue and sighed. "He has no grounds at all. Unless he can find someone to profess that at the hour of midnight, Mr. Darcy was not present at the Netherfield Ball, he has no proof whatsoever. As I mentioned to Mr. Stallard and Colonel Forster, what individual would pay heed to the clock during a ball so as to notice the hour?"

So Mr. Darcy would rather allow himself to be accused of a murder he could not have committed rather than admit to a compromise with her... Elizabeth felt both relieved and insulted.

"I assure you, Mr. Collins, some of us paid very close attention to the clock. It was as good company as could be found at the ball and cheered me greatly with each marking of the hour counting down until such a time as I could depart."

Elizabeth clamped her hand over her mouth. Did Father know of her compromise? No, surely he could not.... Could he?

Father, unable to take her hint to remain silent, continued, "And I can name one other individual who was aware of Mr. Darcy's every move the entire evening."

Elizabeth strained her ears, wishing the hole allowed her to see as well as hear.

"Miss Elizabeth?" a feminine voice from the top of the stairs startled her, causing her to sit upright with a yelp.

Spinning up to her feet, Elizabeth turned to face Mrs. Yeats, who looked at her curiously.

"Are you well?" Mrs. Yeats asked.

"I... yes, I am well." What explanation could she possibly give that would not reveal her impropriety in eavesdropping?

"You appear to have fallen asleep on the stairs. Might I suggest that some moments' rest in your bed is infinitely more refreshing?"

"You are quite right," Elizabeth agreed before Mrs. Yeats could question her further.

Making her way down the hall to her bedchamber, she closed the door behind her with a sigh. Mrs. Yeats was a welcome addition to their family, but she had horribly poor timing.

Elizabeth could not imagine how she was to sleep after what she had heard.

CHAPTER 7

Elizabeth flung the covers off her and groaned. The sun setting outside of her window and the descending darkness in her room increased her frustration. She had not meant to fall asleep. It was becoming a disturbing habit and, lately, the ramifications had been dire.

Breezing down the stairs, she went in search of Father. She had not heard his entire conversation with Mr. Collins, but she had heard enough to increase her anxiety.

His study was empty. So was the drawing room. It was not until her third attempt she found him in the dining room. Father sat at the head of the table with a cup of steaming tea in his hand. He looked blankly out of the window, no doubt enjoying his brief moments of peace before the rest of the family joined him.

"Father?" Elizabeth asked so as not to startle him.

He motioned for her to sit next to him. "You did not sleep long. I daresay your mother and sisters are still partaking of their beauty rest."

"And well they should. I, too, would have slept longer had it not been for some thoughts troubling my mind."

Sliding his spectacles down his nose, Father looked over them at her. "Troubling thoughts? Has it anything to do with what you overheard in the study?" He grinned impishly.

She laughed. "One of these days, you will repair the hole, and then what will I do?"

"I have no secrets from my daughters—especially the sensible ones." He reached over to pat her hand. Did he know of her secret?

Before she could find a way to ask without revealing what she wished to keep hidden, he continued, "What do you think of Mr. Collins' news to— how did he put it?— set aside his happiness and matrimonial bliss in the greater interest of his esteemed patroness, Lady Catherine de Bourgh?"

Elizabeth knew it was a little wicked to smile so completely, but she was too happy not to. "That was the best of news, and my relief on hearing it was immeasurable."

Father chuckled. "I noticed how quickly he directed his attentions to you when Mrs. Bennet implied that Jane was soon to be engaged. At least, now, you will be spared from having to refuse him. It would appear that, unpleasant as he is, Mr. Darcy has saved you from an unwanted match. How fortune he is the nephew to such a highly esteemed lady as Lady Catherine de Bourgh."

Elizabeth laughed at his pompous tone. Indeed, Mr. Darcy had come to her aid. What would Father think if he knew the truth? Would he understand? Did he already know?

"Would you have understood my reasons for refusing him?" Elizabeth asked, her merriness cooling. She did not like keeping secrets— especially from Father. But to admit her refusal extended to Mr. Darcy as well as Mr. Collins would be to admit her compromise. An offer of marriage, even a forced one, was no small matter in a household with five unmarried daughters with meager dowries and no prospects.

Glancing toward the door, Father lowered his voice. "Mr. Collins is as big a fool as his father before him. I could not spend more than five minutes in that man's presence before wishing to be at a tea party with your mother and Aunt Philips— where my ears would bleed from their excessive gossip and nonsense." He chased his shiver with a chuckle before dropping his voice and speaking seriously again. "It is one of my greatest sorrows that his offspring should inherit Longbourn."

A lamp lit in Elizabeth's mind. "Is that why you have not bothered to make repairs or improve the estate since Lydia was born?"

Father blushed like a scolded child. "You have learned my great secret! You are a clever one. I may have to pass my estate on to Mr. Collins, but I will not hand it to him in pristine condition."

"But Father, what if one of us does marry him? I do not think that a match with Mary is too far-fetched."

Father shrugged. "If that happens, then I suppose I would make more of an effort. To tell you the truth, my dear Lizzy, I have so long neglected our property, it has become quite a habit. It will be difficult to break."

"It all comes down to revenge then. You despised Mr. Collins' father, and so you have been doing everything possible to make his son's inheritance difficult."

"Never underestimate the power of revenge," he said in mock gravity. "It makes men act in ways they would not otherwise act."

Like the accusations against Mr. Darcy. Once again, it struck Elizabeth that had she not been with him during the professed time of the crime, even she would have held doubts against him. That he resented Mr. Wickham was obvious to anyone who had seen the two gentlemen near each other.

"That is what has been worrying my mind. I do so wish you would not get involved in this business with Mr. Wickham's murder."

Father's eyebrows bunched up. "Why not? Would you withhold evidence from an investigation which could allow a murderer his liberty?"

"No! Never! My sense of justice would not allow it. However, I cannot help but feel that your testimony would only make Mr. Darcy look guiltier than he already does."

The chair creaked as Father sat back and crossed his arms. "You do not believe that a man like Mr. Darcy is capable of murder?"

"That is not what I mean. A man of fortune and high society is capable of anything. I do, however, have my doubts about the suspicions against Mr. Darcy. I do not believe him guilty."

"On what grounds? Unless you can say with certainty where he was at midnight, you have no reason to doubt the claim against him." He peered over his spectacles at her, inviting her to confide in him.

"It is only… I do not think that Mr. Darcy is the sort of gentleman to resort to such drastic measures."

"Why? Because he is a gentleman? You surprise me, Lizzy. Any man, given sufficient motive, is capable of the worst atrocities. Even Mr. Darcy."

"Yes, however…" She took too long to gather her thoughts. Why was she more concerned about Mr. Darcy— a man she highly disliked— than troubled over learning of Mr. Wickham's sudden death? It made no sense!

Father leaned forward, grasping her chilled hands between his own. "Lizzy, is there something I should know?"

Yes, but how to do admit it?

Mother bustled into the room, waving a sheet of paper in her hand. "Oh, Mr. Bennet, I just heard from Mrs. Philips! Tell the servants to keep the doors locked tight and to post a night watch! There is a murderer in Meryton!"

***

The ladies had already laid down by the time Bingley inquired of them. The gentlemen, not wishing to disturb them unnecessarily, arranged to call back with Mr. Tanner that evening before the hour to dine.

When they did return, Darcy waited in the drawing room along with Mr. and Mrs. Hurst, who had nothing of interest to relate. Mr. Hurst had napped through most of the ball the preceding evening and had nothing to add to anyone else's observations. His interview with Mrs. Hurst had not taken more than ten minutes. Miss Bingley, on the other hand, apparently had much to say.

After a half an hour had passed, Miss Bingley sauntered into the room. She paused in the doorway. Darcy tried not to look interested, but his knee bounced in agitation.

Heaving a loud sigh meant to draw everyone's eye, she said, "What a bothersome ordeal. Mr. Stallard was most understanding, but I have not seen the likes of Mr. Tanner's brusque manners since the last time I was forced to travel by post coach." She shivered at what must have been a repulsive memory.

"Of what did they inquire?" asked Darcy.

She took the opportunity to sit near him. Leaning forward as if they shared an intimate secret, she said, "They asked about you. They wanted to know if I could account for your presence at the hour of midnight. Do not worry. I did not tell them of your indiscretion."

Darcy's blood froze. What did she mean by 'indiscretion'? "Did you tell them you saw me come in from out of doors?"

She smiled and whispered. "I did not. I told them the clock struck twelve just as you passed by me in the entrance hall."

Darcy sat back and squeezed his temples. "I wish you would have been honest with them. If they catch your lie, they will not only distrust anything else you may have told them, but they will also think worse of me."

Shrugging her shoulders, she said in a whisper so quiet, Darcy had to read her pouting lips, "I never get caught. You have no need to worry on my account, Mr. Darcy. If anything, I have helped you escape from an unsuitable marriage."

She knew. Of course, she would perish before breathing a word of it. Darcy supposed she would allow him to hang before she would admit to a compromise which would see Miss Elizabeth installed as the Mistress of Pemberley instead of her. Did Miss Elizabeth value her freedom more than his life? Dear Lord, he hoped it did not come to that!

Miss Bingley placed her fingers on his forearm, an intimacy he rewarded by moving his arm and turning in the settee so as to increase the distance between them.

Unabashed, she continued, "I do not doubt but that I have single-handedly spared you from further questioning by the inept constable. What a tiresome man. He insisted on speaking with the gardener. As if a servant would know anything of import." She scoffed.

Mr. Hurst spoke up. "You ought to hire your own investigator. A more capable professional would make short work of this mess without half the bother."

"What an excellent idea, Mr. Hurst!" said his wife, grasping onto the one intelligent comment he had made in a fortnight.

Darcy had considered it… for all of a minute. An investigator would ask questions Darcy did not want to answer. He had too many secrets. Not only did he fear for Georgiana's reputation, but he now held the future of Miss Elizabeth in his hands. His sense of honor forbade him from betraying her so easily.

"Mr. Darcy does not need an investigator. He is smarter than most of them anyway. He would sooner bring the real murderer to justice than anyone else who could be hired," said Miss Bingley.

He was about to give an answer when Bingley appeared in the doorway. His cravat fell in limp folds down his wrinkled waistcoat. His shoulders sagged in his coat. "Darcy, may I have a word?"

Darcy rose to join him. "Have you not slept at all, Bingley?" he asked as they made their way up the stairs to Bingley's study.

"I have received some distressing news, and my hope is that you will have a clear explanation for it." Bingley pinched his chin, reddening his already mottled skin.

"Distressing news?"

"Yes, from my gardener. While Colonel Forster and the constable were here, the gardener informed me that while he was inspecting the grounds, he found the gravel under the library window disturbed. Mr. Tanner went out to inspect it with him."

Darcy grimaced. What an annoyance. "I suppose he thinks I somehow left the party, traveled the three miles to Meryton, shot Wickham, and returned before anyone noticed I was gone."

"It does seem far-fetched when you put it that way."

"That is because it is. I did not leave Netherfield Park last night."

"But, Darcy, nobody remembers seeing you at that hour. Caroline ensured it by inquiring about your whereabouts several times when you escaped her sight— despite what she told Mr. Stallard. You simply disappeared." He held up his hands. "Now, do not give me that look, Darcy. I do not believe you capable of killing a man, but blast it all if you do not look guilty."

Darcy widened his stance, feeling the blow of accusation hitting him full force. What had started out as a trifling annoyance, of which he was certain to free himself, was growing into a real concern— a fatal one. "Wickham had many enemies. He carried debts all over England, and he had caused the ruin of more than one maiden. When Mr. Stallard told us he had been shot through the chest, I was not surprised."

"What do you plan to do, Darcy? You cannot allow Mr. Tanner to accuse you wrongly. It seems that most of Meryton supports him."

"I know it. I shall simply have to take matters into my own hands." There was no one else he could trust. He could not reveal the basis for his resentment of Wickham, nor could he reveal where he was at the time of his murder.

Bingley poured two drinks and brought them over before the fireplace. "If there is anything I can do to assist, please do not hesitate to ask. You can bet Caroline will do her best to clear your name of fault, although I fear they saw through her falsehood," he added with a worried smile.

"It is best for her not to involve herself— if Mr. Tanner is any indication of the animosity held against me by the villagers." Far worse than Miss Bingley's unwanted interference was the possibility that she could come to harm.

Bingley's eyes grew large. "You do not really think they might go to that extreme, do you?"

"I do not know. Wickham took no time at all in making himself out to be a victim of abuse at my hand." Of course, Darcy had done himself no favors by refusing to dance at the Meryton Assembly.

After some moments of pause, Bingley nodded his head decisively. "I will order the carriage to convey my family to London at the first sign of trouble. Even if Caroline's testimony is needed at the inquest, the distance is not too great for her to return."

"And you? Would you go with them if it comes to that?"

"I shall stay, of course. I am not one to leave a friend in need, nor do I wish to part company from a certain young lady so soon."

"I noticed you paid particular attention to Miss Bennet. She is a fair lady, and I found her manners far superior to those of her family. Is her admiration for you as strong as yours?"

Bingley shuffled his feet. "What do you think, Darcy?"

To be truthful, he believed her indifferent.

Looking down at his hands whilst collecting his thoughts, for it was never easy to be the bearer of bad news, he saw Miss Elizabeth's bite mark on his finger, now encased with a purple bruise. What did he know of the gentle sex? He had not noticed Georgiana's infatuation with Wickham in time to safeguard her from unnecessary heartache. And he did not have sense enough to eliminate Miss Elizabeth from his every thought. She had made her opinion of him as clear as crystal and yet, he admired her still.

"You are a better judge than I am, Bingley." He would say no more on the subject. He knew Miss Elizabeth would have approved.

CHAPTER 8

Bingley was determined to accompany Darcy to Meryton the following morning. He wore a patterned waistcoat with a coat to match the blue swirls on it on the chance they might see Miss Bennet.

"The officers will think you a dandy," Darcy teased him.

"You are one to criticize! I see you took care to wear your dark green riding coat instead of your normal brown. It sets off your black armband nicely. Who are you hoping to impress this morning, Darcy?"

Darcy did not tell Bingley that he had changed his coat three times before settling on the green. It was the same dark color Miss Elizabeth had worn to the Assembly. It sounded foolish to him now, but he hoped she might see him more favorably if he wore a color he knew she liked.

Green suited her, bringing out the rich chestnut of her hair, her honey skin kissed by the sun during her rambles through the countryside, the pink glow to her cheeks…. Like a rose hidden amongst verdant foliage.

"Do you ignore me, Darcy? Or do you plan to make a habit of not answering my questions?"

Startled back to reality, Darcy said breathlessly, "I give no answer because there is none to give, Bingley. Were I to have a satisfying reply, I would gladly share it with you." He must control his foolish thoughts before they carried him too far. He did not love Miss Elizabeth. Admire her, yes. Respect her, absolutely. Love her? It would be the height of stupidity to fall in love with a lady who was tenaciously determined to believe the worst of him.

"Do not be stupid, Darcy. Your manners only make others likely to believe your guilt. You do not always need to say something profound all the time. You come across as pompous and taciturn." Bingley shuffled the reins between his hands.

Darcy forced a laugh. Bingley did not know the half of it. "You are a good friend, Bingley. There are few in England who would speak to me as you do." Miss Elizabeth had been equally honest with him. She was wrong, of course, but she had been honest.

"You need more friends," Bingley replied earnestly.

"I would rather have a few good friends than many false ones. I daresay you are correct in your assessment of the villagers' reaction to my character. However, I refuse to bend to their wishes and have no desire to befriend anyone who expects me to do so. It is impossible to please everyone, and any attempt to do so would only make me miserable."

"So you do not try? Come, Darcy, you are better than that. With this business, you ought to concern yourself more with making a favorable impression. Otherwise, the entire village will set themselves against you."

It grated against Darcy's convictions, but there was some truth to what Bingley said. It was unjust, but people would judge him based on appearances.

"Very well. I will strive to be more amiable where it is appropriate."

The tops of the white barracks' tents peeked over the hill at the side of the village. They would go there first. As Wickham's friend, Mr. Denny would be the best source of information.

He answered their call with a towel draped around his neck, and some shaving cream tracing his side whiskers. Dabbing at his face, he invited them in and motioned for them to sit at a small table adorned with a deck of cards and surrounded by four stools.

"I apologize for calling early, Mr. Denny," began Darcy.

"I had expected you would call. The sooner this unpleasant business is resolved, the better. Tell me, Mr. Darcy, how may I be of service?"

Their call off to a promising start, Darcy said directly, "First, I wish to settle any debt Wickham may have owed you."

Mr. Denny sat down with a thud. "You want to know if Wickham owed me money?"

Darcy laid his hands out against the table. He had nothing to hide, nor any secret motive. "There are more comfortable ways of acquiring this information, but my time is better directed elsewhere at the moment. My intention is to settle his affairs to the best of my ability so that I may focus my energies on discovering the identity of his murderer."

Shaking his head and narrowing his eyes, Mr. Denny said, "But you hated Wickham. You refused him his living."

Would that lie never disappear? "You ought not believe everything you hear. I understand, then, that your friendship with Mr. Wickham was not long-standing?" Darcy's first impression of Mr. Denny was of an honest— albeit naive— chap who would have cut ties with Wickham once his true nature was revealed.

"I met Wickham in London last year. He helped me out of a difficult spot, and we have— or rather had— been friends since."

"I am sorry you lost a friend. I still struggle to comprehend that he is gone." Darcy looked down at his spread hands, momentarily taken aback at the squeezing sensation in his chest. He and Wickham had not always been enemies. There had been a time— though it felt like ages ago— when they had been comrades in boyish mischief. It was why he wore the armband, though others were sure to ridicule him— seeing it as a mockery in celebration of the fall of his foe.

Silence consumed the room, and he felt Mr. Denny's stare. Clenching his fists, Darcy said, "I will not pretend that Wickham and I were on good terms. We were not. However, our discord was not for the reasons you suppose."

Mr. Denny leaned forward on the table. "Then, tell me, why do you care?"

"Aside from my obvious personal interest in seeing his killer discovered, I cannot in good conscience allow for the gravest injustice known to humankind to go unpunished— and all the more so when it has befallen a man I once called my brother."

Leaning back and crossing his arms, Mr. Denny said, "I do not know what to make of you, sir. I know— er, rather, I do not believe that you killed him. I have told Colonel Forster as much, but I can offer no proof of it. You come to me with every intent of acting honorably even though you are under no obligation to do so." Balancing his chair back on two legs, he added, "I will help you where I am able. To answer your question, Wickham did owe me a sizable sum, but he gave me an item of value which I mean to sell the moment I can get leave."

"That is not likely to happen during the course of the investigation. Might I purchase the item from you for the amount owed?" offered Darcy.

Mr. Denny grimaced. "Tis true. Colonel Forster has informed us that no officer will be permitted leave until after the inquest, which Mr. Stallard has scheduled in four days hence. I shall manage until then, but I thank you, Mr. Darcy."

"Did Wickham have any enemies of which you are aware?" pressed Darcy.

"If he did, I did not know them. There were places he would avoid, but that was because he was discreet."

How had Wickham blinded the mind of Mr. Denny, as he had Miss Elizabeth? Darcy wondered how an officer in the militia could be so innocently trusting. It was to be expected of Miss Elizabeth — who no doubt had never had occasion to be exposed to the duplicity common in the higher ranks of society. *How refreshing.*

But he had not called on Mr. Denny to ponder on Miss Elizabeth's finer points. What had they been discussing? Ah, manipulating charm. Though the artful use of charisma had gained Wickham numerous friends, his selfishness had prevented him from keeping most of them. His list of enemies must be longer than Mr. Denny or Darcy supposed. The thought was not comforting.

"Do you think Wickham suspected his life was in danger?" he asked.

"He had never given that impression since meeting up with me to join the militia. However, I do know he was greatly disturbed by a business deal that turned sour over the summer."

Darcy held his breath. He did not know what Mr. Denny knew, but he did not want any hint of the scandal in Ramsgate repeated.

"If I may inquire, what was the nature of his business?" asked Bingley.

Dear Lord, Bingley, stop asking questions!

"I hardly think it signifies," Darcy said casually.

Mr. Denny shrugged his shoulders. "Probably not, and I cannot tell you anything more than what I have said already."

Darcy let out his breath slowly, his relief intense.

"Did Wickham come directly from Ramsgate to here?" Bingley asked, his cheeks pink with self-satisfaction. Darcy wished his well-meaning friend would keep his mouth shut.

"He stayed on in Ramsgate another two months after negotiations fell through, so I knew he was in a bad way when I saw him outside a pawn shop in London. Our meeting was nothing short of providential. He needed an occupation worthy of him, and I was happy to help. In no time at all, arrangements were made, and he scraped up enough for his commission to join me here."

Wickham's blatant dishonesty filled Darcy with disgust, and he pitied Mr. Denny for what he would discover once Wickham's lies were revealed.

Thanking Mr. Denny for his cooperation, Darcy and Bingley departed from the barracks, going to the next best source of information. The inn next to the post. It was a bold move to invade Mr. Tanner's territory, but they had seen the man leave and chose that moment to make inquiries.

A couple of well-placed coins loosened the barmaid's tongue, and Darcy soon learned that Wickham had incurred several debts during his short time in Meryton. As far as she was concerned, Wickham had been a charming gentleman and liked by all who had met him.

Darcy's head ached with injured pride by the time they departed the inn. How could the villagers blindly sing the praises of a lout such as Wickham while they held him, Fitzwilliam Darcy of Pemberley, in derision?

Going across the village square, he saw Mr. Tanner walking their way. It would be impossible to be amiable to that hard-headed man.

"Mr. Darcy. Mr. Bingley. I trust you are not disturbing my guests?" Mr. Tanner snarled, his muscled arms crossed in front of his broad chest.

Mr. Bingley, looking back and forth between the two, spoke quickly, "No, Mr. Tanner. How pleasant to see you. We are merely making some discreet inquiries."

Mr. Tanner raised his chin, leveling his eyes with Darcy. "If I hear of you bribing any of the villagers, I will arrest you. I know a liar when I see one, and I will accept no false witnesses when you are on trial."

"Take care that in judging me without any knowledge of my character, you become the one to spread slander and lies."

"Are you an honorable man then? Is that possible among your set?"

"You are convinced of my guilt based on my rank?" Not even Mr. Collins could have thought of something more absurd.

With a low chuckle that set Darcy's hair on end, Mr. Tanner said, "Me and all of Meryton, sir. Good day to you." He bumped Darcy's shoulder as he charged past. Darcy held his ground.

Bingley looked at him with wide eyes. "We ought not underestimate Mr. Tanner. He means to see you hang."

"He is like an empty ale barrel— full of air. Nothing more." Despite his flippant remark, Darcy felt a cold sweat spread over his body.

CHAPTER 9

Elizabeth stepped out of Aunt Philips' house. Aunt had been a wealth of information, relating to whom Mr. Wickham had owed small sums of money, how charming he had been, and what a pity that such a handsome officer could no longer marry one of her nieces.

Elizabeth had argued that no Bennet sister in her right mind— well, that only left herself, Jane, and probably Mary, but she held hopes that Kitty and Lydia might improve under the guidance of Mrs. Yeats— should want to marry an officer unable to manage his finances, but her common sense fell on deaf ears.

There had been some interesting details mentioned about the state of Mr. Wickham's room…. Details she had not overheard from Mr. Collins regarding his missing pistol.

Deep in thought, Elizabeth walked in the direction of Longbourn. She had slipped out of the house after taking an early breakfast. She had not told anyone where she was going, not wanting any company to distract Aunt Philips with other, less important matters.

"Miss Elizabeth," called a cheerful voice behind her.

She turned to face a grinning Mr. Bingley, followed by a somber Mr. Darcy. For once, she could not blame him for his ill-humor and thought none the worse of him. Under his greatcoat, a dark green jacket stretched over his chest, lending a striking contrast to the dark pools of his eyes. Like the rich coffee she sometimes drank— both bitter in its taste and enticing in its essence. Her mouth began to water at the comparison before she came to her senses in horror of where her thoughts had strayed.

Mr. Bingley stepped forward, his face anxious, "Are you well?"

Lifting her chin and clasping her hands together tightly, she said, "I am well, thank you, Mr. Bingley."

"Are you certain?" he insisted.

Her ears tingled in the heat spreading over her face as Mr. Darcy looked at her silently, unrelentingly.

"Nothing a cup of tea will not cure, I assure you," she said, struggling for air.

Mr. Darcy inclined his head, the corners of his lips quivering. Was he laughing at her? *Ooh, the infernal man!*

In his buttery smooth voice, he said, "I have noticed the heightened color and healthy glow with which exercise blesses you. One might mistake it for a feverish complexion, but it is most becoming."

Elizabeth lost all sense. Otherwise, she would have closed her gaping mouth much sooner. Mr. Darcy had paid her a compliment? She had not known him capable of charm, yet there was nothing else to call his address.

Mr. Bingley, oblivious to the palpitations of her heart, asked, "Are all of the members of your family well? I was anxious holding the ball so close to Miss Bennet's recovery. She did not tire herself, I hope?"

Focusing her full attention on Mr. Bingley, she smiled a bit too enthusiastically and a giggle escaped. For the love of heaven, she was acting like Lydia! Exceedingly aware of herself, and hating Mr. Darcy for making her feel self-conscious, she attempted to ignore the gentleman completely. "Yes, we are all well. Thank you, Mr. Bingley. I do hope your household is equally well?" She would earn no points for clever conversation, but Mr. Bingley did not expect it of her. What a dear man. Mr. Bingley would be kind to Jane... that is, if he proposed.

"As well as can be with this unfortunate affair with Mr. Wickham." He looked to his side at Mr. Darcy.

Like traitorous little balls of metal pulled by a magnet, her eyes followed Mr. Bingley's to settle on Mr. Darcy. The muscles at his temples pulsated where a strand of his hair curled. His broad shoulders tensed up to his ears, and she watched him as he appeared to measure his breaths. She felt his eyes searching her as intently as she searched him. Expecting a condescending glower, she met his gaze directly and promptly lost her breath. The firmness of his chin and the confidence in his steady eyes made him look angry, and dangerous, and… achingly handsome. *Drat Mr. Darcy!*

Forcing herself to look away, Elizabeth said, "How fortuitous that we should meet here today, gentlemen." Collecting her scrambled thoughts, she continued, "I have recently learned some news which may serve to your advantage. I… I also have some unpleasant news of which you should be equally aware."

She flicked her gaze to see Mr. Darcy's reaction, but something over his shoulder caught her attention.

"What is it, Miss Elizabeth?" he asked.

Composing her expression, Elizabeth smiled, "This is not a good place to share information. Mr. Tanner is watching you."

Mr. Darcy grimaced. "I seem to have invoked the wrath of that man."

"If you knew his history, you would understand his motives against you."

Elizabeth knew she held the rapt attention of both Mr. Bingley and Mr. Darcy, but Mr. Tanner watched them too closely. The last thing she wanted was for the constable to uncover their compromise by attaching her to Mr. Darcy. She could not deny her physical attraction to Mr. Darcy, but the kind of love she sought demanded more. Trust. Honor. Respect.

"May we call at Longbourn this afternoon?" he asked.

"You may call, but unless some miracle happens, we will not be allowed to discuss anything of import." She tried to keep a pleasant smile on her face and visible to Mr. Tanner.

"It would give me great pleasure to see for myself that my ball caused no harm to Miss Bennet. And it sounds as if you have a great deal to discuss, which would be impossible to share any other way," said Mr. Bingley, looking at his pocket watch— no doubt counting the time until he would see Jane.

"Until this afternoon, Miss Elizabeth," said Mr. Darcy with a bow.

Elizabeth wanted to turn around as they walked past her, but she forced herself to keep her vision straight ahead of her. She would stop at the post before returning home so as not to be seen leaving with the gentlemen.

"Mr. Tanner," she acknowledged as she walked by.

"Miss Elizabeth," he answered.

Good. He did not stop her to ask any questions. She walked as fast as she could to the post and inquired if she had any letters.

Her heart pounded in her ears so loudly, the postman had to repeat himself more than twice.

After the third try, it grew too awkward to ask him to repeat himself yet again. Smiling and nodding as if she knew precisely what he had said, she was overjoyed when the door opened and she turned to see her sisters and Mrs. Yeats.

"There you are, Lizzy," said Jane, her hand over her heart. She and Mrs. Yeats joined her while Mary, Kitty, and Lydia continued to the counter to post their letters and ask if anything had arrived for them.

"I apologize if I alarmed you, Jane. I wanted to call on Aunt Philips alone."

Mrs. Yeats pursed her lips together, looking very much like she was preparing to give a scolding… which she did once they had gone down the street to the haberdashery, where the distraction of fripperies and fashion magazines occupied her sisters.

Pulling Elizabeth to a far corner, she said, "Miss Elizabeth, a young lady does not walk unattended. I understand matters of propriety are more… shall we say, relaxed… in the country, but need I remind you that there is a murderer about? It is not safe." As if to prove her point, she looked cautiously around the shop, adjusting her bonnet as if its straw could protect her from an assailant.

"I apologize for the fright you suffered. I will take greater care."

Mrs. Yeats squeezed Elizabeth's arm and smiled at her with concerned eyes. "I know you would never give your family unnecessary cause to worry about you, and so I will mention this no more. Your father made it clear to me that I am to give my attention to your younger sisters, but it would distress me greatly should these breaches in propriety continue from you."

"I thank you for your concern. As proof of my understanding, I will wait to return home so that we may all walk together." She wanted to tell Jane about her meeting with Mr. Bingley. It would help the time pass until they called.

At least Mr. Collins was not with them. Odd that. "Where is Mr. Collins?" asked Elizabeth.

Mrs. Yeats straightened her posture and sniffed. "I suggested he make inquiries at the barracks while we went about our business. Miss Bennet had a letter to post. Miss Kitty wanted to re-trim a bonnet with some new ribbon, and Miss Mary wishes to prevent her from adorning it overmuch. She fights a losing battle, I fear, but it provided excuse enough. Miss Lydia, as you see, is surprisingly subdued. Then again, there are no gentlemen present which may account for her docility."

Elizabeth applauded her insight.

"Think nothing of it. Most young ladies' thoughts tend in a similar direction, I have found. As for Mr. Collins... it is not my position to say. However, a gentleman's time is better spent amongst other gentlemen, do you not agree?"

Elizabeth could have hugged Mrs. Yeats.

"Ingenious, madam. I can see how your inclusion into our family will be of great benefit."

A corner of Mrs. Yeats mouth curved up, but other than that, her looks remained staunch— as was expected of a companion.

Lydia did not pay much attention to Elizabeth until she saw a lavender sash she absolutely had to have.

"Oy, Lizzy!" she said, wrapping her arm around Elizabeth's waist and resting her chin on her shoulder. "I have spent all of my pin money, and I simply must have that sash. Do you not think it will look elegant tied around the waist of my white gown? It has such a lovely shimmer to it." She looked longingly at the lilac-colored satin.

"Do you not have one just like it at home?" countered Elizabeth.

Sticking out her lip, Lydia said, "But this one is shinier."

Mrs. Yeats, drawn to Lydia's whiny tone like a bee to honey, said, "Miss Lydia, am I to understand that you have wasted your pin money and seek to borrow another's?"

Lydia jutted out her chin. "I would pay it back."

Elizabeth stifled a chuckle. Lydia still owed her for the ribbons she had bought two days before.

Mrs. Yeats looked at Elizabeth. "Is this true? Has she paid back the coin you have loaned her?"

"One can always hope, Mrs. Yeats, but then again, love hopes all things, does it not?" Elizabeth answered with glee. Her heart rejoiced to see someone attempt to give Lydia some much needed guidance in practical affairs.

Looping her arm through Lydia's, Mrs. Yeats led her away, saying, "A proper lady must be responsible for the contents of her own purse. She does not concern herself with spending the contents of another's…." Her words trailed off as they walked away.

Thus given some quiet, Elizabeth sat in a corner and went over every detail Aunt Philips had shared with her. Nothing was insignificant and everything bore repeating. The remembrance of Mr. Tanner's menacing glare at Mr. Darcy sent chills up Elizabeth's spine. As did the memory of Mr. Darcy's smile when he complimented her— not to mention his intense, coffee-brown eyes.

CHAPTER 10

Elizabeth told no one besides Jane that two unmarried gentlemen would call on them that afternoon. The chaos such an announcement would have provoked would have undermined any preparations they could make to receive them.

And so it was that Mr. Darcy and Mr. Bingley were announced— arousing the entire Bennet family from their boredom-induced comas caused by Mr. Collins' monotonic reading of Fordyce's sermons.

Father closed the book he would have preferred to read during the tedious performance and stood. "See them in, Hill."

Mother rose to her feet at an appalling speed. "What?! No, Hill, give us a moment to prepare ourselves!" Mother scurried from one end of the room and back again. "Kitty, stuff your ribbons and trimmings under this cushion. You ought not leave your things out like this. Mary—"

Unable to think of anything for Mary— who was the only occupant of the room disturbed at the interruption of Mr. Collins' reading of such uplifting words— Mother harrumphed, waved her hand in dismissal, and continued without pause to arrange her daughters, as well as the room.

"Lydia, pinch your cheeks. Lizzy, tighten Jane's ribbon and... for the love of all that is good, Jane, your bosom looks more appealing when you thrust your shoulders back like so..." She demonstrated what she meant, causing Father to clap in appreciation.

Jane's complexion turned an appalling shade of ruby red, and Elizabeth prayed Mother's voice could not be heard through the walls.

The agitation in the room increased until Mrs. Yeats stood. "Mrs. Bennet, might I make a suggestion?" Without waiting for an answer, she continued, "Since your hopes so clearly rest on Miss Bennet to make an advantageous match with Mr. Bingley, perhaps we should allow them some time together. We do not know Mr. Darcy's intentions, but he is well-situated and might suit Miss Elizabeth. If Mr. Bennet stays behind, they will have a chaperone and the opportunity for more intimate conversation."

Elizabeth opened her mouth to protest an attachment to Mr. Darcy, but closed it just as quickly. She had hoped for a chance to speak with him, and doing so in the presence of her mother and younger sisters would have proved impossible.

Mr. Collins did not seem willing to be so easily dismissed. He raised his hand to express as much.

Speaking before he could, Mrs. Yeats continued, "Surely, it would be of great advantage to you for an alliance to form with the nephew of the de Bourgh household. Imagine how you stand to benefit from such an intimate connection— should it come to pass."

"What a wonderful idea! How clever you are, Mrs. Yeats. Hill, see the gentlemen in," said Mother, lining Lydia, Kitty, and Mary next to her by the door Mrs. Yeats stood behind to give room for her charges. Mr. Collins followed them in a daze, clearly dreaming of forming a part of the grand family de Bourgh. Elizabeth thought it was just as likely that the great Lady Catherine would accept Mr. Collins' hand in matrimony than for Mr. Darcy to propose to her. So long as he was not forced to make an offer, that was.

Mr. Bingley walked into the room and soon found himself surrounded by Bennet females. He stepped back and into Mr. Darcy, who held his ground with his usual scowl.

Father stepped forward to receive their guests. "How good of you gentlemen to pay us a call. Mrs. Bennet and Mrs. Yeats were about to accompany my youngest daughters out of doors to enjoy some fresh air."

"Mrs. Yeats?" asked Mr. Bingley.

Father's chest puffed out. "She is the companion to my daughters."

Elizabeth saw the question in Mr. Bingley's eyes. "All of them?" Of course, his manners prevented him from voicing it aloud. He stepped aside, smiling and bobbing his head as each Bennet passed.

Mr. Darcy's eyes were riveted on some invisible object across the wall, giving him a look of haughty concentration which only the bravest— or most ignorant— of individuals would dare interrupt. She wondered how long he had studied that pose before perfecting it.

"Mr. Darcy, we are honored you should visit our humble home," said Mr. Collins as he passed by. *Ignorant it was...*

Elizabeth bit her lips to keep from laughing when Mr. Darcy glared daggers at her senseless cousin. His wrath was wasted on the clergyman, who bowed as he backed out of the room at the insistence of Mother and Mrs. Yeats, who had their arms piled high with shawls and wraps for the girls.

The door closed behind them, and Mr. Bennet motioned for the gentlemen to sit. Mr. Bingley chose a spot on the settee next to Jane, leaving Mr. Darcy to join Elizabeth and Father on the opposite side of the fireplace. It was perfect.

"How sensible of you to take on a companion for your daughters, Mr. Bennet. My young sister has benefited greatly from the company of her most recent companion," said Mr. Darcy politely.

"Most recent? I am unaware of how these things work, Mr. Darcy. Am I supposed to replace the companion every so often or risk my girls perishing from boredom and the companion from an attack of nerves?" He peeked over his spectacles and pinched his lips together to keep from giving himself away.

Elizabeth watched Mr. Darcy's reaction. She knew her father to be teasing, but would he?

Mr. Darcy answered seriously. "Good companions are difficult to come by. We had a horrible experience with the one before her current companion. She was a traitorous woman with no care for my sister."

"How dreadful for you. I am sorry you were troubled by someone who was entrusted with the proper guidance of your beloved sister. However, I am pleased to say that our Mrs. Yeats seems up to the task with my daughters."

"I commend you for it, sir."

That was the second time Mr. Darcy complimented Father. What other surprises would proceed from his mouth?

Father could hold his high humor back no longer. With a chuckle, he said, "Better late than never, I say."

Mr. Darcy did not laugh. Elizabeth had not thought he would. Negligence was no laughing matter to a man such as himself.

"Mr. Bennet, I must thank you for welcoming me into your home. I am in a precarious situation and am performing my own investigation to set matters straight. Mr. Tanner said he received some information from you. Might I inquire about the nature of this information?"

Massaging his chin and frowning deeply, Father said, "How unfortunate Mr. Tanner is privy to that information. At Mr. Collins' insistence, I sent a note to Mr. Stallard and Colonel Forster with what little in the way of observations I could offer. My hope was that they might help you in some way."

"You believe me innocent?"

"Would I have allowed you into my home if I did not? No, Mr. Darcy, if I were a betting man, I would put my money on a hot-blooded officer holding a grudge against Mr. Wickham. I am no detective, but I would inquire after those who claim to be his friends. Often it is the people we are closest to who inflict the most harm."

Mr. Darcy nodded. "I went into Meryton to make inquiries. Mr. Denny was unexpectedly helpful. Mr. Tanner breathed threats, but he has no proof against me."

Elizabeth shook her head. "Mr. Darcy, it would be a mistake to underestimate him."

Mr. Bingley and Jane, who had enjoyed a brief tête-à-tête, turned their heads to listen.

"She is right," Father said. "I only know this because Mrs. Bennet's sister is the greatest gossip this side of the Thames. You see, Mr. Tanner is the firstborn son of a gentleman who had the misfortune of falling in love with a barmaid. The family objected, of course, as highborn families will do. And since life has a way of effecting its injustices against the most defenseless, his father married into a fortune and refused to acknowledge the boy as his own. He and his mother were cast out and shunned."

"The gentleman did nothing in the way of supporting the woman and child?" Mr. Darcy asked, the disgust evident in his tone.

"No doubt he intended to… if he was honorable, which he surely must have been," said Jane in the unknown gentleman's defense.

Father clucked his tongue. "You are too kind, Janey. It could very well be that he intended to, but as happens in most of these cases, the passing of time lightens the error and the sin goes forgotten. It is not a subject Mr. Tanner discusses openly. In fact, it was Mrs. Philips who dug up the dirt on his past and took pride in revealing her discovery all over Meryton." With a chuckle, he added, "What a relief it was to Mr. Tanner when the parson's daughter ran off with a traveling merchant, and he ceased to be the center of attention."

Elizabeth said, so as to keep the conversation on course, "His resentment against the upper classes is well-known in Meryton."

Resentment. That was a sentiment Mr. Darcy would understand. Elizabeth wondered how well he liked being the one to suffer the ill effects of that poisonous emotion.

In case Mr. Darcy had not caught on to her line of reasoning, she added, "It is likely he resents you for the sole reason that you have benefited from everything of which he was denied."

"He is a fool if he thinks harming me will satisfy his need for revenge. It is never as simple as that." He spoke as if he knew from painful experience.

Elizabeth watched the muscles at his jaw clench. With the clear view of his profile, she saw in his rumpled brow, the smoothness of his cheek, and a slight curl at the corner of his lips, a boyish charm which had escaped her notice until then. With a blink, the vulnerable innocence was gone— replaced by a man accustomed to hiding his innermost thoughts and feelings.

Sitting taller and guarding his expression, he asked, "If I may ask, Mr. Bennet, what did you write to Mr. Stallard and Colonel Forster?"

"I told them that, while I could not vouch for your whereabouts at the precise hour of midnight, Miss Bingley likely could. She passed by me as the clock struck the hour, and I heard her ask Mrs. Hurst if she had seen you. She was like a hound on the trail of a fox, and I daresay she could account for your presence at the ball."

Elizabeth groaned. Unless Miss Bingley had lied, Mr. Tanner knew about Mr. Darcy's unexplained reentry into the house from out of doors. He could assume Mr. Darcy had left the ball, shot Mr. Wickham dead, and returned to the ball… unless Elizabeth told the truth.

She looked at Mr. Darcy. He was handsome, there was no denying it. When she had first seen him enter the Meryton Assembly, the sight of him had set her heart aflutter. She could still feel her skin burn where he had held her in the library. Were he to never speak a word to her, Elizabeth felt certain they could live years in a peaceful, if not happy, marriage. But it was not enough.

There had to be another way. She only had to keep her wits about her and find a solution. She had to find the real murderer. If she failed, she would give Mr. Darcy her future and admit the compromise.

She would make sure she did not fail.

CHAPTER 11

"Did you notice anything else which might assist us in our investigation?" Darcy asked. Bingley sat straighter, no doubt deducing that Darcy had included him in his search for the truth. Darcy would not disappoint him by correcting his assumption.

As for his thoughts, they were occupied solely by Miss Elizabeth. She sat pondering already; her eyes keen, her forehead furrowed, and her chin determined. It was an honor to have her on his side, and he believed her every bit as capable as he believed himself of solving the mystery.

"No, I cannot say I recall anything else worthy of note— excepting, of course, Lizzy's unfortunate imprisonment in the library. Thank goodness you inquired after her, or I do not doubt but that she would still be in the Netherfield library!"

Darcy immediately grew defensive. He had not acknowledged Mr. Bennet's previous attempts at humor, and he could not bring himself to do so at this opportunity either. Negligence— especially to a daughter he claimed to favor— was no laughing matter.

"I doubt that. Miss Elizabeth is too well-liked to be allowed to disappear for so great a time," he said, trying— and failing— to keep the gruffness out of his tone.

With a smile which did not reach her eyes, Miss Elizabeth laughed, adding too flippantly, "It is no matter. There is no other place I would rather be locked inside than a library." Her cheeks, though rosy by nature, deepened to a darker shade.

Bingley, never one to allow a conversation to be anything but merry, said, "Tis a pity my library does not have much to offer as yet. I daresay you would have become bored before a day had passed, and Darcy would have discovered you by then. He uses the room more often than I do presently."

Darcy had found her much sooner than that. His limbs tingled as his body reminded him how she had felt pressed against him in the darkness of Bingley's library. He only had to bend slightly, and he could have rested his chin on top of her head. She had fit perfectly in his embrace; her hair had smelled of lavender. Not the overwhelming scent of other ladies who doused themselves in perfume, but a soft perfume which had enticed his senses.

She spoke, dragging him out of his beautiful daydream. "That does not surprise me. Several times, I encountered Mr. Darcy in the library during our stay at Netherfield Park. I have no doubt, Mr. Bingley, but that you will do justice to the mahogany shelves lining the walls, adorning them with books enough to satisfy the most voracious reader."

Much pleased, Bingley said, "Then I shall invite all of your family to admire them when they are properly adorned, as you say." He blushed at Miss Bennet, who blushed at him in return.

Some few minutes passed thus in pleasant exchanges, and Darcy sensed that Miss Elizabeth was more relaxed. Mr. Bennet, too, was improved company now that they spoke of a subject dear to his heart. Darcy even went so far as to invite them to see his library at Pemberley. That brought a smile to Miss Elizabeth's eyes, and he took great pleasure in seeing how her face lit up in excitement. Like the fireworks at Vauxhall Gardens.

An unwelcome figure appeared in the doorway, poking his head into the room and casting a shadow over their lively chatter.

"Mr. Darcy," said Mr. Collins, rubbing his palms against his black breeches.

Mr. Bennet sighed and waved him over to join them. "Please do join us, Mr. Collins. Perhaps you have something worthwhile to share." Looking at Darcy, he added, "Mr. Collins' sole purpose at the moment is to clear your name and, therefore, ensure that the de Bourgh household suffers no disturbance."

Ignorant of Mr. Bennet's sarcastic tone, Mr. Collins passed by Bingley and Miss Bennet, bowing deeply as he approached them.

"Yes, Mr. Darcy, I am at your service. If there is anything at all with which I might assist you, I pray you do not hesitate to ask. Your aunt Lady Catherine de Bourgh would expect as much of me, I am sure, and I consider it an honor to come to your aid in any way, no matter how humble the task." He remained in a half-crouched position, his face growing red with the exertion. Darcy wondered how long the man could hold such a pose.

Miss Elizabeth bit her lips together, and he knew she wondered the same. Mr. Bennet's eyes danced in merriment, accentuated by the reflection of his spectacles. Darcy covered his amusement with a cough.

"Thank you. Your assistance is as welcome now as the last time you offered it," he said when Mr. Collins looked at him expectantly. "The only wish I have at the moment is the same we discussed yesterday— that my aunt not be informed of the recent events here until I can sort them out. I see no need to cause her unnecessary alarm."

Mr. Collins, finally stretching himself up to his full height, pinched his lips together and reached up with his fingers as if to lock them with an invisible key. "You may count on my silence, Mr. Darcy. I will be the soul of discretion. Is there anything else with which I might assist you?"

Darcy could see that Mr. Collins would make a pest of himself unless he was given some task. "I will send a note by messenger should I require your help."

Pleased to have been deigned such an honor, Mr. Collins sat down. "I do have a bit of news which might be of some value. We know you to be incapable of committing such a horrendous sin against your fellow man, and so we are left to wonder who, in fact, murdered Mr. Wickham with his own pistol."

"We are aware of those particulars," said Mr. Bennet, twiddling his fingers impatiently.

Stretching his neck and lifting his head to an exalted height, Mr. Collins continued, "It was through my persistent inquiries amongst the officers I was able to learn that Mr. Wickham owed a tidy sum to none other than Mr. Denny. When I went to confirm the rumor with Mr. Denny, I found him defensive in his manners and particularly close-mouthed. His eyes darted about, and I perceived a layer of sweat which often occurs when a gentleman finds himself in an uncomfortable situation or caught in a falsehood."

The same could be said of men pressed to wear black coats and clerical collars. Mr. Collins dabbed his reddened face with a limp handkerchief.

"Mr. Bingley and I spoke with Mr. Denny as well. He told us about the debt and assured us Mr. Wickham had given him payment. I did not sense any resentment on his behalf— only sadness at having lost a friend." Hopefully that would deter Mr. Collins from badgering Mr. Denny.

Mr. Bennet commented to the crestfallen clergyman, "On that point, I must praise your initiative, sir. It has been my opinion all along that none other than a fellow officer is responsible for what befell poor Mr. Wickham. Of course, I do not think it wise to make accusations without solid proof."

"What sort of proof? We cannot suppose Mr. Wickham's killer will confess openly. The only physical evidence missing is his pistol, and nearly two days have passed. His murderer could have hidden it anywhere by now," said Miss Elizabeth. She brought up a good point. The killer— whoever it was— would not make his identity easily discoverable.

Once again finding a purpose to latch on to, Mr. Collins pronounced, "That is why I will persist in investigating Mr. Denny and any other officer or gentleman who might have harbored resentment against Mr. Wickham. Resentment is, after all, a poisonous sentiment and a powerful motive to wish a man dead. I will not desist until I have uncovered all of Mr. Wickham's secrets."

Darcy swallowed hard, his throat feeling dry though he had drained his teacup. What if Mr. Collins somehow discovered the source of his resentment against Wickham? It was just the sort of information an unwitting, but well-meaning, man would stumble upon.

Mr. Bennet cleared his throat, looking pointedly at Mr. Collins. "Only a certain type of man, I think, would act on it. Most people in life, you will find, resent at least one person, but would never consider killing them."

Mr. Bennet's expression made Darcy wonder about the relationship between himself and Mr. Collins. Perhaps Mr. Collins had best lock his door that night… just in case. Although Mr. Bennet did not seem the sort of man to resort to such extremes. He did not seem to be the sort of man to resort to any extreme at all.

Replacing his handkerchief in his pocket, Mr. Collins rubbed his hands together. "Of course, there is the one question which keeps rising to the fore. Why can no one confirm where you were at the hour of midnight? I have asked many individuals, and not one of them could say with any certainty they had seen you. It is baffling."

Elizabeth's teacup clattered against her plate. "Sorry," she mumbled.

Mr. Bennet considered Darcy closely, his eyes enlarged through the glass of his spectacles. Darcy felt like an insect being examined under a microscope. Was it possible Mr. Bennet knew the truth?

Had Darcy not mastered his composure many years ago, he would have been tempted to squirm in his chair. It was difficult, but he met Mr. Bennet's inspecting gaze through the tense silence which settled over them.

The clock propped on top of the mantelpiece chimed. It was time to depart.

"We do not wish to overstay our welcome. Thank you for receiving us, Mr. Bennet," Darcy said as he rose to his feet.

Mr. Collins wrung his hands. "How distressing. I have so much more to relate. I do not flatter myself to be an exceptional investigator, but some small detail which someone else might overlook could prove to be important, and I so happen to have many such details."

Bingley's face lit up with pleasure. "I have a splendid idea! Mr. Bennet, I would like to invite you, your family, and Mr. Collins to my home to dine this evening. I apologize for the suddenness of my invitation, but I do hope you accept it."

Darcy shot a questioning look at Bingley. He already had a planned dinner party for the evening. An invitation of the female-heavy Bennet family would cause an uneven table. Miss Bingley would be beside herself. Not that Darcy cared, but he did not have the patience to listen to her complain about it all evening.

Bingley continued, looking briefly down at the floor, "I had a party planned for this evening, but I was informed that some of my guests will not be able to attend. The cook has been working all day, and it would be distressing to waste her talents."

Unable to attend? More like they were avoiding him— believing him to be a common criminal. Darcy tensed, angry he should be judged unfavorably by the majority of the village on the pretense that he had chosen not to dance at their silly assembly. Only, now, it did not seem so silly. Perhaps he should have asked a lady or two instead of spurning them all.

He felt Miss Elizabeth's eyes on him, the very lady he had insulted the worst. He regretted it deeply. She had not deserved his biting remarks. She had heard him. He had looked directly at her as he uttered the words he now regretted, "She is tolerable, but not handsome enough to tempt me, and I am in no humor at present to give consequence to young ladies who are slighted by other men." How was he to know she did not hold to the same money-hungry ambitions as her own mother? Still, it was inexcusable of him to have voiced his erroneous view and insult her. The room grew unbearably warm, and Darcy's pulse pounded mercilessly at his temples as he realized how he had wronged her; how profoundly his own words had prejudiced her against him.

It had been convenient to use the deficiencies of others to excuse his behavior, but now he saw himself as she must have seen him. He had not acted as was expected of a gentleman, and never before had he been so painfully aware of his own faults. He was angry. Angry at himself.

Darcy looked at Miss Elizabeth. She stood incredibly still with her hands clenched together, like a child struggling to keep her piece. Could she find it in her heart to forgive him?

"Please do join us, Mr. Bennet. You would be a welcome addition to our table," Darcy said before he could stop himself.

Miss Elizabeth raised her head and met his gaze. She had the finest eyes. Dark, lush eyelashes fluttered over her cheeks when she blinked, adorning her vibrant, chocolate brown eyes.

Through the fog surrounding Darcy, Mr. Bennet said, "We are honored you should consider us worthy company. We accept your invitation, Mr. Bingley, and I thank you."

As Bingley made arrangements, Miss Elizabeth mouthed the words to him, "We need to talk."

She was right. They had a murderer to catch. Though, now, Darcy doubted his ability to think any clear thoughts in her presence.

CHAPTER 12

"Did he propose?" asked Mother, bustling into the drawing room to wrestle with the girls for her position before the fire.

"Move over, Kitty, you are hogging all the warmth," complained Lydia as she rubbed her hands together.

"Hush! I want to hear Jane's answer," hissed Kitty, looking intently at the settee where Jane sat.

Jane smiled demurely. "No, he did not propose. However, he did invite us to dine with them this evening."

Mother clapped her hands and turned around to warm her backside, jostling Mary out of her way with a bump from her plump hip. "Oh, how wonderful! And so soon after the ball! I am certain he will propose tonight. You must wear your best gown and Lydia shall let you borrow from her collection of ribbons."

Lydia's face crumpled up like an angry toddler about to throw a tantrum.

Mrs. Yeats, with an expression of concern, touched Lydia's forehead. "You look feverish, Miss Lydia. Do you feel well?"

"As well as can be expected when you force us out into the cold and when my own mother gives away my ribbons," replied Lydia saucily.

"Lydia, mind your tongue, dear. If it were not for Mrs. Yeats suggestion, Jane would not have secured an invitation for us to dine at Netherfield Park," Mother chided. "Maybe there will be some officers there!"

Mrs. Yeats withdrew her hand. "I will send for a fresh pot of tea. Perhaps I worry over nothing."

To Elizabeth, Lydia looked flushed from being out of doors and irritated that Jane might receive a proposal before she did.

"You are only upset because you have received no gentlemen callers, and Jane is near to securing a proposal. Even Mr. Darcy appears to have taken a fancy to Lizzy," teased Kitty.

"Pshaw! Lizzy can have Mr. Darcy. He is handsome enough, but I could never marry a man who refused to dance," retorted Lydia.

"He danced at the Netherfield Ball," observed Mary dryly.

"Mr. Darcy did seem sensitive to your reactions," Father said to Elizabeth, pushing his spectacles down to perch on the end of his nose. "Do you favor the gentleman?"

"No," she said so emphatically, she felt the need to justify it. "I mean, I do not hold Mr. Darcy in any higher regard than I do any other gentleman." Now, was that entirely true? The guilt twisting her stomach told her it was not.

The stares in the room urged her to continue.

"I will own that he is handsome, as Lydia has observed, but I do not consider him to be a good match for me." She clutched her stomach, which had grown a mind of its own and protested at her every word.

Mother folded her arms. "Why ever not? The gentleman undoubtedly believes himself superior, but I should hope you do not consider him above you. You are a gentleman's daughter and, therefore, you are his equal. If he shows an interest in you, I hope you would do nothing to discourage his attentions."

Oh, if only she knew!

Mrs. Yeats returned to the room with a brew for Lydia, who drank with relish when she tasted it.

"This is delicious," she exclaimed.

"I added some sugar to the herbal tea to make it more agreeable. If you are developing a fever, it should help," Mrs. Yeats once again felt Lydia's forehead.

Elizabeth quietly retreated to her room to ready herself for dinner at Netherfield Park. She could stand no more questions about Mr. Darcy. He was better suited for a lady who gave herself airs. Or was he?

She had seen how easily he had conversed with her father even though he disapproved of his lackadaisical attitude toward life; how he had come to her defense when it was suggested that nobody would notice her absence… She had tried not to show it, but her father's thoughtless comment had stung. Not that he meant any harm by it, but it had pained her all the same. Mr. Darcy had noticed. She was sure of it.

She stared into the contents of her armoire, her fingers tracing the white work on her best muslin dress. The neckline and cinched bodice flattered her slim figure, especially when worn with her gold pendant. The maid could twist a blue ribbon through her hair to complement the flecks in her brown eyes. Did Mr. Darcy like blue?

The patter of footsteps heralded the arrival of her mother. "Lizzy, I want you to wear your best dress. We cannot waste any advantage you might have over Miss Bingley if Mr. Darcy is, indeed, to choose one of you as his wife." She paused only long enough to bark her orders before continuing down the hall to advise and encourage her other daughters.

Elizabeth grimaced at herself in disgust. What had she been doing? Dressing to please Mr. Darcy? With a rebellious resolve, she plucked her favorite cotton gown with long sleeves from her armoire and donned it before she could change her mind. If it was good enough for the Meryton Assembly, it was good enough for dinner at Netherfield Park. It was green.

***

Darcy had no difficulty selecting a waistcoat for dinner, but his cravat was entirely another matter. Either it was too tight or draped down his neck like a turkey's wattle.

What would Miss Elizabeth wear that evening? He still remembered the first time he had seen her. She had worn a green dress, the color of grass before the dew dried from its leaves. Like a breeze of fresh air in a sea of white gowns and low necklines, her modesty and lack of pretension had singled her out in the large ballroom. She had not sought him out or pranced in front of him like competing dancers on the theater stage.

Pulling out a fresh neck cloth, Lawrence, his patient valet, attempted to tie it once again, holding his breath as he folded.

His conscience troubling him for being so bothersome, Darcy said, "That is perfect, Lawrence." An apology would be just as difficult to make with a perfectly tied cravat as with a droopy one.

Darcy's shame bent itself firmly toward determination. He would find a way to speak to Miss Elizabeth and ask— beg her, if he must— for her forgiveness that night.

He descended the stairs to the tune of Miss Bingley attacking the pianoforte. No doubt, she sought to intimidate the Bennets with her accomplishment at the instrument and played in the hope they would arrive in time to hear her performance. It was wasted on Darcy. Georgiana's musical talents, with her soft fingers which glided over the keys, far exceeded Miss Bingley's attempt to dominate it to her will.

He joined the Bingleys and Hursts in the drawing room. Bingley paced in front of the fireplace, pausing every so often to rub his hands together.

Mr. Hurst leaned against one side of the settee, patting his stomach impatiently. Mrs. Hurst, as determined as Miss Bingley to elevate herself above their expected company, embroidered a complicated pastoral scene which would eventually adorn a pillow or be framed to adorn a wall for all to see and compliment.

"Darcy, you do not think me overdressed, do you?" Bingley asked with a pointed look at his eldest sister.

He wore a black coat with matching breeches, a cream shirt and cravat, and a striped blue and gold waistcoat.

"I have seen you wear this before to dinners in town. Why do you doubt yourself now?"

"Louisa thinks the stripes are too elegant for a country dinner party."

Mrs. Hurst paused, stabbing her needle into the fabric. "You need not draw attention to yourself here. There cannot be anyone you seek to impress in this out-of-the-way place. You could take a lesson from Mr. Darcy and wear a solid-colored waistcoat."

Bingley's shoulders sagged under his sister's criticism. There was no doubt she disapproved of Miss Bennet for her brother, although Miss Bennet's manners were superior to her own.

At that, the music stopped. "Mr. Darcy will agree with us, Charles. The Bennets are not the sort of family with whom you should seek an alliance. They would only bring ostracism on you. How would you introduce them to our friends in town?" She giggled, covering her mouth with her gloved hand as if it made her comments any more appropriate.

Darcy bristled at being grouped with Bingley's sisters. Not a week before, he would have agreed with them. That knowledge stung worse than a slap to the face.

Bingley looked at him. "What do you think Darcy?"

What did he think?

He admired Miss Bennet for her delicate politeness and kind disposition. She was every bit a gentlewoman as Georgiana was.

He admired Miss Elizabeth's loyalty. When she had arrived in the soggy weather with a muddy hem to Netherfield Park to care for her sister, Darcy had thought it only a clever device to capture his attention. However, she had practically ignored him for the duration of her stay, only joining the rest of the household when propriety demanded it. When he had engaged her in conversation, she had not been afraid to express her opinions and challenge his in a manner worthy of a rebuttal. There were two occasions where he had to admit, after more careful consideration, that her assessment had been correct, but his pride would not have him admit so aloud at the time.

Purposely evading the question until he could sort through the deluge of thoughts flooding his mind, Darcy simply said, "I like that waistcoat and see no reason for you to change it."

"And Miss Bennet?" Miss Bingley pressed, certain of his support.

Staring at Miss Bingley's haughty face, Darcy's temper pushed all his kind thoughts of the elder Bennet sisters aside, protecting them from any contact with the disgust overtaking him. "Am I your brother's master so that he should bow to my opinion on whom to marry? I would not dare presume to influence a decision he will spend the rest of his life either regretting or delighting in. Should he choose a bride capable of rising above the circumstances in which she was born, I would applaud his choice based on the merits she has earned against the odds. To me, that is a greater recommendation to her character than acceptance from an often hypocritical society."

The butler arrived to announce the arrival of the Bennets before Miss Bingley could raise her jaw from its unflattering position.

Darcy felt so light, only his Hessian boots kept him grounded. It pleased him to see that Miss Elizabeth wore the same green dress she had worn at the Meryton Assembly. Unlike Miss Bingley, her hair was unadorned. The candles in the room shone off her brown curls without the need for pearls or jeweled combs to lend luminescence.

Bingley inquired, "Is Miss Lydia well?"

Darcy had not noticed that the youngest Bennet had not joined them. No wonder it was relatively quiet.

Mrs. Bennet, her hand over her heart, explained, "Oh, my poor Lydia. She had to stay in this evening due to a slight fever. Her companion, Mrs. Yeats, offered to stay with her and call the apothecary should she worsen. She is a sensible woman, and Lydia is in good hands. No doubt, she will be much improved in the morning. All of my girls boast excellent health."

Darcy caught a twinkle in Mr. Bennet's eye as he patted his wife's hand and added, "Yes, dear. Mr. Bingley may rest assured on that point after seeing for himself how soon Jane recovered from her recent illness in this very house."

Mr. Collins gushed, "No doubt, the result of the superior care a household such as this can offer. Being a friend of Mr. Darcy, I feel confident in assuming that no small comfort was spared Miss Bennet."

Looking up to the ceiling to avoid rolling his eyes, Darcy controlled himself and forced his gaze down only to see that his gesture had been observed. A pair of fine eyes danced in amusement. He looked away, embarrassed he had allowed such a slip of decorum.

After a few minutes of meaningless conversation about the weather, dinner was announced. They rose, and Darcy made his way over to Miss Elizabeth to offer her his arm.

Out of the corner of his eye, he saw Mrs. Hurst exchange a meaningful look with her husband who, with a rapidity with which Darcy had not believed him capable, crossed the room and extended his arm to Miss Elizabeth. The scene astonished Darcy so much, he stood frozen in place for a second too long, leaving him with the only three remaining females: Mrs. Hurst, Miss Bingley, and Miss Mary.

Without further hesitation, he offered his arm to Miss Mary. As Bingley's invited guest, it would have been an affront not to do so (although from the huffing sounds emanating from Bingley's sisters, they did not agree). The surprise on Miss Mary's face appeased Darcy's presentiment that dinner would be an agonizingly long event.

CHAPTER 13

Dinner was a drab affair, though Bingley enjoyed himself immensely with Miss Bennet nearby.

Mrs. Bennet's mindless prattle had lulled Mr. Bennet into numb reticence between bouts of witty satire.

Miss Kitty, without her younger sister there to speak enough for the both of them, seemed to be intensely occupied in her own thoughts. She smiled often, and would then look around her self-consciously to see if anyone had noticed. Whatever pleasant musings she pondered, Darcy did not wish to interrupt them. She reminded him of Georgiana with her wistful sighs and gentle expression. How different she was without Miss Lydia's influence.

Mr. Collins regaled Mrs. Hurst with descriptions of the grandeur of Rosings, Lady Catherine's estate. Mrs. Hurst, fascinated with all things exorbitant, listened in fascination.

Miss Elizabeth suffered in silence next to Mr. Hurst, who was much more inclined to make approving remarks and satisfied grunts into his white soup and every course served thereafter than to make conversation with her. Several times, her eyes met Darcy's. He could read her face like a book. He knew when she bit her bottom lip that she dearly wished to laugh. Her eyes would dance in glee. Though she never went so far as to roll her eyes, Darcy knew she wished to. He sensed when her thoughts took a more serious turn. Her brow would furl, and she worried her upper lip.

Miss Mary carried on a conversation without any help from him. He nodded at the appropriate times and encouraged her to continue sermonizing by asking the questions he discerned she would most like to discuss. Never had he met one more suited to the clergy than the young woman seated beside him. Unfortunately, as a woman, her talents could not be realized in a man's profession. How unfair society was. It would be difficult for her to marry, and what else did the world offer a spinster? Nothing but derision. Pity for Miss Mary gave him the patience he needed as the evening wore on. His efforts were rewarded with a pleased smile from Miss Elizabeth, whose loyalty to her sisters never waned.

Finally, the meal concluded, and Miss Bingley led the ladies into the drawing room.

As the door closed behind them, Mr. Collins scooted his chair forward. "Now that the ladies have withdrawn, I feel it is now appropriate for me to tell you, Mr. Darcy, of what I have been able to learn from my meticulous investigation."

Mr. Bennet lit his pipe and leaned back in his chair. "How delicate of you, Mr. Collins, to save the ladies from overhearing news which might taint their sensibilities."

Mr. Collins nodded gravely. "Quite so. I pride myself in being sensitive to their limitations. It is a quality Lady Catherine approves, and one which I seek to cultivate."

Limitations? How dare the clergyman speak of limitations when Miss Elizabeth was more intelligent than most, and Miss Mary had committed entire tomes of sermons to memory. Had he not spent the past few hours listening to them? "I would not have thought to place such limitations on your cousins, Mr. Collins. You might be depriving yourself of some powerful allies."

Mr. Bennet's eyebrows shot up, and he straightened his slumped posture.

Mr. Collins blustered so much, Darcy regretted his attempt to correct him.

"Please, Mr. Collins, tell us what you learned," Darcy continued, before their time was wasted on Mr. Collins' inability to comprehend how a woman could possibly assist him. It was not the clergyman's fault. He only repeated what was commonly believed to be true— even if it was rubbish.

Appeased, Mr. Collins began. "As I told you before, Mr. Wickham's pistol is missing from his quarters. What I was unable to tell you was that I spoke with Colonel Forster himself. I suggested to him that a search be done of all of his soldiers' possessions, a suggestion which he was grateful to receive and fortuitously had already put into practice with Mr. Stallard presiding over the search. He assured me that had he not thought of it, he would soon have been persuaded to do so upon listening to my arguments in favor of the action."

Darcy's mind wandered to the drawing room while Mr. Collins tormented his forbearance with his superfluous wordage. Miss Elizabeth could relate twice the information in the same time.

Struggling to focus on the garrulous clergyman, Darcy sipped his port, and sifted through the abundance of words to find anything pertinent.

Mr. Bennet interrupted, "Mr. Collins, while we appreciate your opinion on Colonel Forster's approval of your advice, we would like to know the answer to the question you raised. Was the weapon found?"

Wiping his brow, Mr. Collins said, "No. It was not."

All that exposition for nothing. Bingley had done well to occupy himself with his own thoughts. He wore a silly grin on his face. Darcy did not need more than one guess to know who he was thinking about.

"Is there any sort of marking on the pistol to identify it as Mr. Wickham's?" Mr. Bennet pressed.

Mr. Collins clearly did not want to own to not knowing the answer, so Darcy interjected, "Yes. His initials are engraved on the barrel."

Rubbing his hands together, Mr. Collins continued, "I did, however, find out that Mr. Wickham had been seen calling on a young lady."

So pleased was Mr. Collins at now having the attention of every gentleman sitting around the table, he sat in silence for some time until Darcy asked, "What can you tell us about the young lady and Mr. Wickham?"

"Ah, I had hoped you would ask. It is none other than Miss Honoria Stallard."

Mr. Bennet removed his pipe. "He set his sights high."

Bingley looked confused. "Why do you say that?"

If Bingley had cared to notice anyone outside of Miss Bennet, he would have remembered two important details about Miss Stallard. Darcy said, "Miss Stallard has ten thousand pounds and is the only daughter of the local magistrate."

Mr. Bennet added, "She stands to inherit her father's estate. Whoever she marries will be considered a fortunate man, though I cannot imagine Mr. Stallard would allow her to attach herself to someone of whom he does not approve."

"Did you confirm the veracity of this information with Miss Stallard?" Darcy asked Mr. Collins. He would have liked to have been present at that conversation.

Mr. Collins flushed cheeks glistened in a smile. "I took the liberty of calling at the Stallards' estate, having established an acquaintance at the ball. I ascertained that Mr. Wickham had called at their household once and had left a favorable impression. He had requested the first dance with Miss Stallard, and so it had been a shock to them when he did not arrive."

"I imagine so," commented Mr. Hurst loudly between sips of port, and startling everyone with his contribution to the conversation.

Mr. Collins recovered and continued, "What surprised me was the lack of feeling Miss Stallard expressed." He looked about them and, thus reassured, said in a low tone, "I know I may trust you with my suspicions, as you are all gentlemen with discretion. At the time, I did not think much of it, but as the day has progressed, it cannot help but strike me as odd that she was able to smile and converse lightly with me when the subject under consideration should have been distressing to her. I do not know if it will amount to much, but I am tempted to ask one of the servants— you know how they talk— if perhaps they had not had a disagreement before the ball."

"You do not mean to imply that Miss Stallard might have killed Mr. Wickham, do you? Pardon my ignorance, please, but would she know how to shoot a pistol?" asked Bingley.

Mr. Bennet chewed on his pipe, then slowly withdrew it from his mouth. "It is possible. She does not strike me as the vengeful sort, but young ladies crossed in love have done worse things." He paused— the sort of pensive pause one makes before pronouncing something of profound importance.

The room fell silent while the gentlemen waited.

Finally, Mr. Bennet's eyes focused, and he looked intensely at Darcy. "Mr. Stallard is our magistrate. If his daughter is involved in this mess, it does not bode well for you, Mr. Darcy."

A numbness overtook Darcy, leaving his fingers as cold as ice. This was the worst news.

"Where was Miss Stallard at midnight?" he whispered.

Mr. Collins winced and pulled his handkerchief out to mop his face. He squirmed like a worm caught between a boy's fingers, waiting for the fishhook to pierce him. It was agonizing to watch, but it was nothing compared to the torment Darcy experienced.

Mr. Bennet said, "Speak up, Mr. Collins."

"I am grateful they received me after the unfortunate accident. As you can imagine, I apologized profusely for my role in Miss Stallard's misfortune. I— You see, it so happened— Well, I— ," he began, his complexion deepening in color with each attempt. With a large huff of breath, he closed his eyes and said, "It is with great shame that I must admit my error. It was I who bumped into Miss

Stallard, causing her to spill her drink down the front of her gown. It was ruined, and she refused my attempts to help her."

"At what time?" Darcy asked, though he feared the answer.

"About eleven o'clock. It was a pity she never returned. I would have apologized much sooner."

***

After some minutes spent in awkward silence in the drawing room, Mrs. Hurst settled in between Mary and Jane, clearly only enduring Mary's company for the sake of avoiding the other Bennet females in the room.

Mother and Kitty were content to talk amongst themselves. It would have been overly rude— even for them— to complain once again for the lack of officers present at the table that evening.

Miss Bingley eased into the chair next to Elizabeth, leaning forward. "Where were you at midnight, Miss Eliza?" she asked plainly, her face pinched.

"I was in the library." Elizabeth offered no extra details. If Miss Bingley wanted them, she could ask.

"I thought you enjoyed dancing. What were you doing in the library during a ball?"

"I had a headache and needed a moment of quiet. It was too cold to venture outside, and so I chose the library." Narrowing her eyes, she continued, "It was the oddest thing, but I had not been in the room long when I found myself locked inside."

The muscles at Miss Bingley's temples twitched in spasms. "Yes, that was unfortunate. My housekeeper took it upon herself to lock the rooms not in use." She looked off into a corner as she spoke, avoiding eye contact.

"Why would she do such a thing?" Elizabeth asked, unwilling to drop the subject too easily.

Feigning disinterest, Miss Bingley shrugged her shoulders. "She considered that some of the guests took advantage of our generosity when a gentleman attempted to ensconce one of the Wedgwood urns from the fireplace mantel in his pocket." She stifled a yawn, further showing how boring she found the subject.

Elizabeth laughed. "I would have liked to have seen that. No pocket is big enough to hide an urn. Surely he was merely admiring it, though I will admit it was badly done for a gentleman to give such an impression."

Picking at her skirts, Miss Bingley sighed. Elizabeth could not help but notice how the red flush of embarrassment crawled up her neck. She could have needled Miss Bingley more, but decided against it in favor of kindness.

"First impressions, I find, are usually accurate, do you not agree?" Miss Bingley asked, looking at Elizabeth from the corner of her eyes.

"No, I cannot say I do," she answered, instantly regretting her quick response. Had she been asked the same question only two days before, she would have readily agreed.

Elizabeth had always believed herself to be an outstanding judge of character, but she had to admit that her attitude toward Mr. Darcy was not what it was at their first meeting. She found herself wanting to like him, but could not give herself over to the idea knowing the abuse Mr. Wickham had suffered at his hand. And yet, she could no longer despise him as she had before.

"Perhaps you lack experience, the society here being limited at best, to correctly judge character." Miss Bingley's sharp voice did not cut Elizabeth too deeply, tottering as she was between two opinions and preferring not to explain from whence her reasoning came.

"How fortunate, then, that you have come to Netherfield so that I might gain the experience to which you refer." Really, kindness only went so far.

"Were you alone in the library?" Miss Bingley hissed, her sharp gaze fierce and desperate.

She knew. And now she sought to find out if Elizabeth would take advantage of it as she undoubtedly would herself.

Mother, who had incredibly good hearing in matters involving available gentlemen, said, "It is too bad an officer was not with you, Lizzy. We would have had a wedding before the end of the year!"

Kitty giggled with Mother. No doubt, they thought a marriage by compromise was romantic.

Elizabeth was glad that ringlets covered her ears. They burned all the more so when Miss Bingley sneered, "I would not think that Miss Elizabeth would resort to entrapping a poor officer when there are far superior gentlemen of fortune about." She looked at Elizabeth through the slits of her eyes, awaiting the reassurance she desired.

Miss Bingley would rather watch Mr. Darcy be accused for a crime she knew him innocent of than to lose him to Elizabeth in a compromise she had unwittingly enabled. That knowledge made Elizabeth clamp her lips shut. Miss Bingley deserved to wallow miserably in her doubts.

"How romantic to marry an officer. They look so handsome in their scarlet coats and gold tassels," sighed Kitty.

"I nearly married an officer, you know," commented Mother, leaving the room in uncomfortable silence.

The door opened, and the gentlemen joined them before Elizabeth could redirect their deteriorating conversation.

"Let us entertain the gentlemen with some music," suggested Mrs. Hurst, looking about for a volunteer.

Mary moved to rise, but Father walked over to her and placed his hand on her shoulder, thus preventing her from standing. Mary looked much put out, but Elizabeth was secretly grateful. As much as Mary practiced, she would only appear foolish compared to Miss Bingley and Mrs. Hurst.

When no one else moved toward the pianoforte, Miss Bingley rose in a flurry of haughty airs. "If no one else will oblige us, then perhaps I shall presume to entertain you."

She crossed directly in front of Mr. Darcy. "Is there anyone who would be so kind as to turn the pages for me?" she asked coquettishly.

Mr. Darcy made no offer, even though Miss Bingley paused long enough for him to have done so.

Mrs. Hurst, always ready to attend to Miss Bingley's cause, bustled to the bench to sit next to her sister when it appeared that Mr. Collins might have offered his assistance.

The gentlemen settled around the instrument, except for Mr. Darcy. He crossed the room to his favorite post— the window by the fireplace. Elizabeth saw the reflection of his face in the glass. Their eyes met and held for the duration of the piece.

When Miss Bingley began another piece, he sat in a chair near Elizabeth, his leg crossed toward her. Aware of his every movement, Elizabeth waited for him to say something.

"Miss Elizabeth," he whispered her name, and she leaned slightly toward him without taking her eyes off Miss Bingley's display of talent.

He continued, "I have learned some information from Mr. Collins which may prove valuable, while it also is detrimental to me. I am interested to hear if it coincides with what you learned from Mrs. Philips."

She heard the strain in his voice and chanced a glance at his face. His eyes caught her, and she could not look away. His forehead creased in worry, and his dark eyes pleaded with her for something she did not understand.

He was innocent, of that she was certain. Therein lay the problem— *only* she was certain. And she was not like Miss Bingley. She could never allow him to face the gallows when it was in her power to free him.

Filling her lungs with air and courage, she whispered, "I know the idea is as disagreeable to you as it is to me, but one word from me can put an end to this."

Holding her breath, she held his firm gaze until she felt she must look away or draw suspicious remarks from their party.

"I cannot ask that of you, knowing your thoughts on the subject. What is left for me to do is to ascertain who is behind this sordid mess before I am charged with a crime we both know I did not commit."

"It has been two days. We do not have much time. The inquest has been arranged for Monday." Oh, if only they could speak freely. Mr. Darcy was intelligent and, with her help, Elizabeth was certain they would soon find Mr. Wickham's murderer.

Mr. Darcy shook his head. "There is no 'we' here. I do not doubt your capabilities, Miss Elizabeth, but

I cannot allow it. How could I ensure your safety were you to discover the truth? Who is to say that whoever murdered Wickham would not do it again?"

"I am cautious."

His eyebrows met together, forming a firm, almost angry, expression against which she instantly rebelled. Who was Mr. Darcy to order her about? She crossed her arms together, forgetting their need for discretion. She hissed, "I am an excellent judge of character. I would know." She realized how silly she sounded, but her pride would not allow her to admit her mistake.

"An excellent judge of character? When you would accuse me— if not for certain events of which we must not speak— of murder? You would not know a murderer if he confessed it to you," Darcy scoffed, returning ire for ire loudly enough that Mr. Bingley turned around to look at them.

Elizabeth clasped her hands in her lap and paid singular attention to Miss Bingley, who now sought to show them all how accomplished her singing voice was.

"Her singing is lovely," she commented to Mr. Bingley, so that he turned back around.

Glaring at Mr. Darcy for doubting her abilities so completely— despite her own growing doubts— she forgot the insult aimed at him on the tip of her tongue when he smiled at her.

"That was ingenious," he whispered.

What a maddening man. She could not justify her haughty anger after he paid her a compliment.

"Thank you," she grumbled.

They sat in silence for several long seconds. Then, he leaned in again. He smelled like everything she loved about nature mixed with the undeniably masculine scents of sandalwood and shaving cream. "We need to talk. Meet me tomorrow at Oakham Mount at the time you normally take your walks?"

Taken aback that he remembered her walking habits, she next considered the obstacles. Mr. Darcy did not know how the arrival of Mrs. Yeats had imposed on her daily exercise. "I will be there," she said, already scheming how she could escape from the house alone.

"Miss Elizabeth, promise me you will not investigate any further?"

Whether it was his nearness, his intoxicating smile, his smooth velvety tone, or his genuine concern, she did not know. But it soothed her, and she answered how she should have before. "I will do my best."

"Why does that not reassure me?" he asked with a sigh, settling into his chair and focusing on the back of Mr. Bingley's head.

The butler entered the room, his steps hesitant as he made his way to the master of Netherfield Park. Cupping his hands around his mouth, he whispered something to Mr. Bingley.

Mr. Bingley sprung from his chair, looked at Mr. Darcy, tugged his hand through his hair, and turned to follow the butler out of the drawing room without so much as a word.

CHAPTER 14

Darcy's unease grew the longer Bingley was gone. Why had he looked at him before he left the room? The butler, too, had appeared quite shaken.

He looked askance at Miss Elizabeth. Shadows from the firelight behind them danced across her face. She chewed the corner of her mouth, and Darcy knew she was planning something. He dearly hoped it did not involve catching Wickham's killer.

Darcy did not doubt her capable of solving the mystery and setting them both at their liberty, but whoever had murdered Wickham had managed to hide himself successfully thus far. If he killed Wickham, then what was to stop him from bringing harm to a curious maiden? And if Miss Stallard was involved, the danger to Miss Elizabeth was far greater. Darcy shivered despite the warmth in the room.

She looked at the door repeatedly, now discontent to chew only on the corner of her mouth as she bit her lips until they were as bright as ripe strawberries. What was she scheming? She shifted her weight forward, as if making to stand. She would not dare! Of course, she had promised him nothing. Had she done so, she would have honored her word.

Before Miss Elizabeth could go out into the entrance hall, he stood. With his firmest stare, he willed her to stay in the drawing room.

She understood his meaning, even if she did not like it.

Crossing quietly to the door, he whipped around it and closed it behind him in one smooth motion.

Bingley had one hand behind his neck as if he suffered from an immense headache. Standing opposite him were Mr. Tanner, Colonel Forster, and Mr. Stallard.

Mr. Tanner bowed mockingly as Darcy joined them. "How good of you to condescend to join us, Mr. Darcy. We are here, after all, to arrest you."

Darcy's glance shot at Mr. Stallard. "What is this?"

The colonel cleared his throat. "We can put it off no longer, Mr. Darcy. The evidence against you continues to mount and, with no other suspects, the people of Meryton demand justice. They are uneasy, and there has been talk of them taking matters into their own hands. Me and my men have been stationed here to promote peace, not to encourage mob behavior."

"We seek to protect you and your friends until we can get to the bottom of this affair," added Mr. Stallard.

"Who would promote such riotous behavior?" Darcy glared at Mr. Tanner, who only lifted his chin in reply.

Darcy pulsed his fists at his side.

"Gentlemen," Bingley interrupted, "let us go into the front parlor lest our voices carry." He signaled the butler and in no time at all, candles lit up the dark room, casting suspicious shadows over their faces as they sat facing each other in the circle of chairs.

Mr. Tanner placed himself directly opposite Darcy, scrutinizing his every move and gesture. It grew increasingly more imperative that Darcy speak before he did. He could not allow for any apparent weakness in front of the man.

Swallowing his growing concern, Darcy asked, "What exactly is the evidence against me? As far as I know, the only evidence is the inability to trace my whereabouts in a crowded ball at the hour of the crime."

"Do you believe yourself so far above the laws which govern us, you feel yourself justified in refusing to give a straightforward answer? Had you answered our inquiries in a forthright manner, I could have taken your word as a gentleman. As it is, your word means nothing when you have given us every reason to doubt you," said Mr. Tanner.

Bingley looked anywhere in the room but at Mr. Tanner.

Mr. Stallard stroked his whiskers and nodded his agreement. "You must admit, Mr. Darcy, that your unwillingness to answer our questions openly does cast an unfavorable light on your testimony. Please do not mistake me, sir. I have made no judgments and will refrain from doing so until we have more evidence. Murder is a serious matter, and I will not send a man to hang unless I am certain of his guilt."

"How reassuring," Darcy muttered.

"Darcy, why can you not tell them what they wish to know? What can you possibly lose when it is your very life which is in danger?" begged Bingley.

An image of Miss Elizabeth flashed before him. Her willingness to give up her freedom to save him made him more determined than ever not to allow it. "What else can I tell them but what I have already said. I was here. I did not leave Netherfield Park."

"What was your dispute about with Lieutenant Wickham the morning of November the twenty-sixth?" asked Mr. Stallard with the firmness of a judge.

If only it were so simple. Could he live with the consequences if he caused the death of Georgiana's hopes by revealing the nature of his quarrel against

Wickham? Any father or older brother would understand it.

Could he chain Miss Elizabeth to an unwanted marriage, certain that her resentment of him would grow over the years to choke out any affection she could possibly feel for him? No, he admired her too greatly to treat her independence so lightly. And he loved his sister more than his own life.

"I will tell you what I have repeatedly said. My quarrel with Mr. Wickham was of a personal nature and as such, I thank you gentlemen to respect my wishes to remain silent on that account as I left him alive and well after our disagreement. I returned to Netherfield, and I did not leave the property until after his murder."

Mr. Tanner leaned forward. "What secrets are you hiding, Mr. Darcy?"

Darcy did not answer, but stared at the constable with the same face he used when playing cards. He would reveal nothing, and judging from Mr. Tanner's consternation, he was successful.

"Darcy," said Bingley, massaging the back of his neck, "is any secret worth risking your life over? I beg you to consider."

Bingley meant well. He was everything kind and innocent. He was the sort to spare the swatting of a fly at a picnic.

"I am innocent of any wrongdoing in this affair, and I trust justice will be done."

"Let me call in an inspector," Bingley persisted.

"No," Darcy answered firmly. He may as well blab the complete story to the occupants of the room than allow for a stranger to poke into his affairs. Georgiana would be ruined and Miss Elizabeth would hate him— and with just cause.

Mr. Stallard sighed. "Then, I am left with no other choice. I had hoped to leave all this unpleasantness behind us, but I must do something lest the villagers decide to take matters into their own hands. I am sure you understand how their unpredictable actions could lead to unnecessary suffering. It is for this motive I put you under arrest, Mr. Darcy. You and the residents of Netherfield Park will be safer if you are in custody. I am sorry."

Was he sorry? Darcy doubted Mr. Stallard's sincerity— especially if Mr. Collins' suspicions proved true. His inclination was to balk, but if what the men said was true, he could cause problems to Bingley and his household if he resisted.

Bingley fell back into his chair, his eyes wide. "You are serious? You will arrest a guest in my home, at this hour?"

"Is it preferable to parade Mr. Darcy through Meryton during the day? We thought to allow him some dignity, given the nature of his arrest and the hostility held against him. I was unaware you had a dinner party, and I deeply regret interrupting their entertainment, but it is better for all concerned that he come with us quietly," said Mr. Stallard.

Holding up his hands, Colonel Forster said, "It is for his protection… and yours, Mr. Bingley. I must do something to maintain order, but arrangements have been made for Mr. Darcy to reside in my quarters until further notice. Please, gentlemen, it pains me greatly, but I have seen what an upset crowd can do. Everyone present at your home at this moment could become a target."

That was all it took for Darcy to decide. He would cooperate. If word of this spread, the Darcy name would run through the gossip mills. But that was a small price to pay. He would prove his character and act honorably to protect those whom he held dear. "That is considerate of you, Colonel."

"It is too considerate," said Mr. Tanner.

With a scowl at the outspoken constable, Mr. Stallard said, "Have your valet pack what you require for the next three days until the inquest."

Colonel Forster asked, "You do not think it preferable to move the date? Surely, the jury will acquit Mr. Darcy. There is no need to drag this on any longer than necessary."

Mr. Stallard considered Darcy from under his hooded eyes. After some pause, he bunched up his chin. "No, Colonel, the inquest stands as it is. The arrangements have already been made."

The gentlemen rose, and with glee, Mr. Tanner pulled out a pair of irons.

That was too much. Darcy balked.

"Mr. Tanner, put those away," ordered Mr. Stallard.

Mr. Tanner jangled the metal together, smacking them against his thick, open hand. If his intent was to irritate Darcy, it worked.

They filed into the entrance hall just as a svelte figure closed the door to the drawing room behind her. Miss Elizabeth stepped toward them and froze, her eyes widening at the sight of the irons clanking in Mr. Tanner's hands. Darcy had no doubt but that the oaf intended to dangle them in front of him during the entire return to Meryton.

"I apologize for interrupting your… meeting, gentlemen," she said, walking toward the stairs. If Darcy knew her at all, she had conjured an excuse to leave the room to satisfy her curiosity. A convenient 'refreshing' would go unquestioned.

Unfortunately, at that moment, Miss Bingley barged out of the door. "Charles, you are neglecting your party terribly and I must insist that you and Mr. Darcy return to us." She propped her hands on her hips and waved her nose in the air, daring Bingley, or anyone else for that matter, to defy her.

When no one else spoke, Darcy said, "I must accompany these gentlemen back to Meryton, but I am certain Bingley would much rather keep your company than his present one."

"Nonsense! Why would you possibly leave at this time of night?" she argued.

Miss Elizabeth, who had stood silently watching, asked, "You must accompany the gentlemen? You have no choice in the matter?"

It was a delicate way to ask the question he could read across her inquisitive face, and Darcy admired her for keeping her wits about her and not causing a scene worse than the one already unfolding in Bingley's front hall.

Mr. Tanner held no such delicacies, as was his habit. "Mr. Darcy is under arrest for the murder of Lieutenant George Wickham, miss. Now, if you will excuse us, we must be on our way. You can return to whatever it is you gentle folks do with your spare time."

Darcy watched the veins in Miss Elizabeth's neck pop out and her shoulders tense. "You would arrest an innocent man?" she challenged, stepping toward Mr. Tanner.

Mr. Stallard placed his hand on Mr. Tanner's shoulder to prevent him from responding. He said, "Miss Elizabeth, do you have any information which would prevent me from putting Mr. Darcy under arrest?"

Darcy watched her intently. She did not hesitate, and would have ruined her future to save him had he allowed her to speak.

"I—" she started.

"How could Miss Elizabeth possibly know what you seek? Granted, she is clever, but I do not think it likely for her to reveal the evidence you require," Darcy interrupted.

Miss Elizabeth had never been a good one to conceal her expression, and her eyes spoke to Darcy as clearly as words at that moment. It made his decision easier to bear. And yet, he could not leave without accomplishing what he had set out to do that evening.

Thinking quickly, and trusting she would understand, he said, "I am sorry for speaking out of turn, Miss Elizabeth. It was unpardonably rude, and I beg your pardon."

He heard Miss Bingley mumble, "A mere interruption hardly merits such an apology."

That was not what Darcy apologized for, but it mattered not. Miss Elizabeth understood him. She knew he regretted having insulted her at the Meryton Assembly. He saw it in her eyes. They softened, and her breath trembled.

He could have spent all night rooted in that same spot, watching the transformation in Miss Elizabeth's eyes. He did not need her to utter the words to know she felt them.

Darcy turned to Bingley, "The best you can do is to return to your party. I apologize if I have ruined your evening."

"I will not give up, Darcy. I will find out who has done this," he said.

Darcy patted his friend's shoulder. "Thank you, my friend."

Miss Elizabeth and Miss Bingley stood behind him, offering their support.

Turning, Darcy said, "Let us go." He had a good many questions to ask Colonel Forster and Mr. Stallard— without the interference of Mr. Tanner.

He did not allow himself to look back as they left the house, but he heard her.

"I forgive you," she said. He had not realized how badly he craved to hear those words from her until she had pronounced them. It was the best parting gift Elizabeth could have offered.

CHAPTER 15

Mr. Darcy had been arrested. The image of him walking between the constable and the colonel burned in Elizabeth's eyes. They had flanked him as if he were a common criminal, but he had walked away with his head held high. And in the midst of all his troubles, he had apologized to her. All the negative thoughts she had ever held against Mr. Darcy had melted into a puddle at her feet, never to rise up in her heart again.

"You are quiet, Lizzy," said Father, as he handed her out of the carriage. They had left Netherfield Park as soon as their carriage could be readied.

"We are all quiet, Papa." She followed Mr. Collins, her mother, and her sisters, who walked in stupors of silence, into their home.

Mrs. Yeats sat near the fire in the drawing room, a book in her hand. She stood as they filed into the room. "Has something happened? Are you well?" she asked, looking between them with concern.

Mother flopped into the nearest chair, fanning her face and leaning against the cushions as if she were so overwhelmed, she could not even hold her head up. "I daresay most of Meryton will call so that they may hear the news." The thought cheered her miraculously. Sitting upright, she added excitedly, "How trying it shall be to have so many callers." Her eyes darted around the drawing room in anticipation of her expected popularity.

"Oh, no, my dear Mrs. Bennet, we must not allow for Mr. Darcy's reputation to be slandered thus," commented an appalled Mr. Collins. For once, Elizabeth agreed with him.

"I certainly will not take the initiative to bring up the subject, but how am I to prevent others from doing so?" responded Mother.

"A fire soon goes out with no fuel to feed it," commented Father. "Mr. Collins is right, Mrs. Bennet. Your social talents are better spent cheering your youngest daughter."

Jane sat on the sofa beside Mrs. Yeats. "How is Lydia?" she asked.

Clapping her hands together, Mother remembered her ill daughter. "Oh, yes, my poor, dear Lydia. I do hope she has recovered enough to receive callers?"

If she were appalled at Mother's priorities, Mrs. Yeats hid it well. Only a hint of sharpness affected her voice. "My guess is that Miss Lydia ate one too many sweets, as I am learning she is prone to do. She was miserable with the stomachache for a couple of hours after you left, but it eventually passed. She is asleep now."

"What a blessing she did not come with us. You, too, Mrs. Yeats, were spared the danger of sharing a table with a murderer." Mother shivered dramatically.

Mr. Collins exclaimed louder than Elizabeth. "Mrs. Bennet, I must insist! Please spread this malignant news no further."

As could be expected, Mrs. Yeats' eyes enlarged at that bit of information.

"Mrs. Bennet," said Father, rolling his eyes, "while it is true there was a sort of arrest this evening, Mr. Bingley explained to us that it is more for Mr. Darcy's protection than a formal accusation. I thank you to remember that when the gossips arrive tomorrow." He looked apologetically at Mr. Collins.

Elizabeth had admired Mr. Bingley's efforts to minimize the scandal, but an arrest was an arrest no matter the motive. It was the most exciting thing to happen in Meryton in a long time, and it would not take long for word to spread and for the villagers to consign Mr. Darcy to the hangman's noose. Nobody would defend him. Nobody liked him. She flexed her hands before her nails bruised her palms.

Mrs. Yeats shook her head. "Am I to understand Mr. Darcy was arrested for the murder of Mr. Wickham? It cannot be! He is from a noble family and has such high manners."

"And yet it was done. Someone killed Mr. Wickham, and who is to say it was not Mr. Darcy?" said Kitty, voicing the self-righteous judgment Elizabeth had expected to hear in Meryton— not from her own sister.

"Kitty!" Elizabeth exclaimed before she could stop herself. "Mr. Darcy is not a murderer. How can you accuse him so easily?"

Kitty folded her arms together defiantly. "The same way you dismiss the idea so easily. Why do you care so much, Lizzy? You cannot know that he did not do it."

Oh, but she did. However, she had already said too much. If Mr. Darcy had prevented her from speaking before the colonel and the constable, he most certainly would not appreciate her revealing the truth to her family. Would he rather dangle from the end of a rope than marry her? Surely, it could not be that bad.

If Mr. Darcy preferred death to a lifetime with her, then she would simply have to solve the murder and, in the process, show him she could be every bit as fierce as the most accomplished lady he would ever meet.

Ready to take on the world, Elizabeth said with feeling, "I do not think it just he has been arrested for a crime that, as yet, nobody can prove he committed. Would not justice be better served if the accused person were considered innocent until proved guilty?" She looked to Father for support.

He bunched up his cheeks. "Perhaps, though I think it would be wise on your part not to voice your opinions outside these walls. Mr. Tanner dislikes Mr. Darcy so intensely, I would not be surprised if he arrests you for coming to the gentleman's defense."

"It is not so much to defend the gentleman, but rather to see justice properly served," said Elizabeth, she said half-heartedly.

"In the end, we all render accounts to God. If it is his will, justice will be carried out," contributed Mary. Kitty nodded her agreement.

Jane, who twisted her fingers in agitation, said, "Would not God want us to help our fellow man when he is in trouble? What of the neighborly Samaritan? I am of the mind that what happened to Mr. Wickham was all one horrible accident. It could be that simple, could it not?"

Father smiled lovingly at her. "My sweet, innocent Janey, I wish it were so simple. However, Mr. Wickham was shot through the heart in his quarters. While he may have suffered a fatal accident whilst, shall we say, cleaning his weapons or from a stray bullet at target practice, it is not likely it would hit him directly in the heart. And then, there is the matter of his pistol— the weapon it is supposed shot him. It is still missing."

Mr. Collins, who had not stopped rubbing his hands together since entering the house, said, "I feel it incumbent upon me to write to Lady Catherine and inform her of what her nephew suffers. She will hire the best investigator in the country and soon enough establish order." He spoke with importance, as if Lady Catherine were a crown judge.

"But Mr. Darcy explicitly asked for you not to inform her. Would it not be best to consult with him first?" objected Elizabeth.

She could see clearly enough that Mr. Collins did not agree with her. Before he could expound on the superiority of Lady Catherine de Bourgh's judgment, she added, "Lady Catherine would, no doubt, do precisely as you say, but would it not be a kindness on your part to inquire first of Mr. Darcy if such assistance is required? He may have a good reason not to inform her of what is transpiring." She did not know this for certain, but Elizabeth sensed that Mr. Darcy hid more than just their compromising situation in the library. He had another secret. There must be someone else involved, for she did not flatter herself that he would risk his life merely to allow her to marry for love.

Mr. Collins considered. "I do believe I will go into Meryton on the morrow to offer some spiritual and moral comfort to Mr. Darcy. And then, if I see the need for it, I will write to Lady Catherine. How sensible of you to suggest a more delicate measure, Cousin Elizabeth. It will please Lady Catherine to know that my relatives are equally concerned over the welfare of her nephew as she would be." His cheeks scrunched his eyes up into a painful looking smile of which Elizabeth did not care to be the recipient.

Father looked at her over his spectacles. "Let us hope all will be resolved soon. Lizzy, I know it is in your nature to be curious, and you will help someone who you believe to be falsely accused... to the detriment of your own safety and reputation, I might add."

"I hardly think expressing my opinion of Mr. Darcy's innocence is damaging to my reputation."

"No, but it stands in stark contrast to the opinion of the majority, and there are those who might question why you feel the need to champion Mr. Darcy's cause when no one else does. You are an intelligent girl, and I will leave it at that. Mrs. Yeats will agree with me."

Elizabeth felt her face flush, and was grateful that the only illumination in the room was the small fireplace and a few lit candles.

"Miss Elizabeth, I do agree with Mr. Bennet," said Mrs. Yeats. "People already have enough fodder for their gossip without adding a dangerous romance to it. Besides, if Mr. Darcy did not...." She shuddered and wrapped her shawl more firmly around her shoulders. "If Mr. Darcy is innocent, it means the criminal is still free to cause harm, and it is no longer safe for you to indulge in the freedoms you formerly enjoyed."

That got Mother's attention. "We shall be murdered in our beds! Mr. Bennet, we must arrange for the servants to stand watch lest we come to harm."

"Nonsense, my dear. So far as we know, the killer is gone. Why would he stay and risk capture?"

"Why, indeed? It would be the height of foolishness to stay nearby and witness the harm he had caused. Unless, he was an officer in the militia," added Mr. Collins.

Father's brows furled together and he pinched his chin. "Hmm. Now that does bring up an interesting point."

"You still think an officer did it?" asked Kitty incredulously.

"It is possible, but no, I am referring to the other bit Mr. Collins said about witnessing the harm done. In a village full of people who dislike the gentleman, it is convenient that *he* was the one arrested. If someone held something against Mr. Darcy, he would provide the perfect scapegoat. A person with a dark bend of the mind would take great pleasure in watching Mr. Darcy suffer."

Elizabeth remembered Mr. Tanner's manners against Mr. Darcy. He had seemed to enjoy the arrest. Did his aggression toward Mr. Darcy have a deeper cause than their difference in social classes? How could she find out without causing more disturbance? If he was the source of the villagers' growing animosity toward Mr. Darcy, he must be stopped.

Warnings or not, Elizabeth would walk into Meryton in the morning to investigate. She would continue where Mr. Darcy was unable. She would discover the identity of the real killer… or die trying, her mind added. She shivered before squaring her shoulders.

No, there would be no more deaths. She would be cautious and walk on the main road instead of cutting through the fields. No one would accost her in plain view of passersby and field hands. She would be safe.

CHAPTER 16

Sleep did not come to Darcy until he had drafted two letters, and then it only came in fits and spurts.

He woke the following morning, his eyes dry from lack of rest, to see that Lawrence had acquired a tub for bathing and was filling it with steaming water.

"The housekeeper was kind enough to allow us the use of the bath, sir. I shall have it ready for you before long," he said as he poured a kettle of hot water into the tub and a waft of steam obscured him from view.

Darcy squeezed the base of his neck, trying to relax his sore muscles. "You are a good man, Lawrence."

Lawrence paused on his way out the door to receive another kettle of water from the footman. "And you are a good man, Mr. Darcy. Why do you permit others to continue to think the worst of you?"

"Do you really think people will believe me if I told them the truth about Wickham now? They have made him into a martyr, and they would hate me all the more for defiling his name after his death."

"Please, sir, you misunderstand me. I would never suggest you expose Miss Darcy to the comments which such a revelation would ensure." He took one step closer to Darcy, clasping his hands before him.

Darcy understood what Lawrence meant. Only he had hoped to avoid the topic.

"Why do I not reveal my whereabouts at the hour it is supposed Wickham was shot?" asked Darcy.

Lawrence looked up. "I have been observing Miss Elizabeth since her stay at Netherfield Park. Please forgive my impertinence, sir, but I noticed how you acted differently toward her. I imagined you esteemed her more than other young ladies, and consequently, I have inquired about her discreetly."

Darcy's head shot up. "To whom have you spoken?"

"Only other servants, and always with the mention of the other Bennets. I never singled her out, knowing you would not appreciate me drawing attention to a preference of yours."

His preference? Was it so obvious to everyone besides him? Certainly, he held Miss Elizabeth in high regard, but for it to be so noticeable disturbed Darcy greatly.

"What were you told?" he asked, indulging in his curiosity.

"Nothing I am certain you have not already ascertained on your own. She is loyal to a fault and speaks truthfully at all times."

Darcy held back a chuckle. Initially, Darcy had thought that Miss Elizabeth's sarcastic remarks had been flirtatious banter. What a fool he had been! She had spoken the truth as she saw it and this revelation, while unflattering to his own character, had earned his trust.

A gripping need to reveal his crippling secret to her overwhelmed him. It was already written. It only needed to be delivered.

"What else?" he asked, craving more.

"She is intelligent. I did not need to hear it from anyone else to know its truth." Raising his head slightly, Lawrence was emboldened enough to say, "She is not intimidated by you, sir."

This time, Darcy chuckled aloud. The sound was strange to his ears, almost as if he had forgotten how to laugh with the tension of the past few days. Nay, not only the past few days. He had worn the burden of secrets and responsibility for years now.

"I suppose it was her disposition toward merriness which inclined me to like her. Miss Elizabeth does not take herself too seriously and would sooner laugh at her own mistakes than allow them to make her bitter. It is refreshing… and distinct to my own tendencies," Darcy spoke softer the more personal his words became.

Lawrence poured another kettle of water into the tub and signaled to Darcy that it was ready.

Darcy had hoped Lawrence would contradict his unflattering assessment of his own character, but he did not. Was he that proud? Apparently, he still had much work to do. His apology to Miss Elizabeth was a start, but it depended on him to continue to cultivate humility.

Lawrence handed him some soap, saying, "She complements you. You could do much worse, sir, if I may be so bold as to blatantly offer my opinion."

The water turned milky-white as Darcy scrubbed his body. "Would that prevent you from offering your opinion anyway, Lawrence?"

Setting the soap aside, Darcy leaned back against the tub and let his muscles melt in the hot water. He opened one eye to catch his valet's reaction and was pleased to see the hint of a smile.

"I do have a favor to ask of you—" began Darcy.

A knock at the door interrupted.

Lawrence opened the door a crack.

"I apologize for the interruption, sir, but Mr. Stallard wishes to speak with Mr. Darcy. Shall I tell him to wait or shall I tell him to return later?" the footman asked.

Lawrence looked over his shoulder at Darcy.

Darcy shrugged his shoulders. Frankly, he did not care what the gentleman decided to do with his time, and he had no wish to see him.

With a sardonic grin, Lawrence told the footman, "If it so pleases Mr. Stallard, he may wait until my master is ready to receive company." He closed the door.

Darcy had always appreciated Lawrence's efficiency and attention to detail, but never before had he felt the same conspiratorial friendship toward his manservant as he felt at that moment.

"You do not like Mr. Stallard?" he asked, rising out of the water and donning the robe Lawrence held up.

"May I speak plainly, sir?"

"Has that stopped you today?"

"It has not, and so I will persist. No, I do not like Mr. Stallard nor his daughter, Miss Stallard. She is a conniving sort of lady, even more so than Miss Bingley, and I have a feeling that this visit will not be to your advantage."

Lawrence did not cease to surprise Darcy. "You disapprove of Miss Bingley as well?"

Clearly exasperated, Darcy spared Lawrence from giving an answer. "I only put up with her because Bingley is a good friend. I hate to think how society would mistreat him were his name not so often associated with mine."

"Mr. Bingley is everything affable and good. I cannot say the same for his sister, though she will keep your secret safe so long as she does not think of a way to use it against you." He gave Darcy a pointed look.

"Do you believe Miss Bingley capable of blackmail?" Darcy did not, but he was learning a lot from his valet, who had observed much more than Darcy had imagined.

"That remains to be seen, sir. Of course, it will not matter much if Mr. Stallard does it first."

Darcy shivered, chilled to the bone. "Let us not make him wait too long, then," he said, donning his pressed clothes in good time.

The letters lay on top of the writing desk. Grabbing the sealed notes and shuffling them in his hands, he said, "You have been with me as my worst fears have come to fruition, and I thank you for guarding my confidence over the years."

"It is an honor to serve you as I served your father before you, sir," Lawrence said with a bow.

"Will you see that Miss Elizabeth receives this?" he held out one envelope.

Taking it and tucking it into his pocket without batting an eyelash, Lawrence said, "I will give it to the Bennets' housekeeper, Mrs. Hill. She feels about Miss Elizabeth as I do about you. She will be discreet."

"Thank you, Lawrence. And please see that this gets sent by messenger. It is of the utmost importance."

Lawrence tucked the second letter in another pocket and nodded. "If you do not need me, I will make arrangements immediately."

It was done. Darcy felt lighter than he had in months. Nothing Mr. Stallard could bring up against him would spoil that.

***

"I missed all of the diversion," complained Lydia, her arms crossed and her bottom lip poking out.

Mrs. Yeats, who walked beside her, said, "It is unbecoming to pout, Miss Lydia. There are better, more ladylike ways of expressing yourself and, until you master them, you would do well to learn the value of silence."

"The one who holds his tongue is considered wise, whereas the one who speaks recklessly is often made the fool," quoted Mary in support.

"What an insightful application of a proverb, Miss Mary," commented Mr. Collins. "Your study of the sermons do you credit."

Mary liked the praise, but she tried very hard not to show it lest she be overtaken by vanity. God forbid!

Elizabeth thought more kindly toward Mr. Collins for giving her sister, who was often overlooked, a bounce to her step as they continued walking toward Meryton. It was a glorious day, and Mother had thought she might need the carriage, and so they had been obliged to walk.

"We so often do what you wish, Lydia, please do not deny us some entertainment when it was your own carelessness which caused you to miss it," said Jane gently. "Besides, it was your wish to walk into Meryton to visit Aunt Philips."

"How convenient we must walk past the militia tents to get to her house." Lydia smiled, flashing her dimples. "I wonder if we will chance upon Mr. Denny."

Kitty's smile disappeared at the mention of that particular officer's name. "You flirt too openly with him."

Lydia smacked her on the arm. "What do you care? You flirt just as I do, and why should we not when we are the youngest, handsomest maidens in Meryton? With their life of self-sacrifice, I consider it my duty to bring the officers cheer."

Elizabeth shook her head. Lydia would be a burden to Father until she married… in which case she would then become a burden to the wretched man who married her.

"You will conduct yourself with proper deportment should we encounter any officers. Allow me to remind you that you are a reflection of the Bennet family name, and it would speak poorly of your education were you to act in any way other than that of a gentleman's daughter. It could even ruin your chances at making an advantageous marriage," said Mrs. Yeats in a matter-of-fact tone.

Jane whispered to Elizabeth, "It is good Mrs. Yeats has learned to speak frankly to Lydia. Such a tone would crush me, but Lydia really does not seem to comprehend anything else."

Elizabeth agreed. "If Lydia has any chance of making a good match, Mrs. Yeats will see to it. Otherwise, she would waste herself on an officer without two shillings to rub together." She inclined her forehead toward Kitty. "You do not think Kitty has fallen for an officer, do you?"

"Kitty has been acting strangely of late. You were not the only one to disappear during the Netherfield Ball, you know. I had been searching for her when Mr. Darcy asked me where you were."

"Really?" This was news to Elizabeth.

Jane lowered her voice all the more. "I stationed myself beside the entrance door after you were let out of the library. It offered the best view of the rooms, and so I saw her come in. She had been walking alone in the gardens with Mr. Denny." Jane gave her a meaningful look.

Elizabeth groaned— both for Kitty's indiscretion, and at the possibility that she and Mr. Denny could have seen Mr. Darcy climb out of the library window.

"So, you see, it is not only Lydia for whom we should be concerned," Jane continued. "Father would be so disappointed were one of his daughters to compromise herself."

Groaning again, though not for the reason Jane supposed, Elizabeth wished more than ever that she had never entered Mr. Bingley's library.

CHAPTER 17

Aunt Philips' drawing room was as warm as an oven, and the gossip exchanged as fresh as steaming bread taken out from the hottest part of it.

Mr. Collins sat as far away from the fireplace as he could without missing any of the conversation. He kept tugging at his collar and dabbing at his face with his sweat-stained handkerchief. Elizabeth felt bad for him. He did not know Aunt would grow too warm just as quickly as she had chilled.

Mere minutes later, Aunt had the maid open the window and a stiff breeze blew through the room to cool her flushed face.

Fanning herself with a fan that matched Mother's, Aunt moved on from the topic of a recent elopement of the butcher's daughter with an officer of low ranking— which had been the source of speculation for at least two days and would provide endless fodder for weeks to come… Or, rather, it would until word of Mr. Darcy's arrest spread. "I heard a bit of news about Mr. Wickham's unfortunate death. Can you guess where he was shot?" she asked, tapping her fan against her chin in her all-knowing manner.

"Oh, I do love a good intrigue!" said Lydia, reaching for another slice of gingerbread.

"I think you have partaken of your aunt's generosity sufficiently," said Mrs. Yeats, causing Lydia's hand to freeze in place before she could snatch the cake.

Mary expressed her disapproval. "It is immoral to discuss disturbing indelicacies openly." She made a point of raising a pocket-sized book of sermons she carried with her for such occasions for all to see. Of course, had she wished not to expose herself to the gossip she was sure to overhear at Aunt Philips', she ought to have stayed at home. Elizabeth knew her reading would be slow as she struggled to overhear their conversation behind her guise of self-righteousness.

Mr. Collins nodded his approval, but he was too interested in saving Lady Catherine de Bourgh's nephew from coming to harm, and so he said nothing to complain of the indiscretion.

"He was shot directly in the heart." Aunt Philips resumed her fanning and sat back in her chair contentedly.

Elizabeth looked around at her sisters, but they all shrugged their shoulders. Mrs. Yeats, no doubt feeling that their current topic was an unladylike one, sighed behind her teacup.

If nobody would ask, Elizabeth would. "We had heard, but what does it signify? If a man is killed, does the location of the shot matter or affect the investigation in any way?"

Aunt gasped at her ignorance. "But, of course, it does. How could you not understand something so obvious when you are the clever one?" she chastised.

The blank stares Aunt Philips received encouraged her to continue and took the sting out of her mild rebuke. "He was shot in the heart. The heart!" she repeated.

She seemed determined to make them understand without having to explain.

Jane attempted to understand. "Perhaps the location of the mortal wound gives some insight toward the motive of the killer? Certainly, if an individual with malicious intent wanted to cause permanent harm, he would shoot his victim in the heart?"

Aunt threw her arms up into the air. "Why does everyone assume it was a man? This detail practically confirms it to me that it very well could have been a woman! To aim at the heart, the seat of passion, is an emotional act which would most likely be done by someone of the feminine sex. Do you not agree?" She gripped the edge of her chair and looked excitedly at each of them, seeking support.

Elizabeth considered. In her mind, it did not make much of a difference where Mr. Wickham had been shot, but she had to admit it was as much a possibility that a woman could have committed the evil deed than for a man to have done it.

Mary was not convinced. "How would a lady know how to shoot a pistol? Are they not very heavy?" she asked.

Elizabeth noticed Kitty fix her gaze firmly onto her lap.

"They are much lighter than a hunting rifle. If a woman with a normal amount of strength were upset enough to cause bodily harm, surely she could find the strength to lift a pistol long enough to shoot it," answered Aunt. "As for it being ready to shoot, my theory is that he left it loaded because he suspected someone meant to do him harm."

Her mind churning with these new details, Elizabeth said, "I suppose it would not be that strange of a thing for a lady to load a firearm. Especially if she lived in a household with gentlemen— a father or brothers— whom she could have observed load their arms repeatedly..." Her words trailed off in thought. Now that the possibility opened before her, the list of suspects grew, muddying the murky water even more than before.

"You do not think Mr. Darcy did it?" Jane asked Aunt.

"A highborn gentleman like Mr. Darcy would never stoop so low as to murder a lowly lieutenant of the militia," Aunt said with authority.

Elizabeth was not so sure the jury at the inquest would agree. She had seen his expression when he left Mr. Wickham's tent after what must have been a heated dispute. What if others had seen him wearing the same dangerous expression?

Mr. Darcy was not a murderer, but he had secrets. And Mr. Wickham knew them. It had likely been a relief to Mr. Darcy to have his enemy disappear from existence. The idea disturbed her greatly. Should not her concern to bring Mr. Wickham's killer to justice be greater than her concern over Mr. Darcy's feelings about the murder of his adversary? She shivered at the thought.

"I am sorry, Lizzy. Let me close the window before you catch a chill." Aunt signaled to the maid, who promptly did as she was bid.

Pouring another serving of tea, Aunt continued, "I am happy none of my nieces have formed unfortunate alliances with any of the officers. Too many of the girls in the village have had their heads turned and are acting in the most appalling ways. It is as if the scarlet red of the militia's coats scatters their brains and all reason with it. But not my nieces. You girls have much more sense than that," she looked at them with pride.

Kitty and Lydia squirmed in their chairs. Little did Aunt know that her sweet nieces would love nothing more than to be compromised by a handsome officer.

Mr. Collins shook his head. "It is shameful. I wonder what their parents are doing to keep their daughters safe from the militia's corrupting influence."

"They are not corrupting! They are here for our protection," defended Kitty, her cheeks burning red.

"My child," said Aunt, "there has not been a murder in Meryton these thirty years, and that one was a domestic dispute and was easily settled. The militia has not been here a month, and already the village is burdened with the murder of one of its officers. I have said it before, and I will say it again, the militia brings more trouble than it is worth, and I will stake my name on it that it was a jealous, spiteful woman who did the deed."

She passed around the teacups and offered more gingerbread. Elizabeth had lost her appetite long ago. The images in her head of bloodstains and the smell of gunpowder only left a place in her queasy stomach for the tea remaining in her cup.

"If you believe it was a female who killed Mr. Wickham, I suppose you have a suspect?" asked Mrs. Yeats.

Aunt smiled. "I thought you would never ask! I have an inkling of an idea, and I have been dying to share it with someone discerning. Idle gossip is dangerous, you know."

"It is, and it shows a great amount of delicacy on your part not to reveal her name and expose her to suspicion if, in the end, she is innocent. However, I do admit to some curiosity on my part and would like to know on what you base your suspicions," said Mrs. Yeats.

Setting down her teacup enthusiastically, Aunt picked up her fan and tapped it against her palm. "I will give no names, but I am certain you will draw the same conclusion I did when you think back to the events of the Netherfield Ball. Mr. Wickham is said to have been murdered around the hour of midnight." She paused, making sure everyone nodded their heads as was appropriate. "Very good. Now, think. Who left the ball in sufficient time to have returned to Meryton before that fateful hour?"

Elizabeth did a mental checklist of all the people she had seen before entering the library. Her memory was a disturbed blur, but she soon fixed on a scene. Calculating the time, her alarm grew as she realized how well it fit the scenario Aunt suggested. It did not take much longer for her sisters to reach a similar conclusion.

"Surely, you do not mean to imply Miss Stallard?" asked Mary in shock, her book closed in her lap.

***

Mr. Stallard's complexion was a shade darker than normal. "How good of you to join me... finally," he said tersely, making Darcy glad he had made the gentleman wait a minute or two longer than necessary. He was certain he bore bad news, and Darcy was in no hurry to rush the inevitable.

"I held no hopes of receiving any callers today. I know where I stand." Darcy sat opposite him.

"Not everyone in the village is against you, Mr. Darcy. I, for one, do not believe you are guilty. Otherwise, I would not have come today, nor would I have taken care to arrange for you to be brought here when no one would be likely to see you."

Darcy held a blank expression, feeling Mr. Stallard's eyes search his face for any indication of emotion. Whatever Mr. Stallard had to tell him, Darcy would not make it easy.

"How good of you to acknowledge my innocence. It is what I am, after all," Darcy said dryly.

"You and I both know it, but I fear the jury at our inquest will not be convinced. They are unaccustomed to good breeding and high manners. Of course, if they vote for this case to go to trial, you stand a good chance of being acquitted. However, the damage done to your name by then would be irreparable."

Mr. Stallard's patronization grated on Darcy's nerves, but he kept his composure. "That may be so, but the people of Meryton are not stupid. When there is no evidence to support the accusations against me, they will draw the correct conclusions." So he hoped. His life depended upon it— if he failed to get to the bottom of this affair before he could be sent to trial.

"You are willing to stake your life on it? You are more optimistic than I believed you to be. Or perhaps I misjudged your character…." Mr. Stallard narrowed his eyes and considered Darcy for some time.

"It would not be the first time I have been misjudged, nor the last," he replied, thinking of Elizabeth. Had she not known him for a fact to be innocent, she would have believed him capable of murder. As it was, she who would have been his worst adversary, was his strongest ally. Her faith in his innocence gave him confidence. He added, "I believe in justice, but I am not so optimistic as to believe that the truth does not need some assistance in revealing itself."

"Indeed," said Mr. Stallard gravely, avoiding looking at Darcy.

What did Mr. Stallard know? Darcy determined to find out what he could if he was forced to suffer through the gentleman's call.

Mr. Stallard exposed his stained teeth in a snarl. "That is my motive in calling on you this morning. I mean to offer you my assistance."

To Darcy, his offer felt more threatening than helpful. It would be wiser to have a witness in the room. "I would hope that if you were in possession of any information, you would reveal it to Colonel Forster and to me."

"Ah, but my business is with you alone. We need not involve Colonel Forster. You see, it is a certainty you would be accused of murder unless some great evidence is revealed to help your cause. Mr. Wickham, despite his debts, was well-liked. He did not yet owe such great sums— having only recently arrived to his commission. And it appears that an honorable gentleman has already taken care to settle his debts, doing so in such a discreet manner, no one would guess it was you. If you cooperate with me, I will make your actions known."

Darcy's heart thundered in his ears. Lawrence had been right about Mr. Stallard. Darcy held his composure, but his stomach churned. He crossed one foot over the other to give the effect of indifference.

"Wickham made friends easily. Whether or not he could keep them is another story entirely."

"Be that as it may, we will never know, will we? Mr. Wickham is dead, and you will hang for his murder unless you allow me to help you."

"How do you mean to do that?" asked Darcy, careful not to sound interested.

"I want you to marry my daughter."

CHAPTER 18

"You want me to marry Miss Stallard?" asked Darcy incredulously. Not once in their short acquaintance had Miss Stallard shown an inkling of liking toward him. In fact, Darcy had assumed her regard lay elsewhere.

"You heard me correctly." Mr. Stallard relaxed his hands against the arm of his chair, smiling as if he had already won.

"What makes you think I would agree to your scheme?" Darcy asked. Not even a guilty verdict would convince him to marry Miss Stallard. There was only one lady who could possibly tempt him... and she did not want him.

Mr. Stallard's fists clenched. "I will be honest with you. I believe we can be of mutual assistance to each other. If you do as I bid and marry my daughter, I can ensure you are not sent to trial. My daughter is handsome and, generally, of a cooperative disposition. She will do you credit in society, and she will add to your coffers with her dowry and inheritance."

Darcy cringed in distaste. "I do not need your money."

"I am pleased to hear it. However, I would wager that you value your life greatly. Your life and an unblemished reputation is what I am offering you. You are hardly in a position to argue or negotiate, though you must see how generous my offer is, the benefits to you being far superior than those you can reciprocate."

"You take advantage of my circumstances, sir," said Darcy, knowing that Mr. Stallard would not want to depart without a guarantee, but being unwilling to give it.

"Be that as it may, it is my dearest wish to see my daughter married well."

"You consider it advantageous for her to marry a man accused of one of the worst crimes known to humankind? You must be thoroughly convinced of my innocence or else you would never consider me for your own daughter. If your conviction is so strong, why am I here under arrest when you could free me this moment? Where is your honor, sir?"

Mr. Stallard laughed. "And risk you leaving without first securing my daughter's future? No, Mr. Darcy, I am not a fool, and I will not lose out on the opportunity presented to me by acting prematurely."

So much for honor. It had been worth a try. "What makes you think Miss Stallard will accept me?"

"She will accept you because I require it of her," Mr. Stallard replied firmly, his eyes hardening.

A chill settled over Darcy. At that moment, Darcy could imagine Mr. Stallard capable of killing a man to suit his wishes. He needed to keep him talking. He needed to learn what he could before Mr. Stallard left.

"You said you would be honest with me, Mr. Stallard, and yet, I do not think you are being entirely truthful. What is your motive in choosing me when Miss Stallard is fully capable of selecting a gentleman to marry of her own choosing?"

Mr. Stallard pressed his white knuckles into the padding of his chair. "This in no way undermines my offer. In fact, it only serves to strengthen it." He paused, his forehead furled for some time before he spoke again. Darcy watched him struggle in silence, taking comfort in the human emotions passing over Mr. Stallard's face.

"My daughter had planned an elopement with Mr. Wickham. I heard of it and, for reasons obvious to gentlemen of our station, I forbade it."

Darcy's pulse quickened. "When did you discover this?"

"The day before the Netherfield Ball," Mr. Stallard answered dryly.

Wickham had only been in Meryton for a week. That was quick work even for him. Unless...

"Wickham's choosing to come to Meryton was no accident, was it?" he ventured, hoping Mr. Stallard would fill in more details.

"No."

"Did he follow her here from Ramsgate?"

A picture formed in Darcy's mind, but he needed a few more details. If his suspicions were correct, Wickham had been a far worse cad than Darcy had thought him. And that was saying much! It also meant that Mr. Stallard benefited from Wickham's death. It meant he was not fit to serve as the magistrate in this case.

As if he could read Darcy's thoughts, Mr. Stallard pinched his lips together and glared at Darcy. "You ask a lot of questions."

"Can you fault me for it when it is my life at risk?" Leaning forward, Darcy narrowed his vision to see only Mr. Stallard's reaction when he said, "I will see Wickham's murderer brought to justice."

Mr. Stallard sat like a stone statue for all the lack of emotion Darcy observed. He revealed nothing. They sat thus, locked in a stalemate, neither gentleman willing to bend before the other.

"I must say I am deeply disappointed in you, Mr. Darcy. I had thought you would be far more reasonable."

Insults were nothing when pronounced by a man undeserving of his good opinion. If the best argument he could come up with was to cut the man he sought to blackmail, then Darcy had gained the upper hand. He would not waste it.

Never wavering in his gaze, Darcy asked, "You refuse to give an answer?"

"I do."

"Then, I refuse to marry your daughter."

Mr. Stallard gripped the arms of his chair so tightly, Darcy expected to hear the wood crack. His pulse, visible to Darcy's eye, pounded at his temples. He rose stiffly to take his leave, bowing to signal his departure, but no words crossed his lips.

Darcy was left to ponder to what lengths a father would go to protect the interests of his only daughter, as well as the dire consequences to himself if his suspicions proved to be true.

***

Lydia huffed. "Well, I never did like Miss Stallard anyway. She is so stuffy and gives herself airs."

"But that is hardly reason enough to commit murder," said Elizabeth, in her way acknowledging and agreeing with Lydia's assessment of Miss Stallard's character. She was worse than Miss Bingley in that regard, though Miss Bingley was more assertive in others.

"Surely, Aunt would not imply such a thing unless she had a solid basis for doing so," said Mary, looking at Aunt Philips in an effort to seek more information without asking for it outright (for that would have been sinful). She was every bit as bad as Aunt Philips and Mother in her thirst for gossip, but Elizabeth was grateful for it. Otherwise, she would have had to ask, and she was always getting chastised for being too inquisitive.

Happily, Aunt obliged, "Oh, I have it from the best of sources, my dears, but I will only tell you in the strictest of confidence." She continued before anyone could utter a word to the contrary. "You see, Miss Stallard's lady's maid is on good terms with my maid, and she told her the most interesting thing." She paused, rubbing her hands together.

These moments of revelation must have brought Aunt great joy and purpose in life. She relished in them, trying Elizabeth's patience and making the wait all the more excruciating.

Finally, Aunt spoke, beginning slowly and dramatically. "As you know, Miss Stallard spent the summer with Lady Pepperwick in Ramsgate."

Lydia huffed and slumped in her chair. "How I should like to spend a summer in Ramsgate! It is dreadfully unfair we do not get to go anywhere."

Aunt continued, "Who do you think she met whilst at Ramsgate but Mr. Wickham?"

Gasps echoed throughout the room. "Our Lieutenant George Wickham?" asked Lydia.

"One and the same. Evidently, they formed an attachment." Aunt pursed her lips and nodded with raised eyebrows.

"They were engaged?" asked Kitty.

"What did Mr. Stallard think of the attachment?" Elizabeth asked, though she knew the answer.

"He was furious, of course. He sent for Miss Stallard and insisted she return directly. Surely, she should have known he would not approve of the arrangement. I have no doubts but that she and Mr. Wickham had planned to elope."

Elizabeth held her breath to keep from breathing too fast. If Miss Stallard had been willing to elope with Mr. Wickham, and Mr. Wickham had followed her to Meryton, Mr. Stallard would have done anything to protect his daughter from marrying a gentleman he considered beneath them.

Would he go so far as to kill? If bloodshed meant that each of her daughters was guaranteed a good match, Elizabeth had no doubt but that her own mother would consider it a viable option. What about Mr. Stallard?

As she arranged the facts along with this recent knowledge, Elizabeth's realization turned her cold. Mr. Stallard was the magistrate. If he murdered Mr. Wickham, then he would do nothing to prevent Mr. Darcy from hanging, thus throwing all hint of suspicion off himself. She rubbed her arms against the chill overwhelming her.

"My inclination on hearing your account is to suppose Mr. Stallard is more involved than Miss Stallard. Why do you presume it was a woman who killed Mr. Wickham?" asked Mrs. Yeats.

Aunt smiled, one eyebrow arching higher than the other. "I saw for myself how Mr. Wickham taught Miss Stallard how to shoot his pistol. She must have been an excellent pupil."

Lydia pouted. "He never taught me how to shoot."

Really? That was all Lydia could think of, as if denying her pleasure was more important than the man's murder?

"Mr. Denny showed me," said Kitty triumphantly. "Do not be so cross, Lydia. It is not as diverting as it sounds. It is heavy and awkward to hold up. I missed the target in the hay and hit the ground in front of it. I smelled the burned powder for hours afterward, and I had no desire to try it more than once."

"I should hope not, Miss Kitty. That was highly improper," reprimanded Mrs. Yeats.

"It was not so heavy you could not hold it up, though, was it Kitty?" asked Aunt, more concerned in proving her theory than in scolding her niece for her breach in propriety.

With a nervous glance at Mrs. Yeats, Kitty answered, "I suppose not. If Mr. Denny had not been teaching me the different parts of the pistol and what they do, I should have been able to hold it steadier in a shorter period of time. It was very educational."

Mrs. Yeats did not appear impressed.

Aunt nodded contentedly. "And there it is, my dears. Miss Stallard knew how to shoot the weapon, and if she felt that Mr. Wickham had crossed her somehow, she had the motive to kill him. She is of the jealous sort and accustomed to getting her way. And there is the convenient detail of her dress at the Netherfield Ball. She could have returned, but she did not."

Could she have done it? Elizabeth would not eliminate any possibility until she found out who was responsible, though her suspicions were more strongly settled on Mr. Stallard.

She had to find some way of warning Mr. Darcy. If either of the Stallards were involved, he stood to take the fall.

She looked about the room, pondering how best to manage an interview with Mr. Darcy without causing more scandal.

Mr. Collins pinched his chin, deep in thought. Of course!

Addressing him, she said, "Mr. Collins, I am interested in hearing your opinion on the value of this information in regards to Lady Catherine de Bourgh's nephew. Would you consider it inappropriate to reveal the topic of our discussion with him if it meant that he could be proved innocent?" Elizabeth held her breath.

Mrs. Yeats interjected. "You must first get permission from the source. Mrs. Philips related this account to us in strict confidence."

Everyone looked at Aunt Philips, who sat like a queen on her throne. Resting her fists on the arms of her chair, as if holding a scepter, she said, "Thank you, Mrs. Yeats. You are quite right, of course, and had I not been interrupted, I would have suggested precisely what my niece has done."

Mr. Collins rose from his chair. "How insightful of you, Mrs. Philips. I am certain a man as discreet as Mr. Darcy can be entrusted with these details, especially when I tell him from which source they came." He added a smile to his compliment to Aunt Philips, who was all too pleased to receive it.

"I have not called on Mrs. Forster in some days," commented Lydia. "I have hopes she will invite me to go with her and Colonel Forster when they return to Brighton in the warmer months."

Elizabeth would make sure that never happened! But calling on Mrs. Forster would put her in the way of Mr. Darcy— especially if Mr. Collins requested an audience with him. That, she would not discourage.

CHAPTER 19

"I feel ill from the heat in Aunt's drawing room," said Jane, her cheeks flushed.

Mrs. Yeats agreed. "Such extremes of hot and cold cannot be healthy for the organism. Perhaps a walk in the cool air will help you feel better?"

"I will go with you," offered Kitty, her gaze sweeping over the empty streets.

Lydia rolled her eyes. "You only hope to see Mr. Denny again. Really, Kitty, if you do not vary in your flirtations, you will be stuck with him."

Kitty did not look as if she minded that much. Elizabeth was uncertain. She was unconvinced Mr. Denny did not know anything about Mr. Wickham's murder. She did not want Kitty seeking out his company until she knew more.

She cast Jane a pleading look, but it was Mrs. Yeats who understood her concern.

"Mr. Collins," said Mrs. Yeats, "since it is your desire to call on Mr. Darcy, perhaps you might accompany Miss Lydia and Miss Elizabeth while they call on Mrs. Forster? I will stay with Miss Bennet to ensure she does not fall ill, and Miss Kitty and Miss Mary shall keep us company."

"What an excellent idea, Mrs. Yeats. I could not very well leave Cousin Jane whilst she is unwell, but duty demands I call on Mr. Darcy and Colonel Forster," Mr. Collins bowed incessantly until Mrs. Yeats led her sisters away, one arm protectively looped through Jane's to hold her steady.

Elizabeth crossed the street with Mr. Collins and Lydia in the direction of Colonel Forster's temporary dwelling, a leased house within a comfortable walking distance to the regiment's tents.

She slowed when she saw Mr. Stallard's tall figure leaving the Forster's residence. He walked stiffly, looking about him as if he did not wish to be seen.

"Good morning, Mr. Stallard," called Mr. Collins when the gentleman turned his back to walk in the opposite direction.

Mr. Stallard's shoulders hunched up to his ears, and he turned around. With a stiff bow, Mr. Stallard greeted them. "You must excuse me. I fear I am late for an appointment and must be on my way. Good day to you," he said with another bow.

He walked away from them in a hurried clip, as was appropriate of a gentleman running late for an appointment. His manners, however, were tense and only added credibility to Aunt Philips' suspicions.

What did Mr. Stallard know about Mr. Wickham's murder? Was he somehow involved? Did he seek to protect his daughter? Was he so despicable as to let Mr. Darcy take the blame?

They were led into the front parlor to await the Forsters.

Being the first one to enter, Elizabeth felt the tension in the room. And she saw him before he could compose himself. Mr. Darcy stood with his elbow propped against the fireplace mantel, his hand buried in his hair. He immediately straightened his posture and lowered his hand, leaving his hair stylishly disheveled. One second later, he had replaced the worry lining his face with a cool mask of calm self-assurance. But she had seen him. She had felt his vulnerability, and her heart ached for him.

If she did not know their compromise to be highly disagreeable to him, she would gladly admit to it to alleviate his anxiety. But he did not want her. Not that she wanted him, she told herself. However, she held his life in her hands and this knowledge brought a great amount of responsibility with it. She did respect him. And she trusted him. How could she not when he so clearly trusted her?

Mr. Collins exchanged enough pleasantries to satisfy their entire group. Lydia ignored them to walk about the room, fully aware that her flirtations were lost on Mr. Darcy and showing thus by her absence of smiles and head-tosses.

Before the purpose of their visit could be stated, the Forsters joined them. Elizabeth went through the motions of greeting them, but it was Mr. Darcy who had captivated her attention with the intimate glimpse he had not meant to give her into his heart. She would not abuse it. Not when she could sense his embarrassment at her having seen it.

Elizabeth compelled herself to look away from him. Shaking her head and clearing her thoughts, she said, "Colonel, we came directly to you from my aunt Philips' home. We are in possession of some information pertaining to Mr. Darcy."

Mr. Collins interrupted her. "Yes, it is our intention to share what we heard in the hopes of being of some assistance."

Lydia, not interested in the least, took Mrs. Forster by the hands. "Please save me from their dull conversation, Mrs. Forster. I have heard of little else these past days, and I would much rather speak of the parties you have attended and of Brighton. I have not spent much time on the coast," she pouted.

Mrs. Forster, who was not much older than Lydia, looked equally pleased to escape the tedious conversation of the older people in the parlor. They walked arm-in-arm to the opposite side of the room, whispering and giggling like girls.

Elizabeth wondered what advantages an older man with heavy responsibilities like Colonel Forster saw in marrying such a young wife who, like Lydia, lived for parties and social activities. Perhaps it was the lightness she brought to their union....

"My love, if there is anything you or your guest require, you must let me attend to you," said the colonel with a warm smile at his wife.

He was rewarded with an equally devoted smile.

"This business has been a hardship for Mrs. Forster, but she bears it expertly," he said in admiration.

Turning to her, he asked, "Miss Elizabeth, would you not feel more comfortable with the ladies?"

She looked over at Lydia and Mrs. Forster whispering and giggling to each other and knew she would certainly not feel comfortable with them, nor did she trust Mr. Collins not to lose the main points of their reason for calling in his deluge of words.

Mr. Darcy spoke before she could answer. "Colonel Forster, Mr. Collins, I should very much like for Miss Elizabeth to stay with us. As a female, she is naturally gifted with certain perceptions and opinions which a male would not consider, or worse, overlook as unimportant."

Never one to contradict a nephew of Lady Catherine de Bourgh, Mr. Collins said, "How insightful of you, Mr. Darcy, to see the natural delicacies of a member of the opposite sex as a strength. I daresay you are correct in thinking so. Were her ladyship here, I have no doubt but that she would see justice served within a se'nnight." For the benefit of Colonel Forster, who had not yet had the privilege of hearing Lady Catherine's praises sung, he added, "Her ladyship, Lady Catherine de Bourgh, possesses such a cunning mind, it is of no surprise her blood relation should see what an average mind does not. It never would have occurred to me to allow a woman to contribute to our conversation, but being thus put to us, I see no other way but to permit my dear cousin to stay."

Colonel Forster acceded hesitantly. It struck Elizabeth that he did so more out of a desire to avoid another lengthy discourse, and she had to thank Mr. Collins' convenient reverence to Lady Catherine, as well as his gratuitous use of words for it.

A knock on the door quieted the room. Lydia, no doubt hoping an officer had come to call, rearranged her skirts. Mrs. Forster, influenced by her guest, did the same.

"Mr. Tanner is here to see you, sir," said the butler, with a stoic face.

Colonel Forster kept his calm, though it was clear to see the intrusion annoyed him. Bunching up his cheeks and sighing, he said, "Very well. See him in."

Mr. Darcy remained standing by the fireplace. He and Mr. Tanner were of the same height and build, but the bitter scowl on Mr. Tanner's face stood in stark contrast to the relaxed calm on Mr. Darcy's.

"Come in, Mr. Tanner. How good of you to call. Please take a seat with us," said Colonel Forster.

Mr. Tanner only sat when Colonel Forster insisted once again. Crossing his arms, he said, "With such goings on as I witnessed here, I took it upon myself to see if all is well in your household, Colonel."

The colonel cleared his throat and pressed his chin down. "Yes, it has been an eventful morning for Mr. Darcy. So long as the truth comes to light, that is what concerns us."

Narrowing his eyes at Mr. Darcy, Mr. Tanner said, "I saw Mr. Stallard leave here in a foul temper. I do not suppose you think he did it, do you?" He said it as if it were too far-fetched of an idea to consider.

"I made no such accusation. He did, however, attempt to blackmail me."

Elizabeth, Mr. Collins, and the colonel gasped aloud.

Mr. Tanner was unconvinced. "You would slander him to make yourself appear innocent?" he accused.

"I am not accustomed to speaking falsehoods, Mr. Tanner. And do not malign the gentleman's intelligence by asking if witnesses were present. He made certain we were alone. You will have to accept my word as truth."

Mr. Tanner closed his mouth, his unuttered question answered.

Having recovered herself, Elizabeth said, "His attempt must have been unsuccessful."

Mr. Darcy nodded.

Colonel Forster ran his hand over his face, massaging his temples. "And in my home, nonetheless. Mr. Darcy, I must apologize. I should have insisted on being present."

"You could not very well have done so to the magistrate. Please do not trouble yourself, Colonel," replied Mr. Darcy. "The details of his demand I will reserve only for you to hear as it concerns a third party I do not wish to involve unless it is necessary."

He did not need to mention Miss Stallard for Elizabeth to suspect what Mr. Stallard was after. Her disgust rose to a new level, and with it, her concern for Mr. Darcy's life intensified.

The colonel nodded in approval. "Very good."

"And me? Am I not to be allowed to know all the facts pertaining to the murder?" asked Mr. Tanner bitterly. Really, his insistent badgering was getting tiresome. Elizabeth had never known him to act so spitefully. Unwavering, yes. But this belligerence was new and all the more annoying because it was undeserved.

Colonel Forster answered in a firm tone, "If it is necessary for you to know, I am certain Mr. Darcy will tell you himself."

Mr. Darcy nodded, growing cooler to the extent Mr. Tanner grew agitated.

She needed to intercede before the purpose of their visit was lost. "If we may, we came to convey some recently learned information."

Colonel Forster waved for her to continue.

Cutting to the chase, she said, "My aunt Philips' maid told my aunt that Mr. Wickham courted Miss Stallard while she was at Ramsgate this past summer. The source being Miss Stallard's lady's maid, my aunt has no reason to doubt its veracity. While Miss Stallard's maid did not admit as much, it was understood from their conversation that Miss Stallard had agreed to elope with Mr. Wickham."

Mr. Darcy's face lit with understanding. "That explains why he came to Meryton. He was not following me. That was an unhappy coincidence; nothing more. He came here for Miss Stallard."

"Against her father's wishes? What did he seek to accomplish with that?" asked Colonel Forster.

"Mr. Wickham was the sort of man to see opportunity in others' weaknesses. If he felt he could extract money from Mr. Stallard by using his daughter against him, he would have delighted in doing so. He could have made Mr. Stallard so miserable, he would have eventually agreed to the match."

"With her inheritance and large dowry," said Elizabeth, shaking her head. She thought she understood Mr. Stallard's motive in blackmailing Mr. Darcy. Naturally, he wanted to see his daughter marry to advantage, and he had a powerful lure to offer. Freedom. Life. A lure which Mr. Darcy had refused.

Elizabeth's traitorous heart filled with elation. Her mind— which she trusted as being far more sane than her heart— told Elizabeth that his refusal of Miss Stallard did not in any way imply he held her in tender regard. Not that she wanted him to....

"It will be simple enough to confirm," said Colonel Forster, once again tugging on his side whiskers, deep in thought.

Mr. Tanner offered, "I will do it. Mr. Stallard has business with his land steward which he expected would keep him busy well into the evening. The servants will not balk at me as they would to their betters. The coachman or the valet would know what happened. I will start there."

"Thank you, Mr. Tanner," said the colonel, coming out of his pensive fog. With alert eyes, he addressed Elizabeth, "Miss Elizabeth, I thank you for this information. However, I must beg you to involve yourself no further. If Mr. Stallard is indeed a participant, either willingly or unwillingly— I shall not judge until I know all of the facts— then you could be in as much danger as Mr. Darcy for what you have revealed to us today. If Mr. Stallard is as innocent as we presume Mr. Darcy to be, then your life is in greater danger still. It would take someone with a keen intellect to have us casting the blame where it is undeserved and providing evidence for it. An individual who would stoop to murder would hold no qualms about doing it again to keep his secret."

His stern gaze locked on her, intent on receiving a guarantee she could not agree to give. While Mr. Darcy was the primary suspect, she could not rest until she found out who was responsible for Mr.

Wickham's death— or until she admitted to their compromise.

Mr. Darcy's soft, pleading voice cut through her tenacious musings. "Miss Elizabeth, please consider. None of us could bear it were you to come to harm. You did well today, but that is where your good intentions must stop."

The entreaty in his eyes nearly cracked her resolve. Almost.

"I will be careful—" she began. Her words choked her throat when Mr. Darcy glared at her. Was he angry? Why should he care what happened to her?

Looking at Mr. Tanner, Mr. Darcy asked, "Is she always this stubborn?"

Stunned at the question, just as she was, Mr. Tanner chuckled. "She is known for it."

Elizabeth clamped her mouth shut, feeling the fumes of her blush radiate from her skin. If it were possible, she would breathe fire.

Rising with what pride she could muster, she said, "We have accomplished our purpose, and we have stayed longer than we ought."

With a parting glare at Mr. Darcy and an added flare of the nostrils for Mr. Tanner, she waited for Mr. Collins and Lydia to join her. They did not delay, though they both stood at a cautious distance from her as they bid their farewells.

Mr. Tanner did not fear her. He moved to join them, offering his arm for her to take. She wanted to slap it away, but took it begrudgingly as they departed.

They had just got outside when Mr. Darcy's manservant called after them. "Pardon me, Miss Elizabeth, but I believe you dropped this." He held a piece of paper in his hand.

Too angry to question him, she took the paper and stuck it in her pocket. "Thank you," she managed to mumble. She was angry with Mr. Darcy and Mr. Tanner, not the manservant. It would not do to take out her wrath on the poor man when he merely sought to be of service.

He turned toward the house and their small party continued toward the square.

"Well done for refusing Mr. Darcy's advances," said Mr. Tanner with a malicious grin.

"Advances?" He must have imbibed too much ale, she considered.

"It is obvious he admires you. I cannot fault him in his concern for your safety, but I have no doubt but that he does it for his own selfish reasons."

Elizabeth dropped her hand and spun to face him, her breath bursting out in angry puffs in the cold air. "You ought to be ashamed of yourself, Mr. Tanner. You have earned the reputation of being honest and honorable in your dealings. You are well-liked in town, and the villagers respect you. Yet you have done nothing but add fuel to their prejudices against Mr. Darcy. If my life is in any danger, it is at your doing! Are you so blind to the facts you still insist on his guilt? You, sir, are the one motivated by a selfish desire to see the downfall of one born into privilege to satisfy your own warped thirst for revenge. Shame on you!"

Mr. Tanner's smile disappeared, and his thick eyebrows knitted together at her rebuke. Softly, he said to Mr. Collins, "See that the ladies arrive home unharmed."

With that, he turned his back to them and trudged across the square to his inn.

CHAPTER 20

"Colonel Forster, you must allow me some freedom."

The colonel gaped at him. "Mr. Darcy, I am being more lenient than I ought to be as it is. Do not forget that my position here is to maintain order and peace. If I were to allow you to roam freely when most of Meryton is convinced of your guilt, not only would I put my own position in jeopardy, but you would likely find yourself in a great deal of danger."

Darcy gritted his teeth. "No more so than I am in now. At least, on my own, I could defend myself."

"And risk another death or injury? No, Mr. Darcy," the colonel said, shaking his head firmly. "That I cannot allow. You are safe in my household, you may rest assured of that. I have men stationed by the front and back doors at all hours."

"I do not doubt your capability nor your good intention in extending your protection to me, but I feel like a man with his hands tied during a battle."

Miss Elizabeth had given no promises, and Darcy knew what that meant. How could he protect her if he could not move about freely?

Mrs. Forster moved closer to them, standing behind her husband's chair and resting her small hand on his shoulder. "Surely, my dear, Mr. Darcy is to be trusted," she said, tracing the gold epaulet marking his rank. "Besides, I find all of this a tremendous bore. While Mr. Darcy remains here, my friends do not call, nor have we been invited to any dinner parties since the Netherfield Ball. I had hoped country life would be more agreeable and provide a nice respite for you, as well as some new acquaintances for me. Of what good is it for us to be here if we cannot socialize?"

He patted her hand. "My love, my first responsibility is to the good people of Meryton and its surrounding estates. Right now, the people are afraid, and if my regiment is not seen to act, they may revolt, causing more trouble to their otherwise peaceful home. I have seen it happen before."

"That does not mean it will happen here," she pouted.

"What of Mr. Darcy's life? I could not live with myself if he or anyone else whom it is in my power to protect were to come to harm," he added in exasperation.

"Can you not protect him, keep the villagers from causing chaos, and allow me to arrange for a little card party?" asked Mrs. Forster as she fiddled with his top button.

"I am sorry, dearest, but it cannot be helped at this moment." Colonel Forster patted her hand, giving a sense of finality to his statement.

"Oh, but surely it could not cause any harm to invite a few select friends. Did we not just entertain the Misses Bennet as well as Mr. Collins? And this just after receiving a call from Mr. Stallard," she persisted.

"Mr. Stallard's visit could hardly be described as a social call, dearest, and he did not come to see us, but rather Mr. Darcy," replied the colonel.

"And the Misses Bennet? I had a lovely chat with Miss Lydia. In fact, I want to ask you before I make mention of it to her and risk getting her hopes up…." She paused, petting his coat sleeve like she would a cat. "When we travel to Brighton, may she keep me company? You are so often busy, and sometimes I am rather lonely."

"Very well, it is an excellent idea," said the colonel with a large sigh and an even larger smile. He seemed pleased to have been able to acquiesce to at least one of the wishes of his young wife.

As they negotiated certain details of Mrs. Forster's plans to include Miss Lydia in their travels in the spring, Darcy considered the uneven match before him, and he wondered why a man such as

Colonel Forster would consider marrying one so young and inexperienced.

While Darcy would not quite call her silly, she lacked a level of maturity the wife of a commanding officer would require. Her manners were friendly and inviting— qualities becoming in society, but perhaps not so welcome in a wife blessed with a handsome face and surrounded by hundreds of men much younger and handsomer than her husband.

Mrs. Forster left the room with a bounce in her step, and Darcy ventured she had achieved her purpose to some degree. She would not remain bored for long.

"Mr. Darcy, what was it you wanted to tell me about Mr. Stallard's attempted blackmail?" asked Colonel Forster, his eyes leaving the doorway his wife had just passed through to focus on Darcy.

"In exchange for my freedom and the disappearance of this macabre mess, he wants me to marry his daughter," said Darcy tersely.

Flabbergasted, Colonel Forster massaged his temples. "I would not believe it if it did not come directly from you, Mr. Darcy. Did he give any indication that he possessed knowledge of the real culprit?"

"He did not. He based his confidence in securing a dismissal of the case against me on his influence over the villagers. He reasoned that they would not convict the man promised in marriage to the magistrate's own daughter."

Colonel Forster dropped his hands. "He does have a point there. Nobody would dare accuse you of murder if the magistrate approved the engagement of his daughter to you. It would show where he stood on the matter so well, nobody would challenge it." He narrowed his eyes at Darcy. "Are you considering his offer?" he asked.

Darcy's controlled manners prevented him from shaking his head vehemently. He took a calming breath, and said, "I cannot agree to a marriage founded on underhanded schemes. Not only would I be unhappy, but Miss Stallard's happiness would forever be denied her if we made such an arrangement."

"Mr. Stallard does not strike me as the sort of man to take kindly to refusal," said Colonel Forster, once again reaching for his whiskers.

"Which is why I dearly wish for some amount of freedom, Colonel. I do not know the extent of Mr. Stallard's involvement, but if what Miss Elizabeth repeated to us is true, then he had sufficient motive to wish Wickham dead. He also had the opportunity, having returned home early from the ball." He stopped, letting the new evidence make an impression on the colonel.

"If I allow you to leave, how do you know he will not take his revenge out on you because you refused his offer? If he is the murderer, what is to stop him? I can ensure you come to no harm here. I would have my men inform me when he called, and I would insist on being present. He would not dare refuse me in my own home."

"I thank you for your concern, Colonel. It is kind of you to value my life as much as I do. However, I am more concerned in clearing my name by discovering the true villain in this affair. And, you no doubt noticed another young lady's interest in this matter... Miss Elizabeth has no one to protect her, and I feel I must warn her to stop making inquiries— something I fear she will not do unless I am in a position to take over to her satisfaction."

Colonel Forster nodded gravely. "I have heard Miss Elizabeth is inquisitive in nature. I do hope she has sense enough not to involve herself more than she already has."

It chafed against Darcy's defenses to have the colonel imply that Miss Elizabeth lacked sense, but he did wish she would stop involving herself.

Darcy said, "It would not surprise me if she called on Miss Stallard to test the veracity of her aunt's story."

Miss Elizabeth had gumption, that was for certain. She would not back down until she heard some reasonable answers. He admired that about her— except where her safety was put in jeopardy. If she were to learn too much... if someone were to harm her.... A dose of panic coursed through his body, tying knots in his stomach until he felt light-headed and nauseated.

Colonel Forster looked at him with the perceptive eyes of a man accustomed to dealing with young men and their most common problem. Women.

"I have to wonder why Miss Elizabeth concerns herself. I understand it from Miss Bingley— you are a good friend of her brother and, until recently, a guest in the home she manages. But Miss Elizabeth is a new acquaintance, is she not?"

Darcy could have avoided the question. It was nothing which pertained to Colonel Forster to know anyhow. But more than anything, Darcy needed his freedom, and he would do nothing to ruin his prospect of it. "You said it yourself. Miss Elizabeth is inquisitive."

Colonel Forster looked unconvinced.

Darcy continued, "I doubt her interest in this gruesome matter is based on any particular regard for me. It likely proceeds from the same ennui of which Mrs. Forster recently admitted to falling victim." The words which had formed so seamlessly in his mind nearly choked him on their pronunciation. Miss Elizabeth was nothing like Mrs. Forster.

"I suppose it is the way of young women nowadays. They are more concerned over their entertainment than of the possibility of suffering any danger."

Such may the case of his own wife, but it chafed Darcy's sense of integrity to allow the same to be implied of Miss Elizabeth. Still, he guarded his tongue lest he worsen matters by coming to her

212

defense. He could not protect her while still trapped in Colonel Forster's home.

The colonel sat in silence for some time. Each passing minute increased Darcy's nerves until he felt he might explode— like a coil held tightly in a hand and let loose.

Finally, after an eternity of waiting, Colonel Forster rose and poured them each a drink. "I am sorry, Mr. Darcy," he said, handing him a snifter of brandy. "I promise you that I will make inquiries. This matter is as important to me as it is to you. But I cannot allow you to leave without first consulting with Mr. Tanner, or before I can determine the extent of Mr. Stallard's involvement. I must beg your patience, sir."

Darcy swallowed his disappointment with the amber liquid, feeling its sting in his throat. He would have to find another way.

His only consolation was a discreet nod from Lawrence as he passed by the open doorway. He had delivered the letter.

CHAPTER 21

"Miss Elizabeth, you must allow me to assist you. Please postpone your call until tomorrow so I may go with you," pleaded Mrs. Yeats for the second time since Elizabeth had stormed into Longbourn, Lydia and Mr. Collins struggling to catch their breath behind her.

How dare Mr. Tanner imply that Mr. Darcy might favor her! Mr. Darcy was the most insufferable man in all of Christendom— well, aside from Mr. Tanner. Granted, Mr. Darcy was more handsome than any gentleman had a right to look, and he had improved in character on further acquaintance. He had acted honorably under the worst adversity....

Elizabeth huffed in anger at herself. She was supposed to make a mental list of Mr. Darcy's numerous faults, not praise his virtues when she was doggedly determined not to like him. Never mind the weakening effect he seemed to have on her knees when he stood close. Or how her heartbeat raced when he whispered to her, and she could feel his breath tickling her skin.

Angered all the more at her perfidious heart, which would have her hope Mr. Tanner was right, Elizabeth dearly wanted to extricate all thoughts of Mr. Darcy from her mind. He simply would not leave her in peace! Bothersome man!

"I promise to be as sensible as the occasion permits," she told Mrs. Yeats. "Jane will be with me," Elizabeth added, as if Jane could prevent her from speaking her mind when it came down to it. "She will ensure I do not trespass decorum by asking unladylike questions."

Elizabeth glanced at Jane, who already looked overwhelmed at the task set before her.

Mrs. Yeats clucked her tongue. "If only your sisters had not arranged for gentlemen callers this afternoon, I would go with you. However, I will admit I trust your judgment much more than I trust theirs, and so, I fear, we must leave it at that."

"It is settled then. You will stay here to chaperone the girls while Jane and I call on Miss Stallard," said Elizabeth firmly. Though she knew the chances of her discovering anything worthy of note was slim, nobody could convince her to change her plans. She had to try.

"Is there nothing I could say which would convince you to delay your plans until the morrow? I am certain I could get much more information out of Miss Stallard's lady's maid than you will out of the lady herself," pleaded Mrs. Yeats yet again.

It was a sound argument, and a valid one, but it would not do. "There is not enough time."

"Time for whom? You speak of this as though you are directly involved when we are well aware you do not even like Mr. Darcy," said Jane, taking sides with Mrs. Yeats. "You ought not involve yourself, Lizzy, and I do not much like being dragged into this sordid affair and creating discord where we do not belong."

Elizabeth reached out to her conflict-averse sister. "I know you only speak out of concern for your headstrong sister but, Jane, I cannot stand aside when I know I can help. I do not trust Mr. Tanner to ask the questions which must be asked, and Colonel Forster already has enough to do. Mr. Darcy is unable to make inquiries, trapped as he is inside the Forsters' home. If I am the only one in a position to ensure justice is done, I must go."

Jane crossed her arms in the most dramatic display of disapproval in her possession. "This is your pride speaking, Lizzy, and you know it. Had Colonel Forster and Mr. Darcy not forbade you from poking your nose where it does not belong, you would not be so…," she took a deep breath, "so… stubborn." Jane's face flushed, and she covered her mouth. "I am sorry. I should not have spoken so plainly."

"Oh, Jane, do not be ashamed of speaking to me so. Sometimes I think you know me better than I know myself. Would you rather stay behind?"

"And let you go by yourself? Certainly not! I cannot offer much in the way of protection, but I scream louder than you do." Her eyes widened. "You do not think he will attack us, do you?"

Even Elizabeth, bold as she felt at that moment, would not call at the Stallards if she thought the master of the house would be at home. "I am not so foolish as to put myself and my own, dear sister in the way of danger. Do you not remember what Mr. Tanner said? That Mr. Stallard will not be at home until well into the evening? We will not see him, and I doubt our visit to Miss Stallard will be so significant she would tell him about it."

Mrs. Yeats watched them, her sharp eyes noticing everything. Her piercing gaze focused on Elizabeth, causing her no small amount of discomfort. "Your motive in helping Mr. Darcy, you claim, is merely in the service of justice? Your aim is to help one who is, albeit temporarily, defenseless?"

"Of course," Elizabeth snapped, wishing she could hide behind something when she felt her cheeks and ears burn.

Exasperated that her body betrayed emotions she adamantly refused to admit to herself, she forced her thoughts away from Mr. Darcy yet again and to the conversation before her. She would have to find out what she could from Miss Stallard, a lady with whom she had never enjoyed the intimacy of friendship. It would be a challenge.

She turned to put on her coat to distract Mrs. Yeats from noticing her complexion, though she was certain Jane had already seen it.

"We will not delay long," she said, pulling Jane with her out the front door.

Elizabeth planned questions— some discreet, some... not so discreet— in her mind, while Jane distracted herself from the unpleasant task before them by speaking of the Bingleys.

Mr. Bingley was everything a gentleman ought to be according to Jane.

They had reached the edge of the Stallards' estate when Jane stopped, wrapping her hand around Elizabeth's arm. "Lizzy, are you certain this is a good idea? How do you possibly hope to extract the kind of information you seek from Miss Stallard?" She lowered her voice. "She has never liked us. She considers our family beneath hers. It will take a miracle for her to confide in us."

Elizabeth knew it. It was why she had encouraged Mr. Collins to stay at Longbourn. If she had any hope of loosening Miss Stallard's tongue, it could not be done with him in the room. "I do not know, Jane, but I will hate myself if I do not try." She tugged Jane's arm, and they resumed walking.

When the gray stones of the Stallards' stately home with its harsh, symmetrical landscape came into view, Elizabeth linked her arm through Jane's.

"Perhaps we should do as Mary would advise us to do, and pray."

Jane bowed her head immediately. After some seconds of silence, she lifted her head and nodded. "All right. If we are to do this, then let us go."

Gaining entry through the gate which kept unwanted visitors out, they walked down the footpath enclosed on either side by strings of poplar trees and up the steps to the front door. A doorman opened the door before they could knock. He left them waiting while he checked to see if Miss Stallard was in and receiving callers.

"Miss Stallard is in the drawing room with some other callers, but she will see you," he said in a monotone.

Drat. Just what she needed. Elizabeth left all of her meticulously prepared questions and leading comments outside as she and Jane went into the drawing room.

Miss Bingley, Mrs. Hurst, and Miss Stallard sat at a table encumbered with refreshments. Miss Stallard, acting the part of a gracious hostess, asked for a fresh pot of tea to be brought in for her newly-arrived guests.

Taking the gesture to be a promising start, Elizabeth pasted a smile on her face and joined the vipers at the table. Miss Bingley and Mrs. Hurst looked as happy to see her and Jane as she felt at seeing them.

"Please join us," said Miss Stallard, opening her hand to the two empty chairs opposite her at the table.

"Thank you. You are very kind," said Jane smoothly. "The weather has been so dreadful of late, has it not? Elizabeth and I felt the need for some good company, and so we decided to call here. How fortunate we should chance upon Mrs. Hurst and Miss Bingley as well."

Thus flattered, the ladies' claws retracted, and Elizabeth would have nodded in appreciation for her sister's diplomacy could she have done so without being noticed.

"Indeed. We would perish from boredom were it not for Miss Stallard. There is precious little society available in Hertfordshire," complained Miss Bingley, making it clear she did not include the Bennets in her definition of society.

Miss Stallard elevated her stubby nose. "It certainly cannot compare to London. It is only at my father's request that I have remained here for as long as I have. Otherwise, I prefer the entertainments afforded in London or Bath at this time of year. My father has a home there as well, did you know?" she added.

Mrs. Hurst looked appropriately impressed. "I did not know. How advantageous indeed!"

"Yes, in the Royal Crescent," Miss Stallard added importantly.

Elizabeth blinked hard so as not to cross her eyes. A house's coveted address was not nearly as fascinating as the state of its library or the characters of its occupants.

"What a pity Mr. Darcy has been forced away from Netherfield Park. I daresay you would have secured Pemberley for yourself before long?" asked Miss Stallard, refilling Miss Bingley's teacup.

Mrs. Hurst said, "My sister is too modest to admit so herself, but I believe she would fill the role well. Such a large estate demands a mistress worthy of the task."

Elizabeth sucked air in through her gritted teeth. They spoke of Mr. Darcy as if he were no more valuable than his property. How odious it would be to have your worth talked about openly by ambitious ladies seeking to improve their situation and greedy mothers anxious to secure their daughters' future… much like her own mother. Her heart sank as realization dawned. Mr. Darcy would have thought that she was no different from all the other social climbers he had avoided thus far. Had he thought her no better than Miss Bingley?

Elizabeth's momentary relapse of empathy was soon overtaken by her pride. If Mr. Darcy could not distinguish the difference between Miss Bingley and herself, then he did not deserve her understanding. Though it was growing increasingly difficult to continue to think poorly of him… and she did not wish for him to think too poorly of her. Drat the man!

Miss Bingley beamed at the praise bestowed upon her. She did not blush at the mention of Mr.

Darcy as Jane did every time Mr. Bingley was mentioned.

Looking straight at Elizabeth, Miss Bingley said, "Mr. Darcy is a man of superior and demanding tastes. He would never marry anyone he considered to be beneath him. I do not consider my progress wasted."

Elizabeth felt the challenge in her remark and refused to look away.

Miss Stallard toppled Miss Bingley's vain presumptions with a harrumph. "We are all ladies here. It is fortunate for you that your brother has disassociated himself from the family's trade, or someone as highborn as Mr. Darcy would not consider you either," she said bluntly.

Perhaps Miss Stallard was not so bad after all. Elizabeth clamped her teeth down on the insides of her cheeks to keep from laughing.

Mrs. Hurst said in her sister's defense, "Times have changed, and I for one am grateful for it. Many of the greatest families in England have their roots in trade, and some have even resorted to dabbling in business in order to maintain their fortunes." She tilted her head to the side and looked at them askance, as if she possessed a great secret, but would not be presumed upon to share it.

It was tempting to allow herself the distraction of the subtle battle taking place between Miss Stallard and Miss Bingley, but Elizabeth had called on Miss Stallard with a purpose, and she would not allow herself to be distracted from it. She turned her attention to Miss Stallard, searching for anything which would denote sadness or mourning at the loss of one she held dear. And she saw it.

Under the lace trimming on her sleeve rested a black ribbon. It was subtly placed, but it was there.

"I am sorry for your loss, Miss Stallard," she said, infusing as much compassion as she could muster into her words.

Miss Stallard instantly grasped her wrist, twirling the ribbon around so that a trinket became visible. It was the painting of an eye. In the second it was visible, Elizabeth noted the intensity of the brown and the thickness of the dark eyebrow framing it. It could have been Mr. Wickham's feature drawn as a remembrance of their forbidden romance.

Drawing her hand to her bosom, Miss Stallard said, "Thank you, Miss Elizabeth. I consider myself fortunate to have secured the love of a gentleman of which other ladies can only dream. It is such a pure emotion, and it really is a pity it should be denied to so many." She elongated her neck and looked down her nose at her unmarried guests, who could not make such a grand claim as she.

With an edge to her tongue, Miss Bingley asked, "If you are so much in love, I wonder why you have not yet married?"

Pulling out a handkerchief and dabbing her eyes, Miss Stallard said, "He met his end, and now death separates us."

Had her words held any warmth of feeling, Elizabeth would have pitied her. She could have offered her condolences freely and meant them.

Jane, overcome by her tender sympathies, said, "How very tragic." Her own eyes brimmed with the tears Miss Stallard failed to summon.

After a meticulously measured silence, Miss Stallard withdrew her dry handkerchief. "It is all for the best, I suppose. As a lady born into privilege, there are certain expectations about the sort of gentleman I should marry."

Elizabeth asked, "Did the gentleman have no fortune?"

"He had an inheritance left to him by a wealthy man who looked upon him as a son. However, when he died, the man's son denied his inheritance. No doubt, the son's jealousy moved him to act out his revenge on one who stood to benefit from his kindness."

Elizabeth set her cup down before she shattered it between her fingers. Mr. Wickham had told her the same, sad story of how he had been abused by the Darcy family. He had told her in confidence. Now, hearing it from the lips of another lady, the secret felt tainted and ugly. Had it merely been a ploy he had used to manipulate the sympathy of ignorant young women? To whom else had he confided the intimate details of his past? It made her angry with herself to recall how readily she had believed him.

Miss Bingley covered her mouth in shock. "I heard a similar account regarding Mr. Wickham. Is he the gentleman?"

Miss Stallard dabbed at her dry eyes again and sniffed into her handkerchief, too overcome with grief to answer Miss Bingley's direct question.

Elizabeth took a deep breath, content she had confirmed the gossip as true. Mr. Wickham had pursued Miss Stallard romantically. The story was too similar for it to be anyone else.

After a few dainty sniffs, Miss Stallard recovered herself enough to stir a teaspoonful of sugar into her cup, clinking the sides of the china as she did so. "Such is the injustice of life. Were it up to my father, he would have me marry Mr. Darcy."

Miss Bingley withdrew her hand from the plate of biscuits over which it had hovered.

"Surely you would not agree to a marriage of convenience when you have been loved by one worthy of your heart," said Mrs. Hurst, her unblinking eyes fixed on Miss Stallard.

A deep voice from the doorway sounded, sending fear rushing through Elizabeth's veins.

"Pardon me for the intrusion," said Mr. Stallard as he entered the room and bowed.

Elizabeth felt Jane's gaze on her, her sister's anxiety adding to her own. He was not supposed to be at home. Oh, this had been a mistake!

Mr. Stallard exchanged a meaningful glance with his daughter. One which had her lift her chin in defiance at the same time as she shrunk ever so slightly in her chair.

It was a good time to take their leave. Unanimously, as if Mr. Bingley's sisters felt the tension in the room too, the ladies at the table stood, uttering empty pleasantries and making their departure.

Frustrated she would not get any more information that day, Elizabeth tried to content herself with the one piece of the puzzle she had acquired. Perhaps Miss Stallard would be more forthcoming the next time she could arrange to speak with her. She had liked the attention. If Elizabeth appealed to her sense of superiority, she might be able to learn something of import.

Miss Bingley and Mrs. Hurst settled into their pony phaeton, and Elizabeth set off down the path with Jane.

The uncomfortable sensation of being watched put Elizabeth's nerves on end. Jane, too, was abnormally quiet. They walked in strained silence down the gravel lane leading to the immense iron gate at the edge of the property. Elizabeth did not know what possessed her to do so, but she looked back.

Whipping back around, she pulled on Jane's arm and picked up her pace. Mr. Stallard stood at the top of the steps, watching them leave.

CHAPTER 22

Bingley walked into the Forsters' parlor looking about him in confusion. He relaxed when he saw Darcy.

"It is good to see you, Bingley," Darcy welcomed.

Sitting cautiously, Bingley replied, "I had to walk past two guards just to get past the entrance. They would not have allowed me to enter had not Mrs. Forster walked by at that moment and insisted they let me pass."

"Colonel Forster takes his profession seriously and has turned his house into a secure prison for me," muttered Darcy, his thoughts wandering to the windows. He had climbed out of one before....

With a chuckle, Bingley asked, "Whatever for? To keep people out or to keep you in?" His face fell. "I apologize, Darcy. This is no laughing matter, and it is good for you to have some protection."

"Nothing has happened at Netherfield, I hope?" asked Darcy.

"Nothing at all, though I have informed Caroline and Louisa that they are to leave if things change for the worse. They wanted to join me, but I encouraged them to call on Miss Stallard instead. She is good company for them."

Darcy tensed, his muscles slowly loosening when he remembered Mr. Stallard would not be at home. He did not think Miss Stallard capable of killing Wickham, but he had doubts about her father.

"You ought to take your family and return to London. When this affair is done, calm will return, and it will be safer for you." He could not tell Bingley directly of his suspicions toward Mr. Stallard without causing panic and needlessly spreading unfounded rumors.

Leaning back in his chair, Bingley said, "And what kind of friend would that make me? I cannot abandon you, and I thank you not to ask it of me. I will not go. Of course, my sisters are free to leave as soon as they wish, so long as things remain calm. Mr. Hurst would convey them safely to town, but they, too, are unwilling to leave when they think they might be of assistance."

Just what he needed. More people snooping into this mess. Darcy held back his disapproval so as not to tread on the good will of his friend.

Instead, Darcy asked with more cheer than he felt, "Have you learned anything?"

Bingley bunched his eyebrows in thought. "I had some of the officers over to dine last night. I included Mr. Denny in the hopes that he might confide something worth knowing during the course of the evening. I even broke out my best Madeira for the occasion." He paused to sigh. "If he knows anything besides what he has already told us, he is not talking."

Darcy nodded. "It is not surprising. Had he nothing to say at all about Wickham? Even some small detail?" As much as Bingley wanted to be of help, Darcy could not trust him to remember that his purpose in inviting the officers had not been merely for a pleasant dinner, but to seek out information.

Bingley thought for a while, rubbing his hand over his chin. "Ah, there was one thing that struck me as interesting. Whether it is of any use at all is another matter, but I will repeat it to you all the same and let you decide. Apparently, Mr. Wickham and Miss Stallard were not new acquaintances."

So it was true. At least part of it. Darcy sat forward in his seat. "When did they meet?"

"They met during the summer at Ramsgate. Mr. Stallard disapproved of their... friendship. He sent for Miss Stallard and forced her to return to his estate." He folded his hands and crossed one foot over the other.

"That is all?" asked Darcy.

Bingley rubbed his chin again. "Yes, I do believe so. It struck me at the time that what Mr. Denny told us gentlemen at the table was significant, not for the information itself, but his conspiratorial manner in telling it. He spoke in low tones, and his eyes darted about. I asked Caroline to encourage Miss Stallard to confirm it. She seemed confident she could get Miss Stallard to talk."

Darcy sat back. "You did well in remembering to tell me of it. Did he give any indication as to why Wickham chose to be stationed here in Meryton?"

Shrugging his shoulders, Bingley said, "I had always assumed Wickham came here in pursuit of you."

Darcy looked at him in shock. He had not told Bingley about what had transpired in Ramsgate.

Bingley held a hand up. "Do not concern yourself, Darcy. I have not discovered your secrets— I do not have the inquisitive sort of mind to figure these things out, and I content myself with simply being your loyal friend. That you have secrets, I know. That they concern Wickham, I have surmised. It does not take great intelligence to know as much, but I have no desire to know any more."

Letting his breath out in a relieved gasp, Darcy ran his fingers through his hair. "What have I done to deserve such a good friend as you are to me, Bingley?"

Bingley smiled. "I may say the same about you. You have done me many more favors in helping me achieve a level of acceptance amongst the gentry— something I never could have accomplished without your assistance. I would be lost in the muddle of leasing properties and establishing myself were it not for your guidance."

Darcy accepted Bingley's explanation. It was true. However, had Bingley been less forthright or in any way secretive, as he had been, Darcy had to admit to himself that his loyalty would have found its limit long ago. Bingley was a much better man than he.

"I want you to know...." Darcy closed his mouth before the words tumbled off his tongue. He paused, collecting himself. He was sincere, but that did not mean he could betray Georgiana— not even to Bingley. However, there was no harm in telling Bingley how he felt.

His heart pounded so vigorously, he felt it in his throat. Taking a deep breath, Darcy continued, "I want you to know how much I value your friendship. Even in these trying circumstances in which I find myself, I am comforted to know you believe me innocent." There, he said it. That had been difficult.

To Darcy's surprise, Bingley grinned. "I know how difficult that must have been for you to say."

With a chuckle, the tension in Darcy's chest lifted and, for a moment, he felt as carefree as he imagined his friend to be. As lighthearted as Miss Elizabeth had been even in the face of her sister's illness. How he admired that quality! The ability to see the humor in life's trials and the grace to maneuver through them with cheer. Miss Elizabeth never lost the twinkle in her eye. Darcy envied her for it.

***

Elizabeth was chilled to the bone by the time they arrived home. Holding her hands up to the lit fire in the drawing room, she pondered the information she had gathered that afternoon. Her intuition, which had immediately taken a liking to Mr. Wickham's charm, was not such an accurate judge of character as she had thought it to be. It was becoming impossible for her to continue to dislike Mr. Darcy as she had so easily done before.

Rubbing her hands together, soaking in the warmth, she and Jane waited downstairs while everyone else occupied themselves in other pursuits. They had entered the house quietly, and Elizabeth enjoyed the brief minutes of peace they had been granted. She had much to ponder.

Hours later, Elizabeth's doubts still warred with her prejudices, her reasonableness with her stubbornness.

She wished she could speak to Mr. Darcy. He was not the sort of man to be carried away by emotions. She admired that about him. He kept his calm no matter how grave the situation.

Of course, she could not help but wish she could crack his stoic exterior. For all of the responsibility he bore— and he bore it well— she felt certain he would benefit greatly by smiling more. Not a polite smile, but the sort of grin which creases the eyes, exposes teeth, and usually prompts laughter. It was a silly wish, but more than anyone she had ever met, Mr. Darcy needed a dose of humor. Perhaps that was his reason for befriending Mr. Bingley.

The clouds covered the stars and smothered the brightness of the moon, making the sky look like spilled ink. Elizabeth shivered despite the warmth in the dining room. Mother had not gone to the extremes of Aunt Philips, but not one wrap was present at the table.

Lydia and Kitty played tug-of-war over Mr. Denny's attentions— though he had departed hours before.

"He sat closer to me than he did to you," boasted Lydia.

Kitty retorted, "With the way you squeezed yourself onto the other end of the sofa, it is no wonder. Were it not for the presence of Mrs. Yeats and Mr. Collins, I do not doubt but that you would have sat on his lap!" Her cheeks burned red, and her eyes glared at her younger sister.

"Why should you both fight over the same gentleman when there are so many handsome officers in the village?" asked Mother.

Pointing her finger at Lydia, Kitty said, "She only fixed her sights on Mr. Denny because she knows he is the one I like best."

"Envy is the root of all evil," Mary spouted.

Before Mr. Collins could expand on Mary's comment, Father opened his hands and said, "Ah, young love. I congratulate the both of you. Next to being married, a girl likes to be crossed a little in love now and then. It is something to think of, and it gives her a sort of distinction among her companions. With officers enough in Meryton to disappoint all the young ladies in the country, I feel optimistic that each of you could have the privilege of being jilted creditably."

Elizabeth had little experience in the subject, but that did not prevent her from expressing her opinion, "And this spoken from a man who suffered from no struggle during his courtship with Mama. Perhaps it does offer some distinction, but I cannot agree that it is a situation in which a lady seeks to be."

Father winked at her and raised his wine glass. Pulling back from the table, he said, "I will retire early tonight. It has been a busy day."

Elizabeth wondered how spending the day hidden in his study could tire him. She had walked into Meryton twice that day, but the shock to her emotions had caused much more fatigue than the physical exercise.

Mr. Collins had told them nothing of import regarding Mr. Denny's visit. Mrs. Yeats had been more intent on maintaining propriety than on asking questions, and so had nothing to relate.

Elizabeth joined the rest of her family in the drawing room after Father left them, but her thoughts were too restless to concentrate on the novel she attempted to read. The light was too poor to do needlework, a task in which the only point she could see was the end of the needle. How an embroidered cushion would communicate her qualifications as a suitable wife was beyond Elizabeth's desire to understand. Why would she want to marry a man who would base such an important decision on trivialities? No, she would marry a decisive, intelligent man. A man with uncompromising values. An honorable gentleman who would never lose her respect. Her vision blurred as she stared out of the black window. The man she imagined was none other than Mr. Darcy. Anybody but him!

Suddenly, the room felt stifling. The giggles her younger sisters emitted, and the droning voice of Mr. Collins reading from his book of sermons, intensified her agitation. Dismissing herself from the room, she went upstairs to the cool and quiet of her bedchamber.

She went over the events of the day, mulling over every detail. There had been a folded piece of paper. Mr. Darcy's valet had given it to her, and she had completely forgotten about it until then. Lighting a candle and opening her bureau, she found the dress she had worn that morning.

Retrieving the paper, she unfolded it to see that it was a letter. It was addressed to her. Flipping over the page, she saw Mr. Darcy's signature, and her skin tingled in anticipation as she sank into her bed to read.

CHAPTER 23

His handwriting was small and bold and perfectly legible. Elizabeth held her breath, her eyes devouring the covered page.

Miss Elizabeth,

My purpose in conveying this message to you is one of hope. I am surrounded by people who believe me guilty of a crime we both know I could not have committed, and I know I have only fueled their prejudices against me by being unwilling to reveal the nature of my quarrel with Wickham. That you believe me innocent is not based on my own merits— of this I am well aware. And yet, I hope. If you will extend to me a measure of the compassion I have seen you display generously to others, please allow me the honor of your friendship whilst you hold this page in your hand. Allow me to unburden myself of the secret which has been weighing on me since Mr. Wickham's arrival to Meryton. If such an imposition is distasteful, then read no further, but my distress is greater than my pride, and I trust no one but you to safeguard my secret.

First and foremost, I must explain my long history with Mr. Wickham. Of what he had particularly accused me, I am ignorant. His accusations have been numerous and varied. Of the truth of what I shall relate, I can summon more than one witness of undoubted veracity.

Mr. Wickham is the son of a very respectable man, who had for many years managed all of the Pemberley estates. His good conduct in the discharge of his trust naturally inclined my father to be of service to him and to liberally bestow his kindness on his godson, George Wickham. My father supported him at school, and afforded him a gentleman's education at Cambridge— an assistance his own father, always poor from the extravagance of his wife, would have been unable to give him. My father was not only fond of Wickham's society, whose manners had always been engaging, but he also held the highest opinion of him, hoping the church would be his profession and intending to provide for him in it.

As for myself, it is many years since I first began to think of Mr. Wickham in a very different manner. I will not speak ill of the dead. Suffice it to say that had my father observed him as I could, in his unguarded moments, he would not have held him in such high esteem.

My father died about five years ago, his attachment to Mr. Wickham so steady to the last that in his will he particularly recommended it to me to promote his advancement in the best manner his profession might allow and, if he took orders, desired that a valuable family

*living might be his as soon as it became vacant. There
was also a legacy of one thousand pounds.*

*Mr. Wickham's own father did not long survive mine,
and within six months from these events, Mr. Wickham
wrote to inform me that, having finally resolved against
taking orders, he hoped I should not think it
unreasonable for him to expect some more immediate
pecuniary advantage in lieu of the position at
Pemberley's parish.*

*He informed me of his intention of studying the law,
and how I must be aware that the interest of one
thousand pounds would be too insufficient a sum to
support him therein. I rather wished than believed him to
be sincere but, at any rate, was perfectly ready to accede
to his proposal. I knew Mr. Wickham ought not to be a
clergyman.*

*The business was therefore soon settled. He resigned
all claim to assistance in the church and accepted in
return the sum of three thousand pounds. All connection
between us seemed now dissolved.*

*I thought too ill of him to invite him to Pemberley or
admit his society in town. I later learned that his life had
become one of idleness and dissipation.*

*For about three years I heard little of him, he still
having sufficient funds on which to live. When that was
squandered, he applied to me again by letter. His
circumstances, he assured me, were exceedingly bad. He
had found the law a most unprofitable study and was
absolutely resolved on being ordained. He then demanded
that I present him the living my father had intended for
him — the living he had exchanged for money three years*

before. You will hardly blame me for refusing to comply with his entreaty or for resisting every repetition of it.

His resentment was in proportion to the distress of his circumstances, and he was doubtless as violent in his abuse of me to others then as he was upon arriving to Meryton. After this period, every appearance of acquaintance was dropped. How he lived, I know not.

However, last summer he was again most painfully thrust on my notice. I must now mention a circumstance which I would wish to forget and which no obligation less than the present should induce me to unfold to any human being. Having said this much, I feel no doubt of your discretion.

My sister, who is more than ten years my junior, was left to the guardianship of my mother's nephew, Colonel Fitzwilliam, and myself.

About a year ago, she was taken from school and settled in an establishment formed for her in London. Last summer, she went with the lady who presided over it, Mrs. Younge, to Ramsgate and thither went Mr. Wickham, undoubtedly by design. There proved to have been a prior acquaintance between him and Mrs. Younge, in whose character we were most unhappily deceived. It was by her connivance and aid he so far recommended himself to Georgiana, whose innocent, affectionate heart believed herself in love and consented to an elopement. She was then but fifteen.

I joined them unexpectedly a day before the intended elopement and Georgiana, unable to support the idea of grieving and offending a brother whom she almost looked to as a father, acknowledged the whole to me. I am *grateful with my every breath that she confided in me. You may imagine what I felt and how I acted. Regard for my sister's feelings and concern over her reputation prevented any public exposure. Mrs. Younge was, of course, removed from Georgiana's charge. We left Ramsgate immediately, but I wrote to Mr. Wickham who, as I understand it, chose to stay at Ramsgate long enough to use his charm to seduce another unsuspecting lady.*

Mr. Wickham's chief object was unquestionably my sister's fortune, which is thirty thousand pounds. But I cannot help supposing that the hope of revenging himself on me was a strong inducement. His revenge would have been complete indeed. My argument with him the day you witnessed my departure from his tent was about Georgiana. He attempted to blackmail me, using his popularity and the threat of her exposure, for money. You must see now why I have refused to reveal the nature of our quarrel.

I will admit to some amount of relief at Mr. Wickham's demise. He can no longer threaten my sister or harm her. However, the way it was done is unforgivable, and I must bring his killer to justice. I will not rest until it is done.

This, Miss Elizabeth, is a faithful narrative of every event in which we have been concerned together regarding Mr. Wickham. I know not in what manner nor under what form of falsehood he had imposed on you, but his success was not to be wondered at. Ignorant as you previously were of everything concerning him, detection could not be in your power and suspicion certainly not in your inclination. You are blameless.

You may wonder why all this was not told you before. My only reply is that my life's experience has taught me not to trust easily and to never allow another any measure of power over me. I would do anything to protect my sister from ruin. She is deserving of happiness, and I could never forgive myself if I failed to protect her.

For the truth of everything here related, I can appeal more particularly to the testimony of Colonel Fitzwilliam, who from our near relationship, constant intimacy, and one of the executors of my father's will, has been unavoidably acquainted with every particular of these transactions. If your abhorrence of me should make my assertions valueless, I pray you might give me the benefit of consulting with him. I have written to him and expect his arrival to Meryton before the inquest. I shall endeavor to find some opportunity of putting this letter in your hands in the course of the morning.

I will only add, God bless you.
Fitzwilliam Darcy

Gasping for air, Elizabeth clutched the letter to her chest. Every bit of hostility she had ever felt toward Mr. Darcy melted away, leaving her light-headed and breathless.

Falling back against the pillows on her bed, she ran her fingers over the paper and closed her eyes. Had Mr. Wickham not poisoned her against Mr. Darcy, would she have understood his character sooner? She groaned as pieces of past conversations came to mind. She had bitten him!

Elizabeth lifted the letter to read it again, the drumming rhythm of her pulse increasing along with her agitation at herself.

A loud crash startled her from her self-deprecation. Shards of glass flew at her face. Bolting upright, she screamed so loudly it hurt her ears.

CHAPTER 24

Forcing her panic aside, Elizabeth gathered her wits and ran to look out of her shattered window. The darkness swallowed up and hid whoever had done it, but she thought she heard the clattering of hooves fading into the distance over the scuffling of feet coming up the stairs.

On the floor, near her feet, lay a brick. 'Murderess' was painted on it with thick, black letters bleeding into its clay like blood soaking into the earth.

Father reached her first. Bursting through her door, his white hair standing on all ends, his nightclothes rumpled, he demanded, "What has happened here? Lizzy, my dearest girl, are you well? You are unharmed?" He strode over to her, unconscious of the glass cracking under his feet, to hold her face between his hands. He lifted her hands up to examine them, but there was nothing to see.

"Father, I am well. I cannot say the same for the window," she added, forcing a smile.

"I do not care a frog's fart about the window. Are you certain you are unharmed?" He only released his hold on her when Jane rushed into the room.

Reaching for her sister, Jane pulled a shard of glass from Elizabeth's hair with a gasp as she took in the damage done to their bedchamber.

"Who would do this?" she asked breathlessly, her eyes roaming the room.

Father leaned down, picking up the brick. "Murderess," he read aloud.

Jane and Father both looked at Elizabeth as if she could explain what had just happened. Alas, she was as clueless as they were.

"Lizzy, what does this mean? Why would anyone accuse you of murdering Mr. Wickham?" he asked.

"I do not know what it means," she said. "I ran to the window, but could see nothing. I think I heard a horse, but I cannot be certain."

Mrs. Yeats entered the room. "Miss Elizabeth?" she asked, her mouth gaping wider the further into the room she drew. She stopped when a piece of glass crunched beneath her foot. She gasped, moving her hand up to her mouth and breathing heavily. "This is awful. Who would do this?"

A shrill cry sounded from downstairs.

Father, in the same soothing voice he had used when Elizabeth was a small child and had scraped her knee, asked, "How is Mrs. Bennet?" to Mrs. Yeats.

Dropping her hand to speak, Mrs. Yeats said, "I saw she was in no position to leave the room, and so I asked Miss Mary if she would stay with her mother and younger sisters. They were growing hysterical, so I offered to come up to ensure all was well while Miss Mary kept them company."

Father nodded approvingly. "Good. I want you to return to them and assure them that Lizzy is well. No harm has been done, only the unfortunate shattering of a window."

He waited until she had left the room, and they heard the wooden stairs squeaking under her weight on the way downstairs.

"I will send Hill in to help clean this mess," he said, one of his hands holding her by the elbow, and his other hand supporting Jane. "We must send for the constable. He needs to know what has transpired."

Jane's eyes widened. "You will not leave us, will you?"

"No. I will send Thomas to fetch Mr. Tanner. He ought to alert Colonel Forster as well." Looking directly at Elizabeth, Father said, "This almost certainly confirms what you have said all along, though I doubt you meant to bring suspicion on yourself, my dearest girl. This casts doubt on Mr. Darcy's guilt. Of course, everyone will know you did not do it. They had better know." He smoothed his wild hair. "What a dreadful mess."

Elizabeth would not argue with him. It was a horrible mess, indeed.

He sent for their manservant, giving specific instructions to go to Colonel Forster's home first, and then to the inn to inform Mr. Tanner of the brick and its damning message. Thomas was pleased to be of service and wasted no time in leaving. Elizabeth heard their carriage horse plodding along as Thomas' voice encouraged it to a gallop.

If only she could have heard more earlier, or seen anything of use. She occupied herself in tending to Father's bleeding feet until Mr. Tanner arrived.

***

A knock at the door loud enough to interrupt Colonel Forster's reading of some military tome Darcy had not been paying attention to, resounded through the drawing room.

Not a minute later, the door opened and a manservant appeared in the doorway wringing his hat in his hands.

"Mr. Thomas to see you, sir. It is a matter of grave importance regarding the Bennet family at Longbourn."

Darcy rose from his chair near the fire as if pulled up by strings. He stepped closer to the manservant, commanding his attention before Colonel Forster had even closed his book. He knew better than to take the lead in the conversation, but Colonel Forster tested his patience.

Finally, the colonel stood and asked, "Do tell us what has happened to bring you here at this late hour? I do hope that the Bennets are well?"

Darcy's eyes never left Thomas. If he so much as flinched or hesitated, Darcy would see it.

"They are in good health, sir," said Thomas quickly enough to placate Darcy's growing dread. "I have come at the request of Mr. Bennet because someone threw a brick through Miss Elizabeth's bedchamber window."

"Dear God," gasped Darcy. "Did she suffer harm?" He needed reassurance.

"Miss Elizabeth is well. The entire household is, as you can imagine, scared."

Colonel Forster, with a forbearing look at Darcy, asked, "Did anyone see who made the assault on their home?"

Thomas slumped his shoulders. "No, sir. More is the pity. I was bringing wood in for the fire when it happened. As for the rest of the household, you will have to ask them yourself. I was told to fetch you and Mr. Tanner, and that is all I know."

Massaging his chin, Colonel Forster said, "You did well. I will accompany you to the inn so that we lose no time."

To his wife, he said, "Do not wait up for me, my love. I will return as soon as I am able." She did not appear affected overmuch.

Darcy fell in behind Colonel Forster.

"Mr. Darcy, do not think you can accompany me," Colonel Forster commanded.

Were Darcy not so determined, he might have felt like a lowly ensign after a rebuke. But nothing would persuade him to remain behind.

"I must go with you. If someone is making threats to the Bennets, Mr. Wickham may not be the only victim. Now that this has happened, who could argue that I am involved? I spent all evening in your company."

The colonel bunched up his chin and furled his brows. After several moments of thought, he raised his head. "Very well. Ready yourself."

With that, Colonel Forster donned his coat and ordered another horse to be readied.

The streets were quiet. It was not a night to inspire an evening walk. It was so dark, Darcy could not see more than a few paces in front of his horse. The air had a decided bite of winter in it.

The inn was warm and smelled of fresh ale. Darcy did not like Mr. Tanner much, but the food he served was good and his beer was decent.

Mr. Tanner was wiping down the bar in the taproom when they walked in. He froze with his arm extended as soon as he saw Darcy.

"What is he doing here?" he demanded.

"He insisted on joining me on urgent business. I had no reason not to comply," said the colonel as he closed the distance to the bar.

"He is not welcome in my establishment," Mr. Tanner growled, speaking to Darcy without addressing him directly.

Darcy was livid. Miss Elizabeth could be in danger, and this fool would rather nurse his grudge when he could go to her aid. "What do you hold against me? What have I ever done to you?"

Mr. Tanner's face twisted with hatred. "You have no idea, have you?"

His answer puzzled Darcy. He had never met Mr. Tanner before his arrival in Meryton, but he would not waste precious time arguing with him. "Enough with your games, Mr. Tanner. The Bennets' home has been attacked."

Mr. Tanner's anger melted away, turning to alarm. "Was anyone harmed?"

Colonel Forster stepped between them. "No one was harmed, but as you can imagine, they are rather shaken. They sent their manservant to fetch us and we ought not delay in going to them."

Nudging his chin toward Darcy, Mr. Tanner asked, "Must he come along?"

Darcy leaned forward. "Try and stop me."

CHAPTER 25

Their horses cut through the fog, their pounding hooves muffled in the thickness of the night. Darcy, his senses at their peak, kept his eyes open for any other riders or late-night walkers until they reached Longbourn. Every candle in the house must have been lit. A fuzzy glow surrounded the house.

Mr. Bennet, his feet wrapped in cloth, greeted them at the door and saw them into the drawing room where Miss Bennet sat next to Miss Elizabeth. Mr. Collins sat gravely nearby.

"Please join us here, gentlemen," said Mr. Bennet, motioning for them to sit, and limping to his chair.

"What happened?" Darcy asked him.

Mr. Bennet waved the matter of as of little import. "Just a few minor cuts from some glass. Nothing of concern."

"You were fortunate, Papa," said Elizabeth, her voice strained.

Darcy's eyes wandered back to Miss Elizabeth. Starting at the top of her head, he searched for cuts, bruises, tears… anything out of place. Aside from her stiff posture and the wringing of her hands, she admirably kept her composure.

Mr. Tanner asked, "Where is the rest of your family?"

Mr. Bennet answered, "I sent my other daughters upstairs, and Mrs. Yeats is tending to Mrs. Bennet, who was overcome by a fit of nerves as you could well imagine. If she does not improve, we shall have to send for the apothecary."

Colonel Forster waved his hand. "I see no need to disturb them, Mr. Bennet. It was thoughtful on your behalf to see to their care under these distressing circumstances."

Mr. Tanner paced about the room, tugging his fingers through his hair. Finally, turning to Mr. Bennet, he said, "I must apologize to you, sir. I have yet to find out who is behind this sordid affair, and now it has affected your family."

Darcy had not known Mr. Tanner capable of speaking without a snarl. He wondered if Mr. Tanner had ever believed him truly guilty or if he only accused Darcy to be bothersome. To see that the rugged man was capable of gentleness came as a shock. To witness some small amount of honor was a relief.

Mr. Bennet rose. Placing his hand on Mr. Tanner's shoulder, he said, "You have done your best as you always do. It is unfortunate, indeed, but it is not your fault." He extended his hand out toward a chair, thus encouraging Mr. Tanner to sit in it.

Colonel Forster shifted his weight. "If I may be so bold, may I inquire what happened?" He looked between Mr. Bennet and Miss Elizabeth.

Miss Elizabeth answered, her tone firm and factual. "I went upstairs to my room after dinner, seeking to retire early. While I was there, a brick flew through my window." She stopped abruptly, her eyes flickering to Darcy.

The colonel asked, "Is there any other detail you remember?"

Miss Elizabeth blinked heavily, as one does when remembering something unpleasant. "I ran to the window once I realized what had happened, but the night was so dark, and the fog hid whoever did this too well. There was a lot of noise by that time in our household, and so I am uncertain if I heard someone riding away or if I merely imagined it." She looked down at her hands and sighed while every eye in the room watched her. Raising her head, she added, "The brick… it is still on the floor of my bedchamber. It… it bears an accusation."

Darcy's heartbeat slowed.

With a huff of breath, she continued, "It says 'Murderess.'" She looked around at them.

"It is, of course, preposterous to think any cousin of mine could act so immorally as to murder anyone," said Mr. Collins.

Darcy ground his teeth at the clergyman's self-interested comment, but he could not disagree with him. Miss Elizabeth could not possibly have murdered Wickham. He knew where she had been at the time of his murder.

Mr. Tanner slapped his thigh. "I will not have it. This is too much." He popped up from his seat and resumed pacing in front of the window.

Colonel Forster frowned deeply and tugged at his side whiskers. "This is distressing. Do you have any notion of who might have acted against you in this manner?" he asked.

Miss Bennet, who had been quietly sitting next to her sister with one arm draped around Miss Elizabeth's shoulders said, "Lizzy and I share a room. I do not think it wise to assume the message was meant only for her."

Whipping her face around to her sister, Elizabeth exclaimed, "Jane! No."

Mr. Collins nodded his head approvingly. "It is true, and I am proud to hear my cousin admit to it. For that matter, any or all of the females in this household are under suspicion."

Darcy glared at Mr. Collins. He ought to keep his mouth shut.

"What are you implying, Mr. Collins?" asked Mr. Tanner, his voice gruff. "In an effort to prove your self-righteousness, are you willing to cast suspicion on all of your female relatives?" He shook his head, not bothering to disguise the disgust on his face.

Mr. Tanner's eyes darted over to Darcy and they met for some seconds. Darcy held his gaze steady. He had nothing to hide, nor did he feel defensive of himself when all of his focus was on the Bennet family. With a furl of the brow, Mr. Tanner looked away.

Colonel Forster addressed Mr. Bennet. "With your permission, and that of your daughters, of course, I would like to inspect the room and the grounds under the bedchamber window."

Leaning forward, and nearly tumbling out of his chair when he attempted to bow, Mr. Collins, asked, "Might I be of service?"

Colonel Forster inhaled deeply, his lips pursed together.

Darcy opened his mouth to suggest Mr. Collins take charge of the inspection outside, but Colonel Forster beat him to it.

"How kind of you to offer, Mr. Collins. As you are more familiar with the area, I think you would be of considerable use outside. If you could find a boot print, or anything the individual may have dropped, it could be enough to solve this mystery."

Darcy dearly wanted to laugh at the look on Mr. Collins' face. No doubt, he had hoped for a more prestigious task. Miss Elizabeth cleared her throat and kept her eyes fixed on the floor in front of her.

Mr. Bennet sent the manservant out with Mr. Collins, lantern in hand, lest the clergyman get lost in the fog. Once they had disappeared out of doors, Mr. Bennet said, "Let us go upstairs then. We did our best not to disturb anything. I did pick up the brick to read the writing on it, but I placed it where it fell."

"Papa, are you well enough?" Miss Elizabeth asked, looking at his feet.

Mr. Bennet hobbled toward the door. "I have been comfortable for most of my life, Lizzy. A little discomfort might be good for me."

He led the way up the stairs, followed by Colonel Forster and Mr. Tanner. Darcy held back so Miss Elizabeth and Miss Bennet could pass in front of him.

"Thank you, Mr. Darcy," she said as she passed by. Her eyes lingered on his, communicating so much more than her words. Had she read his letter?

"My pleasure," he replied, wishing he could ask more. Say more. But they had to continue up the stairs. He followed so closely, he could appreciate the curls defying her hair pins at the base of her neck. He could not rightly explain how powerful the urge was to ensure her safety— nor how deeply he wished to hold her in his embrace so nothing could ever harm her again.

Glass crunched under their feet as they entered the modest-sized room. The window was opposite the door and a stiff breeze blasted in, chilling him with cold and worry as his gaze followed a trail down to the floor and he saw the condemning message painted on the brick.

The colonel and Mr. Tanner poked around, but there really was very little to see.

In one glance Darcy took inventory of his surroundings. Without a second guess, he could tell which part of the room belonged to Miss Elizabeth.

The table on her side of the bed held a candle burned down to nothing more than a wick. Three books lay on top of the table.

The contents of the table on the opposite side of the bed were not nearly so interesting, and Darcy wasted no time on them. What was a hairbrush to a book of poetry? Darcy squinted to see the title of the second tome better. A book of political satire. Not exactly the preferred reading material of most young ladies, but, then again… Miss Elizabeth was not a typical young lady.

"There is nothing more to see here," declared Colonel Forster, interrupting Darcy's tender thoughts. What would she think if she saw his room at Pemberley? Would she notice the stack of books always by his bedside? Would she take interest in his views and welcome the opportunity to expand her own? She would love Pemberley. He would love showing his home to her.

In an intruding voice, Colonel Forster said, "That is all then. We will leave you to rest. I must see Mr. Darcy back to my home, and I am certain Mr. Tanner is anxious to return to his inn."

A door opened and a weepy voice from the hallway said, "Colonel Forster, am I to understand that you will allow my daughters to be attacked again without extending your protection to them in the same manner you have done with Mr. Darcy?" Mrs. Bennet sniffed.

***

Elizabeth closed her eyes, hoping in vain her mother would go away. It had never worked in the past, and she had no reason to think it would do so then either… for all that she dearly wished it.

At least Elizabeth had had sense enough to conceal Mr. Darcy's letter up her sleeve before anyone had noticed. Mother would have loved to have caught her with a letter from an unmarried man. She would have insisted that Mr. Darcy purchase a special license and would have seen them married before the inquest.

Sighing in resignation while the gentlemen overcame their shock at her mother's suggestion, Elizabeth said, "Mother, the trouble is done. Jane and I shall sleep well so long as we can cover the window to keep out the cold."

"On top of fearing for your life, I am to fret you shall catch your death of a cold? No, child, it will not do. My nerves cannot endure it. Tell her it is so, Mr. Bennet! I cannot bear it! Oh, the sufferings of a mother!" she exclaimed through sobs.

Father stepped into the hallway, where Mother held a handkerchief wadded up by her face and a wrap clutched around her shoulders.

Lydia stamped to her door and cracked it open. Elizabeth saw the edge of her nightgown peek through the bottom of the door and prayed she would open it no further. "If Lizzy and Jane get to stay with the Forsters, then I demand to go to! My life is in just as much danger as hers, and I am too pretty to die so young! Imagine if a shard of glass had cut my face!" She began to sob violently.

Lydia's outburst fueled Mother's hysteria until the two of them became inconsolable in a matter of seconds. Father inhaled deeply, his cheeks puffing out as he exhaled. He knew their routine well.

Colonel Forster, unaccustomed to such dramatics, stood with his jaw open. In a profession where he was surrounded by men day in and day out, it must come as quite a shock to deal with a house full of temperamental women.

Elizabeth swallowed her chuckles, preferring it to the embarrassment she also felt.

Controlling her emotions enough to speak, Mother said, "None of us shall rest well tonight, and how are we to receive all of our callers on the morrow?"

Mr. Tanner rubbed his hand over his face. "I agree with Mrs. Bennet."

Mother's reaction was instant and nothing short of a miracle. Tears dried and her wailing ceased completely.

"Hush, Lydia! How can we listen to Mr. Tanner's voice of reason when you carry on so?" she exclaimed, adding, "Please, sir, convince these gentlemen to offer their protection to my beloved daughter."

Mr. Tanner said, "Someone has it in for Miss Elizabeth, and until we find out who it is, she could be in danger. I have an empty room at the inn for her and Miss Bennet, but I am unable to keep a vigilant watch while attending to my duties." He looked expectantly at Colonel Forster. As did Mother.

Mr. Darcy was silent. His face gave nothing away— unlike her own, which she could feel burned in mortification.

CHAPTER 26

Elizabeth crept down the stairs, feeling like an intruder with each step. Her room had been cold, but the bed had been warm and comfortable. She had to admit she would not have slept so well in her own room at Longbourn. Here, at the Forsters', she could look out of her window and see an officer standing in front of the back door. The sight offered a sense of security, and when she awoke the following morning to see another officer stationed there, her fear subsided.

Father and Mr. Collins had stayed at Longbourn. Mother had insisted that the house was unsafe, and so she and the rest of their household had spent the night with Aunt Philips. Elizabeth felt better knowing they were nearby.

Following her grumbling stomach and her nose, Elizabeth found the breakfast room. It was a cramped space, but the curtains were open and offered a view of the soggy streets through the glass.

Mr. Darcy sat at the table, a plate in front of him. He bumped against the table in his haste to stand. "You are awake early," he said in greeting.

"I may say the same of you." She looked around her, but saw no one else.

He motioned to the chair opposite him. "Please have a seat, Miss Elizabeth. The door is open and with the servants wandering in and out of the room, I hardly think it inappropriate for us to break our fast together."

"Have you seen Colonel or Mrs. Forster?"

"I have not, but I suspect the colonel is out. Mrs. Forster, I have learned in my brief stay here, prefers to take her breakfast upstairs."

A servant passed by the door, nodded when she saw Elizabeth at the table, and scurried away—Elizabeth hoped in the direction of the kitchen. She was dreadfully hungry. And dreadfully nervous. Now that she held no resentment against Mr. Darcy, she felt uncertain in his company.

Mr. Darcy did not take a bite from his own plate until her own breakfast was served a minute later. They sat across from each other, the silence growing increasingly heavy as the minutes passed. Why was this so difficult? How much easier it had been when she had hated him…

"Did you sleep well?" he asked, buttering a roll of bread and reaching for the preserves.

"I did," she answered, reaching her hand out for the jar of preserves when he had finished. "And you?"

"Yes, thank you."

Her teeth sank into the soft bread, still warm from the oven, and moaned before she remembered with whom she sat at the table.

Opening her eyes and stopping herself short, she heard Mr. Darcy laugh.

"It is good bread. Please do not let my presence diminish your enjoyment."

Thus encouraged, she took another bite, savoring the sweet flavors, but keeping her pleasure mute.

When she had finished half of a roll and could think more clearly, she sat back in her chair and sipped her coffee. Scrunching her face up at the bitter taste, she reached for the sugar bowl at the same time Mr. Darcy pushed it toward her. She pulled back her hand, surprised at his gesture.

"I remember how you take your coffee… from your stay at Netherfield," he explained.

"Oh," was all she managed to say, wishing she could think of a clever retort, but none came. So she put a teaspoon of sugar in her coffee and stirred, wondering why Mr. Darcy would remember such an insignificant detail about her. He probably remembered every curt word of hers against him, too. And she had never had an opportunity to apologize… until now.

"Mr. Darcy, I read your letter. I…," she looked for servants before continuing. "… I am sorry for biting your finger." Now, that was not what she had planned to say. Embarrassed, she lowered her chin. She did not want Mr. Darcy to see her blush.

With a frustrated sigh at her inability to speak as easily as she had before, Elizabeth stared into her coffee cup. When Mr. Darcy did not reply, she got curious and looked up at him. She was not prepared for what she saw.

His eyes brimmed with mirth, his lips trembling. Elizabeth had always thought him exceptionally handsome— What woman with a beating heart would not?— but his entire face glowed in happiness. His eyes brightened like fireworks in a dark sky, crinkling upwards in the corners. He parted his lips, no longer struggling to hold in his merriment, and the throaty laughter which emanated from him carried away all of Elizabeth's apprehensions. It was so contagious, she soon joined him.

He held his hand out for her to see. There were two neat, purple marks just below his knuckle. "As you see, Miss Elizabeth, I shall live. Considering the circumstances, I rather admired your reaction at the time— painful though it was for me." He chuckled again, and Elizabeth bit her bottom lip to restrain her laughter.

"I am sorry," she repeated, this time allowing her eyes to fix on his.

Mr. Darcy waved his hand. "You need not apologize. I should have told you the truth about

Wickham sooner. For that, it is I who should apologize."

She shook her head. "The timing of the telling should not have mattered. I insulted your character, and my conscience has tormented me ever since. I cast my judgment against you based on unfounded prejudice. I had always taken pride in my ability to measure a person's character, and now I see how mistaken I have been. It makes me doubt how helpful I can be to you, and yet, I must not fail."

"The ball was only three days ago." Mr. Darcy spoke softly, his eyebrows pressing up in concern.

Elizabeth sighed and twirled her cup. "But it feels as if it has been an eternity ago. And still, I am no closer to finding out who really did kill Mr. Wickham. Have you found out anything? I do not imagine it is easy to continue making inquiries while you are stuck here." Imagine that. Mr. Darcy stuck. Those words did not belong together. A man such as he would not be presumed upon to stay unless he wished it. Hmm... now that was something. "Why *do* you stay here?" she asked.

He smiled. "Right now, I am enjoying my stay."

How had she not appreciated the cleft in his chin before or the dimple that deepened in his cheek as he smiled? She felt a blush creep up her neck. Mr. Darcy was flirting with her. Such a mixture of pride and pleasure surged through her and muddled her thoughts so that she wondered if she would ever be able to utter a sensible sentence again. Thankfully, it passed. So long as she did not look at him again, she would manage.

He cleared his throat. "All pleasantries aside, Miss Elizabeth, I am only here because I hold life in high regard. I did not want to put Bingley and his household in jeopardy. While my freedom is limited, Colonel Forster has been a gracious host and keeps me informed of any advances in his search."

Elizabeth bowed her head, her cheeks burning with heat. "I realize how disagreeable the consequences of what happened in the library are to you," she paused to catch her breath, hoping he would interrupt her. Hoping he would deny her assumption.

When he did not, she continued, her chest tightening, "However, I also value life. Mine, as well as yours. If it comes down to it, I will tell Colonel Forster what happened the night of the ball."

"I would only think it disagreeable to the degree in which you do," Mr. Darcy said, his brow furrowed. He muttered, "Do not think I place more value on my life than I do on your freedom and my sister's reputation. Were it not for the confounded secrets I must take with me to the grave, I would long since have liberated myself from this burden."

He could not mean it. Then again, when had Mr. Darcy ever said anything he did not wish to express?

"Surely, in my case, you cannot mean it. For your sister, I would do the same in your situation, and I am honored all the more for your sharing it with me. Such loyalty should be commended, not sacrificed for the freedom of one who has acted ungratefully toward the giver as I have."

"Of what use is life without freedom?" he asked, the intensity of his gaze burning her cheeks.

"And of what use is freedom without life?" she countered. She searched his face, but he revealed nothing. How did he do it?

"What of your happiness?" he asked. "Would you be willing to settle to a life of mediocre complacency if I were to reveal the truth of our circumstances?"

She came so near to exclaiming, "Yes," she forced herself to look away from him before he read her thoughts. Unlike him, she had never been good at disguising her feelings. There was still much she would like to learn about Mr. Darcy, but that was the trouble. She *wanted* to learn more about him.

If only he felt the same about her, she felt confident love would grow where respect and trust thrived. But she was too simple. She despised disguise of any sort, and had never learned the art of flirtation as other, more sophisticated ladies had. There were too many reasons why he should not attach himself to her.

Finally, she looked up. He had asked a sincere question, and he deserved a sincere answer. "I would make the most of it. If happiness is possible, I would soon discover it and nurture it."

Her eyes prickled, making her angry with herself. Why should she feel inclined to shed tears at a time like this? How foolish she felt. How foolish she must seem to Mr. Darcy. She tried to push away her emotions. She told herself, as she had so many times before, that she did not care in the least what Mr. Darcy thought of her. Therein lay the problem. She cared. It disturbed her greatly to feel how deeply she cared.

***

Why did it bother him so much to hear Miss Elizabeth insist they would be unhappy together? Would she give him no encouragement at all? Despite everything she knew, despite her knowledge of the truth and his attempts to reveal his character to her, did she despise him yet?

Darcy filled his lungs and exhaled, counting the seconds as his breath left him. No, Miss Elizabeth did not despise him. He could have read it on her face if she still held him in derision. He had seen the expression on her face too many times not to recognize it now.

To think there was a time when he had thought her brutal honesty to be an exercise in the mastery of flirtation. But he knew better now. She could not flirt properly if her life depended upon it, nor would she offer him hope where there was none.

Her answer ought to have pleased him. Indeed, it made him think all the better of her. The same tenacity with which she had stubbornly misjudged him before would serve as a blessing if she directed it toward their mutual happiness. He would do anything to make her happy. He loved her with his whole being. Her voice was his favorite sound; her smile, his favorite sight. She filled his senses and for the first time in his memory, he felt complete. Like a sunrise in his heart, Darcy's love for Elizabeth awakened his hope, filling his soul with warmth and joy until it overflowed.

Darcy fought to keep his face neutral.

He could not declare himself if she did not return his affection. His heart ached with pent up emotion, but he could bear it better than he could her refusal. It was too soon, and he loved her too much to risk making a premature declaration merely to appease his ardent heart.

"I promise you, Miss Elizabeth, I would exert no less effort than you would."

He watched the flush in her cheeks intensify, brightening her fine eyes to sparkling gems of amber. A hint of a smile curled the corners of her lips. His mind filled with questions he wanted to ask and conversations he wanted to have with her. It would take a lifetime. He could not envision a better way to spend his life.

Like rainclouds at a picnic, Mrs. Forster slipped into the room. "Good morning, Mr. Darcy. Miss Elizabeth," she said cheerfully.

Why had she not taken breakfast in her room as she had before? The lightness in the room disturbed, Darcy mumbled something polite before turning his attention to his plate once again.

CHAPTER 27

The morning was replete with unwanted callers. First, Mrs. Forster had interrupted his comfortable tête-à-tête with Miss Elizabeth, and now they found themselves in the company of Mr. Stallard and Mr. Tanner.

Mr. Stallard had the audacity to look shocked at the events of the previous evening. He pretended sincere concern over Miss Elizabeth's safety. In Darcy's opinion, he was nothing more than a superb actor. Darcy watched his every move for signs of insincerity. Fortunately, Colonel Forster had joined them to witness the interview.

"Miss Elizabeth, I cannot express my dismay enough. This is a sordid affair, and as far as I can tell, one in which you should have no involvement," said Mr. Stallard for the second time since he had entered the Forsters' drawing room.

Mr. Tanner sat in the chair next to him, his arms crossed. He glared at everyone in the room as if he trusted no one. Perhaps he had more sense than Darcy originally gave him credit for— except, of course, when his glares were targeted at him.

Colonel Forster, who stood near the fireplace took a step forward, commanding everyone's attention. "Miss Elizabeth," he asked, his hands open and his voice soft, "do you have any enemies who might have acted against you? Or, perhaps less likely, might you have stumbled upon some valuable and therefore incriminating information regarding the identity of Lieutenant Wickham's murderer?"

Miss Elizabeth shook her head. "If I have enemies, I do not know them. And I fear I have discovered nothing of use about the investigation or I should have told you or Mr. Tanner directly."

Darcy could not help but notice how she excluded Mr. Stallard.

"Have you any indication at all as to why someone would accuse you in a manner meant to startle all in your household?" asked Mr. Tanner, one fist balled up inside the other. He looked as Darcy felt. Were the identity of the assaulter to be found, Darcy would have to hold his fists as tightly as Mr. Tanner did.

"No. I have spent all night and this morning trying to think who might do such a thing, and I have nothing more than unfounded suspicions." Her eyes flickered to Mr. Stallard.

The man, whose guilt grew by the minute, said in mock innocence, "Nothing good can come of a female involving herself in a man's work. Miss

Elizabeth, I must insist for your own wellbeing that you not make any more inquiries. Allow the men to do their work."

Miss Elizabeth swallowed hard, and Darcy watched her eyes flash in anger. He could hardly blame her. She was one of the more intelligent people in the room— her startling misjudgment of his own character aside, although she had not been entirely in the wrong… He observed her struggle. She twisted her hands in her lap, her knuckles white.

He could watch her suffer no longer. "Miss Elizabeth, while I cannot agree a female is any less qualified to investigate a murder, I will agree with Mr. Stallard that you should cease to inquire into it further. The incident you suffered from last night may have nothing to do with Mr. Wickham's murder, but until we know for certain, you ought not make yourself a target by continuing to ask questions where perhaps they are not welcome. Your life is infinitely more valuable than that."

Darcy felt Mr. Tanner's gaze boring into him, but he did not care. He would not allow Miss Elizabeth to come to any harm if he could prevent it.

She loosened her clutched fingers, and her shoulders relaxed. However, she said nothing in the way of a reassurance.

With a chuckle, Mr. Tanner said, "If you gentlemen think you can get Miss Elizabeth to stop doing what she has set her mind to do, then you have sorely mistaken her character."

Despite himself, Darcy smiled. It was true. He ought to have known better, but even knowing how his plea would be received would not stop him from insisting.

"Be that so, and I have no doubt but that it is, Mr. Tanner, I know I speak for myself, if not for everyone present in this room, when I say I do not wish for her to come to any harm."

Heads nodded— all except Miss Elizabeth's, that is.

She inhaled deeply, letting her breath out with a swoosh. "Very well, I thank you all for your concern and shall strive not to do or say anything to bring on any more attacks." She looked around the room, her eyes settling on him.

Darcy shook his head and smiled. She had made no promise, nor would she. He knew her too well. She would be more discreet than she had been before, but nothing could prevent her from involving herself. Her eyes smiled back at him in acknowledgment of their shared understanding.

"Miss Elizabeth, you have made it clear from the beginning you believed Mr. Darcy innocent of Lieutenant Wickham's murder. Why?" asked Mr. Tanner.

Only then did she look away from Darcy. He shivered when her warm gaze departed from him.

"I simply know he is not the sort of gentleman to resort to such a drastic action," she shrugged her shoulders as if her words were of little import.

Mr. Tanner leaned forward. "You are known through all of Meryton for being an excellent judge of character. What was it that led you to dismiss Mr. Darcy so decidedly from having committed the crime?"

She bowed her head. "I once believed myself to be an excellent judge of character. Perhaps you will believe my intuition is correct when I tell you my first impression of Mr. Darcy. It was not a favorable one." Looking up, she smiled impishly. "The truth is I did not like him at all."

Darcy ground his teeth and pressed his lips together to keep from laughing at the shocked silence surrounding them. Measuring eyes searched him for a reaction, but it was finally Mr. Tanner who broke the silence.

With a loud guffaw which startled Darcy, leaving him unsettled, Mr. Tanner said, "I have always known you to speak the truth, but I never expected to hear you say it so plainly where he could not help but hear you."

She looked at Darcy, her pupils sparkling with mischief and merriment. "Why should I hide my opinion of the gentleman— especially when he insulted me to my face on our first meeting?"

Darcy cringed. He had made no secret of his opinion of her at the Meryton Assembly. Overly fatigued and annoyed, he had insulted Miss Elizabeth's vanity so that she could not help but overhear him. He had thought his behavior justified at the time, but he had come to learn how kindness could never be too heavily bestowed.

Her eyes darkened and settled into a calm somberness. "I will also be the first to admit how completely my opinion of Mr. Darcy has changed." She paused, breaking their silent exchange to look at Mr. Tanner. "Mr. Darcy is as honorable as you are, Mr. Tanner. In fact, now that I think of it, you both share similar virtues."

Darcy sat back. What could he possibly have in common with Mr. Tanner— a man who had taken such an instant dislike to him and who still seemed determined to find fault with him?

Mr. Tanner's grin disappeared so quickly, Darcy doubted he had ever heard his laughter. Except he had sounded so alike someone… someone he had not heard these many years. Darcy examined his face until their eyes met, and Mr. Tanner glared at him. Evidently, he did not appreciate the comparison either.

Colonel Forster cleared his throat, commanding their attention. "This is most unfortunate. Not for you, of course, Mr. Darcy," he added quickly, "but for the fact that it appears we no longer have a principal suspect for the crime of Mr. Wickham's murder. Mind you, I did not believe it to be you from the beginning. A gentleman would hardly mix in like company with an officer such as Lieutenant Wickham." He bunched his cheeks in a scowl.

It struck Darcy that he had never considered what Colonel Forster thought of Wickham. He had been so new to the regiment, Darcy had assumed Wickham would do as he always had done— win everyone over with his charm until he was found out. Only, Colonel Forster did not speak of Wickham as one to be admired. Darcy admired his intuition at judging his nemesis' character more accurately than most.

"Will you continue to offer Mr. Darcy shelter? He is still under suspicion," said Mr. Stallard.

Colonel Forster answered without hesitation. "So long as he is in need of it, he is welcome to stay here. He made it clear to me when he accepted my offer that he did so more in an interest to protect his friends at Netherfield Park than for his own benefit. He has been a considerate guest and may stay as long as he pleases."

Darcy nodded his thanks to the colonel.

Mr. Stallard continued, "That is considerate of you, Colonel, as well as of you, Mr. Darcy. I should like to extend my hospitality to Miss Elizabeth. My daughter, I should think, would be more suitable company for her than Mr. Darcy."

Over his dead body! Until Darcy cleared Mr. Stallard of all wrongdoing, he would not trust him to protect Miss Elizabeth.

Before he could voice his concerns, she spoke. "I thank you for your kind offer, and I have no doubt but that I would enjoy the company of Miss Stallard as much as she would enjoy mine. However, my family knows I am *here* and they will come to visit me soon. I suspect they will not delay in calling, and it would distress them greatly to find I am not here when this is where they expect me— especially after the events of last night."

"Of course. However, I can easily arrange for my carriage to transport you and anything you require to my estate after their call. You would have sufficient time to inform them."

Darcy spoke the first thought to come to mind. "There is no need. Now that sufficient doubt has been cast on my perceived guilt, I think it only right for me to be the one to leave. Miss Elizabeth has been through enough in the past few hours, and I intend to cause her no further trouble. I will stay at Mr. Tanner's inn."

He had to swallow down the chuckle that almost escaped him at the shocked look on Mr. Tanner's face. "Do you have a room you can spare for me?"

When he recovered, Mr. Tanner nodded. "Aye."

"Then it is settled. I will have my things removed to the inn, and Miss Elizabeth may continue here undisturbed." He addressed her. "Does that suit you?"

He read the relief in her eyes as clearly as a voiced reassurance.

Colonel Forster cleared his throat. "Excellent plan. Now, that brings us back around to our more urgent matter. Who killed Lieutenant Wickham?"

Darcy had some questions for Mr. Stallard and there was no time like the present.

CHAPTER 28

"Where were you the night of Mr. Wickham's murder?" Mr. Darcy asked, his dark eyes settled firmly on the magistrate.

Elizabeth held her breath. Mr. Stallard would not take kindly to the implication behind Mr. Darcy's question.

Puffing out his chest, Mr. Stallard replied, "Unlike you, Mr. Darcy, everyone knows where I was. I returned home with my daughter when her dress was ruined. I did not leave my estate until Mr. Tanner came for me after Mr. Wickham had been murdered in his barracks."

Mr. Tanner fixed his eyes on his hands, his neck turned in such a way that his ear would not lose one word. As the village constable, he answered to Mr. Stallard. However, as a man with a reputation for strongly held values and honesty, he would seek the truth… no matter who was involved.

Elizabeth watched the men, her eyes darting back and forth between them so as not to miss a twitch.

Colonel Forster stood between them like a parent standing between quarreling children. He watched them every bit as closely as she did.

Mr. Darcy added, "My intention is not to offend you, Mr. Stallard. After all, I, too, am a gentleman and have been wrongly accused. My purpose is merely to state the facts before these witnesses so that we may have the assurance our peers, at least, are free of guilt."

Somewhat appeased, but not entirely convinced, Mr. Stallard said, "Very well. I will answer your questions if you will tell us, once and for all, where you were at the hour of Mr. Wickham's murder." He sneered, and Elizabeth clenched her hands together and bit her tongue to keep from replying in like manner. An answer from her would only draw suspicion. Besides, Mr. Darcy did not need her help. Mr. Stallard did not know Mr. Darcy very well if he thought he had laid a trap.

"I did not leave Netherfield Park," Mr. Darcy replied, his eyes and voice level.

"Nobody recalls seeing you," challenged Mr. Stallard.

"I will not bother to deny it. It is true nobody has testified to my whereabouts. However, while it hurts my pride to have my presence unnoticed at a crowded ball, it does not change its veracity." He lowered his chin and his voice. "It is not my custom to be intimidated by circumstances, no matter how unfavorable. I would no sooner speak a lie than bend to the will of others." His piercing gaze made Mr. Stallard squirm in his chair.

Elizabeth had to think to close her mouth.

Mr. Stallard's eyes narrowed, and his nostrils widened as he huffed his disapproval from his uncomfortable chair. Mr. Darcy, on the other hand, sat as calm as a man at his leisure. Elizabeth admired his control. She could never accomplish such a superior level of composure.

"I believe it," said Mr. Tanner in a growl which made apparent how badly he wished not to utter the words. "I have made my opinion of Mr. Darcy clear from the beginning, but even I will admit he has not acted or spoken in deceit."

Only then did Mr. Darcy look away from Mr. Stallard, his eyes widening at Mr. Tanner.

"Besides," Mr. Tanner added in a lighter tone, "with the message written on the brick sent through Miss Elizabeth's window, my suspicions lie elsewhere."

Colonel Forster, as quick as a whip, asked, "Who?"

Mr. Tanner looked at his hands again, his chin working from side to side. Finally, he pressed his fingers together and looked from person to person about the room. Elizabeth held her breath so long, she had to gasp for air.

"I do not believe this is merely a simple murder we are trying to solve. There are too many pieces which do not fit. There are too many people involved. Too many people with too many blasted secrets."

"Too many people involved? What do you mean, Mr. Tanner? As far as I can discern, it was a simple case of revenge against a young man who had too many enemies." Colonel Forster folded his arms and shook his head gravely, continuing, "I would never minimize the value of Lieutenant Wickham's life, but the world will not suffer from the loss of it."

His words filled Elizabeth with melancholy, and she dared not look at Mr. Darcy, though she struggled against the impulse to do just that. She could think of one person who would mourn his loss, even though he had attempted to bring her to ruin. The heart of an innocent maiden in love with a scoundrel was more traitorous than the murderer who ultimately took Mr. Wickham's life. Elizabeth ached for Miss Darcy, just as she knew Mr. Darcy did.

Mr. Tanner offered no argument. "Be that so, I sense there is more at stake than one murder." He looked intently at Mr. Stallard, who had only just recovered his complexion.

"If you would speak more clearly, perhaps we might be of assistance. We are, after all, working together to find out who is responsible," suggested the colonel.

Mr. Tanner pursed his lips, his attention captured by Mr. Stallard still. "I will ask one question. What do we know of Mrs. Yeats?"

Elizabeth gasped. What did Mrs. Yeats have to do with anything?

"I never met her before she arrived in Meryton," offered Mr. Stallard quickly.

"Nor I," added the colonel.

Mr. Darcy shook his head. "I could not identify her were she to walk into this room. I must have met her at Longbourn, but I do not recall having seen her face."

All heads turned to Elizabeth. She rose her chin in defense of the lady, but stopped before she uttered a word when she realized how little she really knew of Mrs. Yeats. Where had she come from? Aunt Philips had mentioned a tragic story tracing her origins and employ, but Elizabeth could not recall anything specific which could recommend her.

"I am afraid I know very little about her. However, I expect we will see her when my family calls during the day. Perhaps we can find out more then?"

Details— things so small she had not noticed them before loomed before her. Lydia's strange illness and even stranger quick recovery. Mrs. Yeats' disappearance whenever they had callers. Her tendency to stand with her back to windows and behind doors. Her watchfulness. Elizabeth's pulse raced as it struck her. "You do not think the message was meant for her, do you?"

She stared at Mr. Tanner, her heart pounding in her throat. What if the murderess lived with her family? Clutching her stomach, she breathed deeply to abate the acid rising in her throat.

"I do think the message was meant for her, though I have reason to believe her innocent of that particular crime," he said, his vision flickering over to Mr. Stallard once again. Crossing his thick arms, he leaned back against his chair. "I question her motive in coming here."

***

Darcy watched Mr. Stallard, but every other sense in his possession focused on Miss Elizabeth. Her breath came in muffled bursts. How he wished he would have paid more attention to the companion when he had called at Longbourn with Bingley. He had been too preoccupied with his own thoughts to give any attention to a servant. What a brute he had been. He might have noticed something telling— something which could have protected Miss Elizabeth… if Mrs. Yeats was found out to be someone other than who she claimed to be.

Mr. Stallard's eyebrows flinched at the mention of Mrs. Yeats. By the second mention of her, he had his hands clasped firmly together and had assumed a relaxed pose. It was too forced.

What did Mr. Tanner suspect? Darcy would make it his business to find out. Miss Elizabeth would have no peace until Mrs. Yeats' name was cleared of any reproach which could affect her family.

More convinced than ever of Mr. Stallard's involvement, and trusting that the gentleman would reveal nothing unless under duress, Darcy said, "If there is nothing else to be considered until the Bennets call, might I suggest we return to our dwellings until they arrive?" He wanted as great a distance as was possible between Mr. Stallard and Miss Elizabeth, and he now had several questions for Mr. Tanner. He did not look forward to their conversation, but the constable had voiced a major concern. More was involved than Mr. Wickham's murder, and Darcy aimed to get to the bottom of it before anyone else was wrongly accused or… worse.

The gentlemen stood, as did Miss Elizabeth. She did not sway or swoon as a weaker female would have taken opportunity to do. She clasped her hand over her heart, looking out the window, her arched eyebrows knit together in anxiety. His determination intensified on observing her suffering.

"Do you wish for me to go to Longbourn? I can speak with your father," he said quietly as the men filed out of Colonel Forster's drawing room.

"I expect them here soon. However, if they do not arrive..." She bit her lips together and inhaled sharply.

He looked at the clock. "I will go if they do not call within the half hour."

"Thank you, Mr. Darcy."

She had no idea how lovely his name sounded on her lips. Gone was the bite in her tone with which she had formerly addressed him. Gone were her defenses, and with that, Darcy felt a heightened sense of responsibility toward her. Not that she was weak. Not in the least. But she was vulnerable. She would not hesitate to put herself in a dangerous situation to protect her family and friends. He felt honored to have won a fraction of her loyalty, but he could not allow their budding friendship to cause her harm.

"Are you coming with me, or not?" voiced Mr. Tanner impatiently.

"Yes." Darcy blinked and returned her smile, withdrawing slowly from the room. He did not want to leave.

Lawrence stood next to Mr. Tanner awaiting instructions, which Darcy gave him in short order. He would pack Darcy's trunk and bring it over in a cart to the inn where they would stay until it was safe to return to Bingley's estate.

Mr. Tanner trudged across the square so quickly, Darcy had to stretch his legs to keep up.

The post coach having recently departed, the taproom was empty. A barmaid scrubbed the tables, a broom leaning against the wall near her.

Intent on asking Mr. Tanner what his suspicions were concerning Mrs. Yeats, it took Darcy by surprise when the bulky man whirled around to face him, his arms crossed and his fists tightened.

"Miss Elizabeth is not one of your loose country maidens to fool with. If you so much as lay a hand on her, I swear your own family will not recognize you when I am done with you."

Rage coursed through Darcy's veins. What kind of a cad did Mr. Tanner think he was? "I would never do Miss Elizabeth the injustice of treating her with anything less than the utmost respect."

Mr. Tanner scoffed, a cold laugh setting Darcy's nerves on fire. "I know gentlemen like you. You are all the same." He stepped forward, closing the gap between them.

Darcy made to step around him. The man was unreasonable, and his time could be used to far better advantage than in listening to bitter insults.

"Or do you think yourself too good for her?" Mr. Tanner asked, narrowing his eyes to slits. "She is a pretty little thing…"

"Do not speak of her," Darcy warned. His fingers tingled and his muscles tensed.

"She would be quite the conquest…"

Darcy did not let him finish his vile speech. Heaving all of his weight into his arm, he packed a blow so hard to Mr. Tanner's face, the man went sprawling back, breaking a chair as he crashed to the floor.

Darcy had warned him.

CHAPTER 29

Darcy's knuckles stung and stabs of pain raced up his forearm. Mr. Tanner had felt it too. He held the side of his face, the skin already swollen and red under his calloused fingers.

Stepping to the side to give himself more time to react should Mr. Tanner decide to retaliate, it surprised Darcy to hear a guttural chuckle where threats should have been made.

Wiggling his jaw from side to side, Mr. Tanner said, "I underestimated you, I see."

Still irate, Darcy said, "Never speak slightingly about Miss Elizabeth. She is a lady, and as someone who has known her for most of his life, I expected more from you. She deserves your respect, sir."

Dropping his hands from his face, Mr. Tanner sprung to his feet and stood to his full height. "You have it on my honor, Mr. Darcy. I hold Miss Elizabeth in the highest regard and only said what I did to see what your intentions toward her were."

"You have a strange way of going about it," Darcy complained.

Mr. Tanner nodded. "We are from different worlds, Mr. Darcy, but I felt your sincerity." He reached up and winced as he touched his puckered cheek.

Going around the counter, he pulled out two tankards, filling them to the brim and setting one before Darcy. What a strange man. One moment he acted as if he hated Darcy, and the next moment he offered him beer. Still, Darcy was grateful for the drink. Raising his glass, he drank.

"We can see everyone who drives into Meryton from that direction," said Mr. Tanner, pointing out of the window at the front of his building. "We will not miss the Bennets' carriage."

Darcy sat on a stool facing the window and the front door. "You see everything going on from here," he observed.

"Aye. It is why the villagers continue to elect me as their constable. Not a thing goes on in Meryton I do not eventually hear about." He pulled more tankards and glasses out from under the counter along with a clean, white linen. Wiping the rims carefully one by one, he continued, "That is what has me so puzzled about Mr. Wickham's murder. He seemed like an amiable sort, but I have seen too many of his kind. They are accustomed to living a life of leisure at the expense of others and feel the world owes them a living."

He did not need to say anything more for Darcy to understand his meaning. He had thought Darcy was the same— a comparison which Darcy could not allow. "Wickham grew up on my family's estate at Pemberley. Being my father's godson, he was given more advantages than he could have hoped for without Father's patronage."

Mr. Tanner gripped a glass so tightly, Darcy feared he would break it.

When he said nothing, Darcy continued. "Instead of using the opportunities given him to establish himself in a gentlemanly occupation, he resorted to manipulations and scheming devices so he could live a life of leisure whilst pursuing all the vices he could presume to afford."

"Your father put up with it?" Mr. Tanner asked.

Darcy felt his shoulders tense. Father's leniency where Wickham was concerned had been one of the many bones of contention they had debated over the years. "He did." He offered no excuses. There were none.

Mr. Tanner set down the glass he had polished to transparency. "You did not approve?"

"Of course not. Wickham was given all the advantages of a gentleman without any of the responsibilities. It ruined him."

"What do you hold against him, if I may be so bold as to inquire?"

Darcy considered Mr. Tanner. It was an honest question lacking accusation.

"I cannot give details. However, he hurt someone vulnerable. A young lady innocent in the ways of the world." Darcy's chest tightened at the memory of Georgiana's tears when he had separated them. She had resented him at first, believing herself in love. She had been convinced Wickham loved her in return. When she realized his attachment depended on his need for her dowry, it had been devastating.

"A relative?" pressed Mr. Tanner.

"My little sister," said Darcy, tossing back the rest of his ale. He could not explain why he said it, but he knew his secret was as safe with Mr. Tanner as it was with Miss Elizabeth.

Mr. Tanner leaned against the counter, strangling the linen in his fist.

"You have a younger sister?" Darcy ventured.

Such a look of pain crossed Mr. Tanner's features, Darcy regretted the question.

"Aye," he said softly.

"Then you understand what it is like. I remember when she was born. She was so small and defenseless, yet she latched onto my finger with the strength of a vise. I was a lad then, but I promised I would not let anyone or anything harm her. When Wickham was found shot through the heart, all I could think was that he could no longer hurt her." He stopped, his throat tight.

"What is her name?" Mr. Tanner asked tenderly.

"Georgiana."

Mr. Tanner nodded. "A daughter named Georgiana and a godson named George. I wonder why your father did not name his firstborn after him as well." His voice carried an edge to it, but he was not as defensive as he had been.

Darcy sighed. "My father's vanity had its limits, thank the heavens and all that is good. I would have loathed to share the same Christian name as Wickham."

Darcy heard the clopping of hooves and the jingles of harnesses.

Mr. Tanner stretched his neck to better see. "It is Mr. Bennet," he observed.

Sighing in relief, Darcy watched the carriage as it crossed the square in the direction of Colonel Forster's home. Now that Miss Elizabeth's anxiety would soon be soothed, he could ask what he had intended to Mr. Tanner.

"You said you have suspicions. Do you care to share them?" he asked.

Mr. Tanner narrowed his eyes, taking up another tankard to polish.

After some long seconds, he said, "I will only be honest with you if you are honest with me."

"Very well."

"Why have you been so elusive about your whereabouts the night of the Netherfield Ball? I sense you are hiding something, but I am equally convinced it was not you who killed Mr. Wickham."

Darcy grimaced. "Are there not enough leads to pursue? If you are convinced of my innocence, then why do you wish to know?"

"To forever smother my doubts. There will be some who will argue that you arranged for the brick to be thrown through Miss Elizabeth's window in an effort to distract us from you..."

Darcy's pulse pounded. "Whoever did that is a coward and deserves to be found out and punished."

"I agree."

Darcy weighed his options. "I will own that I do have a secret, but it is not mine alone. Otherwise, I would have been more forthcoming from the start."

"You do realize how your refusal to cooperate was our main reason for suspecting you?"

"I do. It changes nothing. I would no sooner prove disloyal to a friend for my own convenience than I suspect you would."

He watched Mr. Tanner intently. His eyes remained steady, encouraging Darcy to continue. "Can I trust you to keep a secret for the benefit of a lady you respect?" He knew he had probably already said too much, but he would say no more without a guarantee.

Mr. Tanner said, "On my honor. Especially if it involves Miss Elizabeth, as I suspect it does."

Having no greater possession to swear by, Darcy was content. "If you break your promise and so much as whisper a word of what I am about to tell you, I will deny it. I will dig up the one thing you wish to keep hidden about yourself, and I will use it against you so your word could not stand against mine. Even here in Meryton."

Folding his arms, Mr. Tanner said, "Unlike you, I do not have any secrets."

"Everyone has secrets," Darcy countered.

They stared each other until Mr. Tanner blinked. Tossing up his hands, he said, "Very well. You have my guarantee of silence."

There was no going back now. To be sure, it would be a relief to tell someone he could trust. Mr. Tanner of all people. "The clock struck midnight while I was in Mr. Bingley's library. The same library into which Miss Elizabeth, minutes before, had disappeared. She had fallen asleep on the sofa and before we could escape from our compromising situation, Mr. Bingley's housekeeper locked the room."

"But you are partial to Miss Elizabeth. She would have to marry you if it were found out."

Darcy pounded his fist against the counter. "Of course I am partial to her! She is everything my mother trained me to avoid in a lady: opinionated, clever, knowledgeable on subjects she ought not to be…. I have always thought her handsome, but it did not take long before I admired her mind even more than her beauty. To win the admiration of a lady such as she occupies my every thought, my every dream. But I cannot take away her freedom to choose whom she would bless with her love."

"You put her welfare ahead of your own?" asked Mr. Tanner, incredulity lacing his question with doubt.

"I am depending on you to do the same for her sake. We were alone in the library for too long to avoid a compromise, and her only hope is that my whereabouts remain vague."

Mr. Tanner ran his hand through his hair, then leaned against the counter on his elbows. With a smile in his crinkled eyes, he said, "How did you get out if you were locked in?"

Darcy could not hold back his grin as he remembered how they had argued. It had been a battle of wills which he had ultimately won— but only barely and with a bite mark. "I jumped out of the window and walked in through the front door as if I had stepped outside for some fresh air."

"Hmm… the gardener was right. Nobody saw you?"

"Miss Bingley saw me come in."

Mr. Tanner's eye, by now, had turned a dark shade of violet. He winced as his cheeks bunched up, but nothing could stop his laughter. He roared as loud as his cousin Richard.

Darcy chuckled, but the matter was still too serious to indulge in with much glee.

Finally catching his breath, Mr. Tanner said, "You are not at all what I supposed you to be, Mr. Darcy."

"I can only hope you mean that as a compliment. Now, I have held nothing back from you, we can solve this mystery once and for all. What can you tell me about Mrs. Yeats and what does she have to do with Mr. Stallard?"

CHAPTER 30

Mrs. Forster was disappointed when Kitty and Lydia did not join them, choosing to remain with Aunt Philips. She endured the company of Mary with dreamy glances out of the window and long-suffering sighs.

Elizabeth was glad to see her family without the distraction of her younger sisters.

"How did you convince Mr. Collins to stay behind?" she asked Father.

With a crooked grin and a low chuckle, Father said, "It was easier than I thought it should be. Thankfully, his determination to identify who the murderer is and to protect his inheritance at Longbourn is far greater than his concern for your safety."

Elizabeth laughed. "I am grateful for that!"

"As am I, Lizzy. It is bad enough to know a fool shall inherit my estate, but it is worse for me to think he intends to marry one of my daughters when this trouble is resolved."

Mother, who had been admiring Mrs. Forster's drawing room until that moment, exclaimed, "Mr. Bennet! You say the most astounding things! Of course he should marry one of our girls. Would you have us cast out of our home when you are no longer here to protect us?"

Father knew better than to answer. She would not hear reason.

"What if he proposes to Jane before Mr. Bingley has the chance?" asked Elizabeth in a low voice meant to exclude Mrs. Forster from the intimate subject at hand.

Jane's cheeks flushed pink, but she watched Mother with the attention of a hawk. So did Elizabeth. She would not see the happiness of her sister ruined by a bumbling clergyman whose only recommendation was the security he could provide them at their father's death.

Mother sniffed. "Mr. Collins would do no such thing."

Everyone looked at her. As the eldest daughter, Jane would naturally be his first choice, despite the hints Mother had given to discourage that particular match.

Looking around guiltily, Mother whispered, "I had hinted at it discreetly before, but I wanted to be certain Mr. Collins would leave you be so Mr. Bingley could court you. There may have been mention of a wedding…."

Jane squeezed her eyes shut, her face flaming red.

"You told a falsehood to a man of God?" exclaimed Mary, her complexion deepening to match Jane's.

Mother shrugged her shoulders. What did a little lie matter to her when she had five unmarried daughters? Elizabeth knew she ought to be as shocked as her sisters, but she understood Mother's concern too well.

"Now, where is Mr. Darcy? Have you been able to spend some time with him?" Mother asked, her eyes glued to the door she hoped he would walk through.

"He is not here," replied Elizabeth, sad to displease her mother so much. Sad he had gone. Even though she was safe under the colonel's roof, with guards posted at all entrances, she felt Mr. Darcy's absence more than she had believed possible. The air was heavier. The rooms were colder.

"What! He is not here? Where is he then?" Mother said, plopping her fists on her round hips. She muttered, "After all I did to send her here. After all of my work to put them together."

Elizabeth sighed. Mother spoke as if nobody could hear her. Poor Mrs. Forster. What she must think of them!

Father bunched his cheeks up, and looked at Mother under his bushy, white eyebrows. "It must be such a burden to you, my love, to manipulate affairs so well only to have your work undone."

Mother fanned her face with her hand. "You have no idea what I suffer, Mr. Bennet. If only I could see my girls settled."

She did appear to be suffering at that moment. Her cheeks flushed, and she continued flapping her hand in front of her face by the fireplace.

Feeling it best to change the subject to one more agreeable to their hostess, Elizabeth asked, "Why did Lydia and Kitty not come?"

Mary's face pinched, and Jane looked out of the window facing the street with a sigh.

Mother perked up in her chair. "They stayed to help Mrs. Philips. She is to have a card party this afternoon, and she has invited several officers. I am certain Mr. Denny shall propose to one of them!"

"You do not know to whom he will propose? Has he not shown a preference?" asked Elizabeth, her question biting with sarcasm.

Father added, "It is of no matter, Lizzy. Whether he chooses Lydia or Kitty, I shall give my blessing gladly. He must lack sense to want a silly wife, and so it does not signify which one he shall choose for both are equally silly."

"You cannot mean that, Father. How would they live?" she asked.

Father rolled his eyes, gazing beyond the ceiling. "They shall have to live on the ardor of their affection, myself being unable to give them anything more than my blessing."

"Love is the most sacred of all emotions, but it will not put bread on the table," mumbled Mary.

Elizabeth had to agree. The tender emotion could so easily turn into hatred when the stomach grew hungry and there was no money to pay the rent. And she doubted Lydia— and quite possibly Kitty as well— loved Mr. Denny. Theirs would be a superficial attachment which would fade with their looks as the years passed. Elizabeth refused to settle for a man to whom she could not give her complete heart. A man she could trust implicitly with her being, with whom she longed to share every waking moment.

Mrs. Forster left the room to request tea with cakes and sandwiches, and Mother prattled in the background. Elizabeth was too wrapped up in her thoughts to pay her much attention. That was, until Mother said Mr. Darcy's name.

"What?" asked Elizabeth when it became clear that Mother expected an answer.

"I said that with an estate the size of Pemberley and ten thousand pounds a year, Mr. Darcy's wife would never have to suffer want. I daresay he would take care of his family… and the family of the wife he chooses to marry."

Grimacing in distaste, Elizabeth replied, "Mr. Darcy is not the sort of man to allow himself to be taken advantage of. I doubt he would be content to marry simply for convenience, otherwise he would have married by now."

Father looked at her so intently, she struggled to keep her composure. "He sounds very similar to someone else I know, do you not agree?"

She swallowed hard. "Perhaps, though a few commonalities hardly guarantee a strong foundation on which a strong love and respect may grow."

He sat back, crossing his arms and his feet leisurely. "True, but I have known happy marriages to flourish on less."

Elizabeth tried not to let her father's questions disturb her. She admired Mr. Darcy, but her opinion of him was so recently changed and there was yet much about him she wished to know. If their secret was found out, it would not be the end of the world. Not anymore. But that was not how she wanted to start a marriage. She wanted complete, whole-souled, unhindered love. Was that too much to hope for?

"Let us not speak of the heart now. Our concern is for Lizzy's welfare," said Jane, her soothing voice like a balm on Elizabeth's turbulent heart.

"Yes, I mean to call on Miss Stallard again today," she said.

"Will you be allowed?" asked Mary.

"I should think so. I am not accused of any crime and am only here for my safety. I hardly see the danger in calling on Miss Stallard to ask her some questions." She did not voice her suspicions toward Mr. Stallard, but decided she had best not call unaccompanied. What a pity Mrs. Yeats was too occupied with Kitty and Lydia. Aunt Philips could not go either, as she had a card party at her home.

"I will go with you," offered Father. Quickly, he added, "I have not conversed much with Mr. Stallard of late, and it would be a neighborly gesture to pay a call."

Grateful for his thoughtfulness in discerning her predicament, Elizabeth thanked him.

"Tis I who should thank you. You have given me an excuse to forgo your aunt's card party, and I shall return home at a much more convenient hour."

So much for thoughtfulness. On the bright side, she would not be trapped indoors all day, and Father was infinitely better company than Mrs. Forster, who would no doubt be cross when she heard about the card party to which she had not yet been invited.

A fresh tea service was brought in, followed by Mrs. Forster.

"Please stay a while longer and enjoy a repast," she said. While she and Elizabeth did not hold many common interests, Mrs. Forster was an excellent hostess.

Biscuits and sandwiches were passed around on china saucers along with steaming cups of tea. The conversation turned to the more socially acceptable topics of the weather and, naturally, to Aunt's card party.

Turning to Elizabeth, Mrs. Forster said, "I only received an invitation today, but forgot to make mention of it in my excitement. It has been ages since we have enjoyed a party, and I need your help in selecting the best dress for the occasion."

Forcing her mouth into a smile, Elizabeth muttered something agreeable. As a guest in Mrs. Forster's home, she could not refuse to accompany her. She only hoped Miss Stallard would be present at Aunt's home or she would be forced to wait another day to ask her questions.

Father accepted their change of plans. Tipping his cup to drain the last of his tea, he set it down. "We should depart so you can ready yourselves for this afternoon's entertainments." To Elizabeth, he said with a meaningful glance, "We will see you there. We will make our call together on the morrow."

There was nothing else to be done. Straightening her shoulders in resignation, she waited for the hours to pass.

The only excitement was the removal of Mr. Darcy's trunk to Mr. Tanner's inn and Colonel Forster's return to the house to prepare for Aunt's card party. He seemed to be as excited as Mrs. Forster.

Elizabeth thought she might float away with all the tea she had sipped during the day, but she took the cup the colonel offered politely, savoring a hearty drink of the beverage in her mouth so she would not appear rude to drink it so slowly. It was a horrible mistake. The tea was so bitter, it was all she could do to swallow it.

The magnitude of her mistake spread through her body as quickly as the blurred numbness which followed.

"It was you," she said, her speech slurring. Her tongue felt thick in her mouth.

"You finally figured it out," the colonel said with a bow. He had the audacity to be proud of it. "I admit I held little hope of avoiding suspicion this long, but Mr. Darcy's valet will soon find Mr. Wickham's pistol when he unpacks his master's trunk." He shrugged his shoulders. "It will not take them long to realize I am the only person who could have put it there. Tis a pity. I had hoped not to have to involve you." He took a step toward her, a rope in his hands.

She raised her heavy arm to throw her teacup at him. The liquid doused his coat, the cup bouncing off him harmlessly.

CHAPTER 31

Lawrence did not delay in arriving at Mr. Tanner's inn, placing Darcy's trunk where he could easily unpack it as soon as he had ensured the room was suitable for his master.

Mr. Tanner watched in amusement as the gentleman's gentleman carried out his duties. "He will not find anything lacking and will soon have nothing to do," he commented confidently.

Darcy smiled at Mr. Tanner. He was beginning to understand his gruff manners and straight speech. "Then I shall have to send him to the shop for a razor or a comb. He does not like to be idle, and should protest if I so much as hint he take some time for himself."

"You have attempted to do so? I daresay that is not a common practice among highborn gentleman."

"I would much rather live by my own rules than adopt someone else's. You seem to me to be the sort of fellow to live by your own values…" He said it like a question, letting his words trail off so Mr. Tanner could finish the idea if he were so inclined. Somehow it seemed more polite than asking directly. He did not want to pry, but he was curious.

"Aye. I learned long ago a man must act as he best sees fit. Otherwise, as I have observed, one must suffer the torments of a guilty conscience or risk hardening the conscience so much from abuse that one loses all sense of what is right and wrong." He stared out of the window. "My father was such a man. He rarely gave much thought to others. He was too absorbed in his own world to give consideration to others."

There was a bitterness to his tone which stunned Darcy. When Mr. Tanner looked at him, he was a man divided between an anger Darcy did not understand and a desire to be understood.

The door opened, bringing in a rush of winter weather and a smiling Bingley.

"Darcy! There you are! I had thought to find you at Colonel Forster's, but I was told you are now here," said Bingley in all of his joviality. "And good day to you, too, Mr. Tanner. I hope you do not find your new guest too cumbersome," he added with a grin. He could not miss Mr. Tanner's impressive black eye, but he said nothing. Only a small wince betrayed his composure.

Mr. Tanner, his face and voice devoid of all emotion, said, "That remains to be seen."

Darcy nearly choked in his effort not to laugh at Bingley's reaction.

Bingley looked between the two gentlemen. He would not allow his friend to be maligned in any way, but he avoided confrontation like the pox — especially from an impressively proportioned man like Mr. Tanner. "Say here, Mr. Tanner…" he mumbled.

Shaking his head, Darcy alleviated his well-intentioned friend's anxiety with a clap on the back. "Pull up a chair, Bingley. Mr. Tanner, please pour him a tankard of your fine ale."

"He looks to need it," Mr. Tanner said, removing the cork from the barrel and filling a tankard to the brim.

"You were only teasing?" asked Bingley, reaching out for the drink offered to him. "I ought to have known, but you know how dashed uncomfortable I get when there is an altercation."

"I do, and let me assure you that Mr. Tanner and I are now on amiable terms." He received an affirming nod from the constable.

"Ah, good. The world would benefit greatly if we all got along."

Bingley's incessant optimism cheered Darcy, lightening his worries so he believed that all would end well — if only for a moment.

Darcy was too realistic to believe anything but a shrewd mind and keen eye for detail would explain the events of the past few days. Now that someone had involved Miss Elizabeth, Darcy was unshakable in his purpose to find out who had attempted to cause her, or someone in her household, harm. If he were to believe Mr. Tanner, the message had been meant for Mrs. Yeats. But why?

Mr. Tanner said, "What brings you into Meryton, Mr. Bingley?"

"Yes, that." Bingley looked around the room sheepishly. "You see, I… Well, I felt entirely useless. I do not have the sort of clever mind necessary to be of any assistance in an investigation. What is more, it was my own sister who could have caused you more trouble by concealing information which I am certain only made you appear guilty of hiding something of importance. I mean to say, you were hiding something, but I know you well enough to be certain it is not related to the murder…"

Before Bingley could go off on an unrelated tangent, Darcy asked, "What did you do? You are explaining yourself in a roundabout way as if you are guilty of something, but you have yet to say what it is."

Sucking in air, and holding it, Bingley said in a burst, "I wrote to Colonel Fitzwilliam. Please do not be angry with me, Darcy. I could think of no other way to help you, and it looked very bad for you when I wrote."

"When did you write?"

"I sent him a letter by messenger yesterday," responded Bingley, downcast.

"Then Richard will ride all the harder having received two urgent messages in one day. Do not trouble yourself, Bingley. I wrote to him as well."

Richard would arrive that same day, of that Darcy was certain. He would ride his big, black stallion from London at a gallop, slowing only when his horse required it.

Bingley slumped in his chair in relief, drinking deeply from his tankard. "You have no idea how glad I am to hear that."

For Mr. Tanner's benefit, Darcy added, "Colonel Fitzwilliam is my cousin. Richard is the sort of man you want on your side in a battle. Besides me, he is my sister's guardian."

"Will he require a room?"

"Do you have another available?"

"One of my guests is leaving on the post coach this afternoon. He may have the room once the maid has seen to it. It should be arriving shortly."

Mr. Tanner busied himself about his work while Darcy filled Bingley in on what he had missed.

As Mr. Tanner had predicted, Lawrence soon had nothing to do. He came downstairs.

"The room is simply furnished, but it is clean," he commented.

It occurred to Darcy that his valet looked pale. As if he needed some exercise. What he would give for a ride over the countryside, but he could not leave Meryton. Not with Miss Elizabeth across the square and a murderer on the loose. Far be it from him to

309

deny his man exercise merely because he could not venture far.

"Lawrence, I do believe my green riding coat is still at Netherfield Park. I would like for you to fetch it."

Lawrence took to the idea with great enthusiasm, asking if there was anything else he should bring or see to whilst at Netherfield Park. Darcy obliged by adding a few more items to his list.

"I have not yet unpacked. Do you wish for me to do so before I leave?" asked Lawrence.

"No. I would rather you go with Bingley."

Bingley nodded. "I am ready to leave. You will send for me if I may be of any assistance?" he asked Darcy.

Mr. Tanner returned, bringing with him two steaming mugs of black coffee. He set them down only after Bingley refused them politely, not wishing to delay any longer. Mr. Hurst was to escort his sisters back to London, given the Bennets' recent fright, and his presence was required at Netherfield Park.

"I will get the horses," said Bingley, departing with good cheer.

"Do you take sugar or cream?" Mr. Tanner asked, sitting next to Darcy so he could still see out the window at the front of his inn.

"No. Thank you," Darcy accepted the coffee and blew on it before taking a sip. It was good and strong— precisely how he liked it.

At the door, Lawrence turned around, wearing a contented expression. "This is how I had always hoped it would be. The connection between you is too strong for you to have remained foes."

"Connection?" asked Darcy.

Mr. Tanner went pale and fidgeted in his seat.

"I fear I have spoken out of turn, sir. My deepest apologies." Lawrence frowned at Mr. Tanner, nodding at him as if to move him to do something, and departed without another word.

"What did he mean by that?" Darcy asked Mr. Tanner. A suspicion sprouted in his mind, gripping him both with excitement and the worst shame he had ever known.

Mr. Tanner set his mug down, continuing to spin it slowly around. "Have you ever heard of a lady named Clarissa Dent?" he finally asked.

Darcy made to deny having ever heard that particular name before, but something in Mr. Tanner's eyes made him consider longer than he needed to. What he answered was of importance, and he would not treat the question lightly.

He pondered, thinking back to his youth at Pemberley, his schooling at Eton and Cambridge, his travels around the country for education and business.... Still, he could not recall ever hearing that name.

"No, I cannot say I have. I am sorry."

The hurt spread over Mr. Tanner's face so that it was impossible to ignore.

"Was there never any mention of…" Mr. Tanner wrapped his hands around his mug of coffee, his fingers turning white at the pressure. He looked up at Darcy and swallowed hard.

"Whatever you have to say will not become any easier to utter by delaying in saying it." Darcy wished to end Mr. Tanner's agony. And he needed to hear it.

"Did Mr. Darcy, your father, say nothing of his life before marrying Lady Anne?"

"Not that I can recall." His father never spoke of his indiscretions. Darcy's heartbeat hurt his chest.

"He never told you he had another son?" Mr. Tanner stared into him, willing him not to have to say the words he had kept hidden his entire life. In a look, his brother concealed nothing and revealed everything.

CHAPTER 32

Darcy slowed his words, his heart thudding so violently, he thought he might choke. "We are brothers."

Mr. Tanner nodded. "I am the illegitimate firstborn of George Darcy with a barmaid his family refused to allow him to marry."

The sadness in his voice was like a stab to Darcy's gut. There was nothing he could say to right the lifetime of wrongs done against Mr. Tanner. Questions boiled within Darcy, but he did not feel he had the right to ask them when the memory clearly caused his brother pain. His brother.

"I would not have said anything," Tanner said.

"I am glad you did. I can—"

"You can do nothing! I have done well enough on my own," Tanner growled, pounding his fist on the table in a magnificent display of Darcy pride. How had he not seen it before?

Knowing especially well how to deal with that particular trait, Darcy said, "Very well. I will respect your wishes… for now. Until you decide how you want to proceed, you must allow me to address you as a friend. It would please me for you to do the same."

The front door opened and Mr. Denny slipped inside, peeking out of the window, then ducking out of its view. Seeing them, he nearly stumbled over his feet in his haste to join them at the table.

"Mr. Darcy, you must help me!" He leaned against the table, too agitated to sit.

Tanner moved over to the window. "What are they doing?" he muttered as he looked out of the glass. More loudly, he added, "I see Miss Lydia, Miss Kitty, and Mrs. Yeats standing by the coach. There appears to be an altercation."

Mr. Denny groaned. "I could not go through with it. Mrs. Yeats made all the arrangements for us, and I am certain we should be happier than most, but I could not start our life together this way. And then *she* found out about it!"

Darcy did his best to interpret what was not said. "You were going to elope with…?"

"With Miss Kitty. I love her dearly, but Miss Lydia insists that I love *her*! She cannot accept how I could possibly choose Kitty over her. Mr. Darcy, please, you must help me or I will never be free of her!"

Darcy crossed his arms, leaning back in his chair. "You ought never to have encouraged Miss Lydia in the first place. The consequences have caught up with you, and you must face them."

"I hardly encouraged her at all! She only focused her attention on me when I made it clear I preferred Kitty over her." Mr. Denny's desperation grew the more he talked.

Tanner jerked his thumb at the window. "This is the sort of domestic dispute in which one does best not to involve himself. It never ends well."

Passengers from the recently arrived coach poured into the inn, chattering about the scene outside in hushed voices. Tanner's workers set about their business efficiently.

"But you must help me!" Mr. Denny insisted. "I saw you leave through the library window," he hissed in a voice loud enough to draw some eyes.

Darcy kept himself from bolting out of his chair. A hasty reaction would only call more attention to them. Slowly, he sat forward, resting his hands against the table. "Kindly keep your voice down, and tell me why you have chosen now to tell me what you saw."

Mr. Denny obliged. In a whisper, he said, "I have not said anything for fear of being discovered in an equally awkward position."

Tanner joined them, standing between Darcy and Mr. Denny, thus blocking the view of several passengers with his large frame.

Darcy raised his eyebrows, encouraging Mr. Denny to continue.

His cheeks coloring to the same scarlet shade of his coat, Mr. Denny said sheepishly, "I was alone with Miss Kitty. Mr. Bingley's garden has a nicely placed statue where we talked— I swear on my honor we *only* talked— without interruption from Miss Lydia."

"Did Miss Kitty see me?"

"No. Her back was to the house."

Darcy relaxed slightly. "I thank you for your discretion."

Standing upright, Mr. Denny asked, "Does that mean you will help me?"

"We had best interrupt their dispute before the ladies get into the carriage," said Tanner.

Darcy stood, clamping his hand on Mr. Denny's shoulder. "I will help you *if* you speak with Mr. Bennet. Miss Kitty is very young."

"I promise. Indeed, I wished to do so instead of sneaking off as if we were ashamed of our attachment, but Miss Lydia is like a bur on my coat and Mrs. Yeats was insistent."

Darcy followed Tanner and Mr. Denny to the coach.

He asked, "The lady in the middle is Mrs. Yeats?" Her back was turned to them, and he could not see her face.

Only a few paces from the post coach, the lady turned and Darcy froze mid-step. "You!" he roared between clenched teeth.

The lady turned to run, but he caught her arm before she could escape. She writhed like the evil serpent she was. Miss Lydia swooned, forcing Mr. Denny to catch her before she landed in the pile of horse manure at her feet.

"I would have let her drop," remarked Tanner, without deviating his gaze from Darcy and his captive.

Darcy needed to explain, and the Bennet girls needed to be dealt with. There were too many people milling about. The inn was too crowded. That only left one place.

Tightening his grip lest she escape, Darcy marched across the square to Colonel Forster's home. He would lay bare her sins, and by God she would pay for them.

He listened with half an ear to Miss Kitty and Miss Lydia's incessant bickering. Mr. Denny could not get a word in until Tanner's patience had hit its limit.

They had reached the garden gate to Colonel Forster's house, when Tanner bellowed, "Enough! The two of you will hold your tongues until you are asked to speak."

Darcy stopped in the middle of the footpath. The guards which had been present on a constant rotation were nowhere to be seen. The hair on Darcy's arm stood on end. He looked around, but not a soul was in sight. No one opened the door to receive them. He knocked once, and when there was no response, he pounded on the door. Still nothing. It was all wrong.

Tanner paced in the lawn, looking from right to left. "It is empty."

Scenarios and explanations ran through Darcy's mind, each one dismissed as soon as it appeared. There was no excuse for this. Even if they had left early for Mrs. Philips' card party, there would be someone around to ask. The house looked abandoned.

Shoving the vile woman toward Mr. Denny, Darcy said, "Do not let her out of your sight. Take her back to the inn along with Miss Kitty and Miss Lydia. Nobody leaves until we return with Miss Elizabeth."

Darcy raced around the house, the sound of Tanner giving instructions fading as he ran.

The door to the stable was open.

"What do you think has happened?" asked Tanner, hastening up from behind him.

"I do not know, but something is horribly wrong. Why is nobody here? And look, the coach is gone."

"Hallo there?" called a man. It was an officer.

There was no time for pleasantries. "Where have they gone?" asked Darcy.

"The colonel? I saw his coach leave some minutes ago."

"Did you see who was with him?"

"I did not, but I did think it strange for him to be driving his own coach. He seemed to be in a hurry, and so I assumed the Missus had taken ill."

Apprehension seized Darcy. Moving across the lawn toward the village stables, he asked one final question. "In what direction did he go?"

"Toward London."

"Tanner, why did we not see him?" Darcy asked.

"He must have gone around the square."

Colonel Forster had not wanted to be seen.

Darcy was grateful he had not returned his favorite stallion to Netherfield Park. The horse pranced in his stall when he approached. They would lose no time. Tanner joined him, tossing a saddle onto a dark chestnut mount and cinching the girth.

"Can he keep up?" Darcy asked.

The beast pawed the ground as if he understood Darcy's doubts. "Brutus will keep up with your fancy blood horse, Darcy. Let us go!" He jolted forward as his horse took off at a canter.

Once they reached the edge of the village, there was no restraint. They galloped so hard, it pulled tears from Darcy's eyes, and he had to squint and blink to see clearly.

All this time, it had been Colonel Forster. Darcy recalled every conversation; every interaction with the colonel. Had Elizabeth found him out? Is that why he kidnapped her? What did he plan to do with her?

Darcy's indignation bordered on madness, and his horse responded to his frenzied emotions by galloping faster than he ever had before.

They passed a man he suspected to be his cousin Colonel Fitzwilliam riding toward Meryton. Darcy would not slow down to make sure.

He heard Richard shout and saw him turn his horse around before Darcy lost sight of him. Good. Richard would have his sword and pistol. Darcy had nothing other than his bare hands.

Of course, if Colonel Forster touched a hair on Elizabeth's head, his hands would be all he would need. With a shout, he urged his horse on.

CHAPTER 33

"Why did you murder Mr. Wickham?" Elizabeth had asked while she still could.

He had looked at Mrs. Forster, who was slumped against the settee, her empty teacup dangling from her finger.

"If I cannot have her whole heart, then nobody can," he had said with all the warmth of a statue.

Elizabeth wondered how a man so cold could deceive them for as long as he had.

She had been too weak to prevent him from tying her hands together. She had screamed, but he soon silenced her with the handkerchief. She remembered hoping he had not used the handkerchief before stuffing it into her mouth.

Had she lost consciousness? How long had they been traveling? It was not yet dark outside, but it would be soon. A fine spray of moisture covered the windows.

Elizabeth fought against the stupor, fueling her anger against the colonel to keep herself and Mrs. Forster alive. He had killed Mr. Wickham and was content to let Mr. Darcy hang for it! He had drugged her and his own wife! He had kidnapped them! Colonel Forster's list of sins grew, and her mind awakened with the addition of each one.

Now, Elizabeth found herself kneeling on the floor of the coach, her legs too numb and her knees too sore to move immediately. Mrs. Forster lay motionless on the cushioned seat above her.

Gathering her wits, Elizabeth calmed her breathing and assessed her situation. Her feet were free, but even if she could get out of the carriage, she did not trust her legs to hold her weight. Her mind might have some sharpness to it, but her body lay like a lifeless lump.

Colonel Forster must have been in a hurry, for he had tied her hands in front of her. Reaching up, she pulled the handkerchief out of her mouth. There. That was one less obstacle to overcome. Her throat was sore, but she could muster a good scream when the time was right.

Carefully, so as not to shake the carriage and draw his attention, she slid up the seat to look out of the window. Nothing but open, empty fields.

Panting at the exertion, she eliminated all thoughts of a quick escape. Even if she managed to jump from the carriage into the fields, she could not run. She doubted she could even walk. And then there was Mrs. Forster. She could not just leave her.

"Think, Lizzy, think! Use your brain!" she mumbled to herself. Lifting her hands to her mouth, she pulled on the rope tying them with her teeth until her arms got too heavy. What had been in that tea?

Unwilling to give up, she propped her feet up against the seat in front of her and leaned forward to reach the rope. It was clumsy work, and she toppled over too many times to count, but finally the rope loosened, and she pulled her hands free.

The skin around her wrists was chafed and raw. It looked worse than it felt... for now. That would change once the effects of the drug had run their course.

Sliding closer to the door, she wiggled the handle. The door clicked open. Could she jump? As the ground sped by at an alarming rate, she clutched her stomach at the thought. If no better idea occurred to her soon, it would have to do.

She considered Mrs. Forster. She was no bigger than her, a fact for which Elizabeth was grateful. She would gather her strength, hold Mrs. Forster as closely as she could and, in one mighty leap, she would pray for the best and jump. Neither of them weighed much. If she chose a rough patch of road, there was the possibility— though slight— that Colonel Forster would not feel the carriage lighten. The fog would make it difficult for him to find them if he did notice.

Elizabeth huffed in frustration. Too many possibilities and maybes. Was there no other option?

She looked at the door again. Maybe, just maybe, there was a passing rider who had the keen eyesight necessary to see her through the foggy dusk. One could dream. If not a rider, then she wished for a good, heavy rain. Falling into mud, while unpleasant, would provide a much softer landing than the packed earth of the road.

Opening the door just an inch more to see if any other travelers were about (anything to keep from breaking her neck and Mrs. Forster's by taking a risky jump which Colonel Forster would certainly be able to feel), she peeked her head out and looked in the only direction in which she could see without toppling over.

Her hair whirled around her face and stung her eyes. Grabbing the loose strands and pulling them back with one leaden hand, she tried again.

And she saw him. She blinked hard, ensuring herself he was not a dream.

He shouted so loudly, Colonel Forster must have heard him. Before Elizabeth could shift her weight back and away from her precarious position, the coach scratched and creaked to stop, sending her lurching against the open door and bruising her ribs as she smacked against it.

***

Darcy's heart leapt from his chest as he saw Elizabeth dangle headfirst from the carriage, her face dangerously close to the ruts in the road.

"Stop!" He shouted so loudly, the clomping of the horses' hooves and the carriage wheels grinding over the packed dirt road faded like whispers.

"Get down!" clamored Richard.

Just above Elizabeth, Darcy saw the flash of a pistol at the same time Tanner rammed his horse into him, sending Darcy against Richard. The crack of the shot echoed through the fog and Tanner's mount screamed.

Darcy's stallion careened to the side, and he grabbed at the mane to keep his seat. Tanner's horse shrieked, tossing its head wildly, tangling his bridle in Darcy's stirrup and smearing something wet and hot down his leg.

"Tanner, are you shot?" Darcy kicked his foot free and hurled himself down, holding the reins closely to his horse's head to steady the animal, and trusting Richard not to let his horse trample him.

"I am unharmed. Go!"

Needing no more reassurance or encouragement than that, Darcy ran to Elizabeth. She lay in a ball on the dirt. He heard Richard click the cock of his pistol.

Colonel Forster jumped from the footboard, weapon in hand. "Stop!" he ordered, pointing his pistol at Elizabeth.

Darcy reached his arm out to warn Richard.

"Stop right there or I will shoot her." The colonel grabbed at her arm and yanked her to her feet.

"If you harm her, we will shoot. My cousin is an excellent shot. He will not miss," threatened Darcy.

Elizabeth staggered on her feet, waving back and forth. Her face was dirty, but he saw no blood. Colonel Forster grabbed her around the neck, and she screamed so loudly, it made Darcy's ears ring.

The colonel smacked his hand on top of her mouth, and Darcy knew what would happen. He was close enough to see it in her determined eyes. With a fierceness and enthusiasm he was privileged to witness, she sunk her teeth into Colonel Forster's fingers.

The gloves he wore were no protection against the sharpness with which Elizabeth's teeth pinched his flesh. Darcy knew the feeling all too well and it filled him with pride.

Promptly pushing her away, the colonel yelped in pain, his pistol misfiring in the process.

"Grab him!" Darcy shouted as he reached for Elizabeth. He caught her just before she hit the ground.

Richard kept his pistol on the colonel. "Put your arms behind your head and kneel," he boomed in a voice demanding swift obedience.

Tanner joined Richard, leading the horses. "Tend to your lady, Darcy. We will take care of Forster." As if he thought Darcy capable of doing anything else.

Kneeling on the ground, Darcy cradled Elizabeth in his arms.

"My limbs feel like lead. He drugged my tea," she explained with a slurred voice.

Gently, he pushed her hair away from her face, stroking her skin until the tightness in his chest grew unbearable. "Did he hurt you?"

"No more than is visible to the eyes." She snickered. "I must be a frightful sight."

To him, she had never been more beautiful. Her dirt-smeared face did not diminish her humor or tenacity, and nothing could dim the sparks in her eyes. Were he to consider only his feelings, he would have declared himself that moment.

"I thought I would lose you," he whispered more to himself than to her.

She sighed and mumbled, "You will not be rid of me so easily, Mr. Darcy. So long as I have my teeth…"

Darcy laughed from the bottom of his lungs. "You would show a sense of humor at a time like this." He loved her for it.

"Darcy, are you going to make yourself useful?" asked Richard sarcastically. He had tied Colonel Forster's hands behind his back and now stood beside him with the tip of his sword poking the criminal's neck.

Casting him an annoyed glare, Darcy lifted Elizabeth, nestling her head against his shoulder. "I see you two have everything under control."

Richard rolled his eyes and addressed Tanner. "By the by, I am Colonel Richard Fitzwilliam of His Majesty's Army, at your service." Jerking his head in Darcy's direction, he added, "I am the handsomer, cleverer, and far more charming one."

Tanner chuckled. "I am happy to meet you, Colonel. I am Jonathan Tanner, the innkeeper at Meryton."

"And my brother," added Darcy, delighting in the shock on Richard's face. Tanner grumbled and wrinkled his face in displeasure. It did not bother Darcy in the least. He would have to get used to his family, and there was no better time than the present to start.

"Tanner, you will have to learn to put up with us. I will only tell Richard and Georgiana about you, but you must allow me to claim you as my brother to the people closest to me. For God's sake, you pushed me out of the way of Forster's bullet. Had you not done so, it would have been my face he hit instead of your horse."

Elizabeth gasped. Reaching up, her fingers glossing over his face as soft as a feather, she wrapped her fingers around the hair at the base of his neck.

"Poor old boy. He does not much like the hole in his ear, but he will live. He is a tough one," said Tanner. Darcy would have smiled had he been in better possession of his senses.

He saw the concern in Elizabeth's eyes when they met his, and she let her hand drop. "I am sorry, Mr.

Darcy. I only needed to be certain you were not hurt. If you will put me down, I think I might be able to walk. I did not drink much of it."

Darcy was not so confident. Nodding to Colonel Forster, he asked, "What did you give her?"

Richard removed the gag from around his mouth. "Answer the question."

Colonel Forster stretched his lips and cleared his throat. "It was only laudanum."

"*Only* laudanum?" Darcy growled. "Tie him up, Richard. Tanner, when we return to Meryton, can we gather everyone at your inn?"

Tanner nodded, but Darcy's attention was soon drawn to Miss Elizabeth. Her eyes were as large as tea saucers.

"Mrs. Forster!" she exclaimed, struggling in his arms to get to her feet.

He set her down, but kept his arm around her waist. She was not strong enough yet.

Leading him to the carriage, she opened the door. Mrs. Forster lay quietly on the cushioned seat. Too quietly.

Reaching forward with his opposite hand, Darcy felt her skin, pulling his hand back sharply. "She is dead."

Colonel Forster sunk to his knees and wept.

"We will stop at the coroner's on the way. Let us go."

CHAPTER 34

Mr. Darcy's valet greeted them with an ashen face when they finally arrived at the inn. "Mr. Darcy, I found this at the bottom of your trunk." It was a pistol with the initials GW engraved on the sideplate. "If only I had seen it earlier, we would have known who put it there."

Taking the weapon from his trembling hand, Mr. Darcy said gently, "It is done now. Do not forget it was at my suggestion you put off unpacking. You are not to blame. Now we know why the colonel left when he did."

Elizabeth said, "He must have placed it in your trunk when it was almost certain you would be found guilty." She shivered, deeply troubled at the ease with which the colonel would have discarded another life.

Mr. Darcy took her by the arm. "You are shaking. Tanner, we must see to Miss Elizabeth."

A second later, the housekeeper whisked her away, swatting Mr. Darcy from their side with her plump hands. "I will tend to the lady, Mr. Darcy." When he made to follow, she dared him with a glare to take a step closer.

Chuckling, Mr. Tanner slapped Mr. Darcy on the back. "Miss Elizabeth is in good hands with Mrs. Molly. You had best leave them be."

Taking her upstairs, Mrs. Molly lost no time. She helped Elizabeth clean up at a wash basin, straightening her hair and brushing her dress.

On their return, Mr. Tanner settled Elizabeth at a table in the corner. Bringing her coffee and a plate of beef stew, he insisted she eat— a demand with which she was more than willing to comply.

It seemed that all of Meryton was crowded into the room. Father sat beside her with an overjoyed Mr. Denny, who after receiving permission to marry Kitty, was only kept at their table in case he was called upon to testify. His eyes strayed to the door many times, no doubt longing to be with Kitty at Aunt Philips' party.

Colonel Fitzwilliam, Mr. Tanner, and Mr. Darcy stood at the front of the room, each of them the epitome of seriousness with their arms crossed and stern expressions. Three cousins.

Now that she knew about their relationship, she wondered how she had not seen it before. Mr. Tanner bore a stronger resemblance to Mr. Darcy than Colonel Fitzwilliam did. But they were there nonetheless. Watching the three of them standing shoulder to shoulder, full of confidence and power, was an impressive sight.

Colonel Fitzwilliam represented the authority in the room, Mr. Stallard no longer qualified to do so. With a booming voice, Colonel Fitzwilliam said, "Let us begin. Given that the proof against these offenders is irrefutable, we shall hear their testimony before the witnesses present before conveying them to Hertford to await the next available assize."

Colonel Forster sat in the front row next to Mr. Stallard, his shoulders bent and his head bowed. When his name was called, he did not bother to raise it.

"Are you guilty of the murder of Lieutenant George Wickham and of your wife, Mrs. Helen Forster?"

The colonel nodded his head, his shoulders shaking.

"Speak up, man!"

"Yes. I never meant to hurt her. She was the love of my life." The colonel took a deep, shaking breath. "I have nothing to live for and would sooner take my own life than live with the knowledge that I have taken hers."

"Then you may as well unburden yourself before these witnesses," suggested Colonel Fitzwilliam. "Tell us why you killed Lieutenant Wickham."

Colonel Forster looked up, addressing the three men before him loudly enough for everyone in the room to hear. "In celebration of our wedding anniversary, I gave Helen a necklace of my design. I spared no expense, and she said she loved it." He paused, and Elizabeth could feel his struggle. "You can imagine my surprise when, one evening, I asked her to wear it only to learn she had misplaced it. I later found out she had given it to Lieutenant Wickham— a man she had only recently met."

Mr. Denny sat up in his seat, his jaw wide open.

Colonel Fitzwilliam asked, "Is that why you killed Mr. Wickham?"

"I was consumed with jealousy. It had never been easy to have such a pretty wife, but this was the first time she had given me reason to suspect something more than an innocent flirtation with one of my officers. It was nothing for me to slip away from the Netherfield Ball. He claimed not to have the necklace. Knowing men of his sort, I assumed he had already sold it for the money. I was so enraged, and he had so carelessly left his pistol on the table, I picked it up and shot him."

Mr. Denny stood, his entire body shaking. "I know about the necklace," he said, turning everyone's attention to him.

With a nod from Colonel Fitzwilliam to continue, he said, "Wickham owed me some money. A sizable sum. The day of the ball, he gave me the necklace so I might sell it."

"Is the necklace still in your possession, Mr. Denny?" asked Colonel Fitzwilliam.

"Yes. Not being able to get leave during the investigation, I chose to keep it. Not long ago, I gave it as a gift to the young lady I plan to marry. I am sorry. I did not know where it had come from, only that it would cover the amount Wickham owed me."

Mr. Darcy said, "Under the circumstances, I think it best for you to return the necklace to Colonel Forster." Elizabeth agreed. If Kitty knew her necklace had once belonged to the deceased Mrs. Forster, she would never be able to wear it.

Colonel Forster stood, spinning on his feet to face Mr. Denny. "No! I never wish to see that necklace again. You must let your young lady keep it. Tell her nothing of how you acquired it, but let her cherish it as my dear wife never did."

He crumpled into his seat, covering his face with his hands.

"You had best sit down too, Mr. Denny," Father whispered. "You can sell it later and buy Kitty something you know she would like. Keep no secrets from your wife."

Touched by his sage, loving advice, Elizabeth smiled at her father. Had he left it at that, her hopes that her parents' love ran deeper than she supposed would have been confirmed. Unfortunately, he leaned toward her, adding, "I have never had to keep secrets from your mother. She does not understand half of what I say and does not care to listen to the other half." He chuckled and relaxed back into his chair.

Rolling her eyes, Elizabeth focused her attention back to the front of the room. To Mr. Darcy precisely. She felt a strong pull toward him, but what if it proved to be merely a passing fancy? There had been a time when her father and mother had loved each other enough to marry, but it had not taken long for them to realize their attachment had been based on fleeting fancy. Mr. Darcy stirred her in ways which left her breathless and weakened her knees, but would it last? Could he love her until death did them part?

Mr. Darcy looked up at her. His eyes were as soft as a caress, and she could almost feel his arms around her, his gentle hands grazing her face when she had been too weak to stand. She had wished he would hold her thus for a lifetime. It was the most secure place she had known. She could not bear it if she gave him her heart, and he grew weary of her as her father had tired of Mother.

Father pointed to the front of the room. "Now this is what I want to know about."

Mrs. Yeats was next. Elizabeth sensed the animosity between her and Mr. Darcy as clearly as if it were another person in the room.

"Will you state your real name?" asked Colonel Fitzwilliam.

"Mrs. Louisa Younge."

Elizabeth gasped. She was the same woman who had nearly ruined Miss Darcy!

"Why did you assume a name?"

"I could not find work. Mr. Darcy saw to that," she stated venomously.

"Why did you come to Meryton?"

Addressing Mr. Darcy, she said, "Do not flatter yourself that I came to beg from you. I did not know you were in Hertfordshire until I had already arrived. I came here because Mr. Wickham had promised he would take care of me if I helped him woo a young lady in possession of a generous dowry. I knew the risks involved if we were found out, and made him guarantee I would be provided for should we be discovered. He failed to keep his end of our bargain, but he proved helpful in other ways..." she let her voice trail off suggestively as she looked at Mr. Stallard.

Shifting in his seat, Mr. Stallard kept silent while Mrs. Younge continued. "You see, a business transaction failed to meet up to our expectations this past summer at Ramsgate. In need of a position, I schemed a new plan with Mr. Wickham, who found himself in dire need of a small fortune. We selected a promising young lady— handsome and with a sizable dowry. Only, Mr. Stallard found out about it and insisted his daughter return home. To Meryton."

Mr. Darcy asked, "Mr. Stallard, did this woman attempt to blackmail you?"

His face flaming red, Mr. Stallard responded. "She is a viper and not to be trusted. Yes, she threatened to expose my daughter to ridicule unless I paid her a weekly salary."

"Until you stopped paying!" Mrs. Younge declared to the room. She looked around with a smug expression, taking notable pleasure in watching his embarrassment.

"I had already mortgaged my estate! Where else was I supposed to get money?"

"Is that why you came to me?" Mr. Darcy asked him in a low voice.

Mr. Stallard nodded. "I am ruined. It was my last resort, and one of which I am deeply ashamed. My humiliation is complete, and so I will lay bare my offenses." Rising from his seat, he looked at Elizabeth. "Driven to madness by this woman," he pointed at Mrs. Younge, "I did something of which I must beg your pardon, Miss Elizabeth."

She held her breath.

"It was I who broke your window. Had I known you were in the room, I would have chosen a different window. I had hoped it would land in *her* room, but my desperation to rid myself of her led me to act rashly. I am sorry. I will see the damages repaired before I must leave my home."

Mrs. Younge complained, "Is he to receive no punishment at all for what he did?"

"Fair enough question," said Colonel Fitzwilliam. "What does the lady affected think?" He looked at Elizabeth kindly.

She knew her answer. "Mr. Stallard went to great lengths to keep his daughter's indiscretion disguised and his circumstances secret. I believe that when he is called to testify in Hertford, and he has to repeat what he has told us this evening to a room crowded with curious onlookers, it will be punishment enough. No harm outside of the broken window, a fright, and a few cuts has been done."

"That is all?" Mrs. Younge asked in disgust.

"Would you have me send him to the gallows just to please you? I would rather sleep with a peaceful conscience than indulge in revenge and end up a bitter, lonely woman."

Elizabeth saw Mr. Darcy's nod of approval, and that was enough for her.

Mrs. Younge sneered, "I ought to have poisoned you too when I had the chance."

Colonel Fitzwilliam bellowed, "Too? You openly admit you poisoned an individual?"

Realizing her mistake, Mrs. Young made a point of clamping her lips shut.

It all made much more sense now. Speaking up, Elizabeth answered for her. "She poisoned my sister Lydia to avoid attending a dinner at Netherfield Park. Mr. Darcy would have recognized her immediately. Why did you stay on with us when you risked discovery at every turn?"

"It brought me pleasure to watch Mr. Darcy suffer. I had already accepted a position in your household when he was accused of murder, and I wanted nothing more than to watch him as he dangled from the end of a rope."

Oh, she was evil!

Mr. Darcy interrupted her before she could spout any more venom, "Mrs. Younge, you do realize the punishment for attempted murder is far worse than extortion and fraud? Your resentment has worsened your own fate."

"It was not attempted murder! I only slipped enough arsenic into her tea to give her a stomachache!"

Unmoved, Colonel Fitzwilliam said, "You can attempt to convince the jury of that, madam." To the crowd assembled, he added, "Very good, then. At first light, we will transport the prisoners to Hertford where they can rot in prison until their trial." To Colonel Forster and Mrs. Younge, he said, "May God have mercy on your souls. I doubt either of you will find much sympathy in this room."

The meeting came to an end, and everyone filed out of the inn, leaving Father sitting beside her.

"Mr. Bingley has kindly offered the use of his carriage to convey us home. A bath and a proper night's rest will do you well. Are you strong enough to stand on your own?" He stood, offering his arm, unaware of the welcome figure approaching them from behind.

"Mr. Bennet," said Mr. Darcy. "Might I have a word with you and Miss Elizabeth?"

CHAPTER 35

"Of course, Mr. Darcy. It has been a rather exciting day, has it not?" Father said, sitting down.

"My admiration for Miss Elizabeth has grown through these trying times. If it is agreeable to you, I should very much like to call on the morrow… and every day thereafter."

Elizabeth had not realized how tense she was until her shoulders relaxed. He was giving her time! He wanted to call on her!

Father's eyes darted around the room. Leaning forward, he said, "You do know, Mr. Darcy, I could insist you marry my Lizzy."

"You knew?" Elizabeth asked excitably.

"Yes. I did not say anything because, of all of my girls, I know you would have the most difficulty allowing yourself to fall in love. You demand too much. But I do believe this young man here is more stubborn than even you are, my dear girl." He pushed his spectacles down and looked at Mr.

Darcy. "I apologize if I have given cause for offense."

Mr. Darcy had the grace to laugh. "None taken."

"I do have a question, though, if you do not mind...," continued Father. Elizabeth winced, wishing he would keep silent before he insulted Mr. Darcy again. What would he call him next? Proud?

"Ask what you will."

"My family has many faults, and you are not a fool to be unaware of them. There are dozens of reasons why you should not want to potentially attach yourself to my family. Why do you stay? Why my Lizzy?"

"Though there be numerous reasons to leave, I only need one to stay. My future is entirely in her hands."

Hope gripped Elizabeth so hard, it left her speechless. Would he always put her wishes before his own? Humbled to the core he valued her enough to allow her to choose him— or not— her doubts faded away like dust in the wind.

Only four days had passed since that fateful night in Mr. Bingley's library, but it may as well have been a lifetime. Elizabeth's opinion of Mr. Darcy was so extremely opposite to what it had once been, and her heart palpitated in anticipation of what tomorrow would bring.

"I would like very much for you to call on the morrow," she said, her smile deepening to the same extent of his grin.

Through tribulation, he had overcome his pride, and she had learned to see beyond her prejudices. It made her wonder what the future would bring. If their past was any indication, it would be exciting. For the present, she was happy to fall in love with Mr. Darcy.

THE END

(And so Mr. Darcy and Miss Elizabeth lived happily ever after... or so we hope. Courtship is all fun and games until someone else gets murdered...)

Thank you!

Thank you for reading *The Honorable Mr. Darcy.* This story was a blast to write and the characters were so disappointed when it was done, I gave in to their insistence and have begun plotting their next story. (Charlotte Lucas was especially miffed to not be included in this story. She can be very demanding!) I can't very well end a story before seeing Mr. Darcy and his Lizzy to the altar, and so… their story will continue.

I want to give special thanks to you, dear reader, for choosing my book and spending your precious time in reading it.

Muito obrigada to Rita, who has a gift for pointing out plot holes and makes sure there are swoon-worthy moments in the romance.

Thank you to Anji for catching my Americanisms and keeping my vocabulary true to period. Your knowledge of the Regency era is inspiring.

Thank you, Betty, for keeping my commas in line. (They're such divas and think the book is all about them. Without your help, dear lady, they would take over!)

Muchísimas gracias to Renán, my greatest supporter and constant encourager. You've helped me unravel more tangled plots than I like to admit to.

Thank you, Dad and Mom (J Dawn King, as some of you know her), for keeping me on track. I love our 'shop talks' and it's the coolest thing ever to write along with you.

And last, but certainly not least, thank you, Mammy, for always believing that I could do this. You're the original storyteller in our family.

There are many others whom I wish to thank, but this novel would double in size, and so I'll shout, "THANK YOU!" I appreciate all of you.

I hope you enjoyed reading my latest story. It was a joy to write. Please let me know what you thought and help other readers find my book by leaving a review on Amazon and recommending it to your friends!

If you would like to know when my next book is available, you can:

* sign up for my new release newsletter at www.jenniferjoywrites.com (I ONLY send out a newsletter to   announce a new release. No spam!)

* follow me on twitter at @JenJoywrites

* friend my Facebook page at facebook.com/JenJoywrites

* follow my Author page on Amazon at amazon.com/author/jenniferjoy

About the Author

When Jennifer isn't busy dreaming up new adventures for her favorite Jane Austen characters, she is teaching English, reading, perfecting her doughnut recipe, or taking her kids to the park.

Her wish is to continue to write sweet romances and mysteries with happy endings for years to come.

She currently lives in Ecuador with her husband and twins. All of them are fluent in Spanglish.

Right now, Jennifer is imagining how a courtship with such a turbulent beginning can possibly lead to a smooth Happily-Ever-After for Darcy and Elizabeth. She senses there's more trouble to come and promises to keep a detailed account of events (because, let's face it, it makes for fun reading!).

Other Books by Jennifer Joy

Darcy's Ultimatum: The Cousins Series, Book 1
Anne's Adversity: The Cousins Series, Book 2
The Colonel's Challenge: The Cousins Series, Book 3
Earning Darcy's Trust
Accusing Elizabeth
Love Never Fails
Win, Lose, or Darcy

Printed in Great Britain
by Amazon